DISCARD

f

Fountains of
Youth

Stephen Ausherman

Livingston Press
at
University of West Alabama

copyright © 2006 Stephen Ausherman
All rights reserved, including electronic text
ISBN 1-931982-55-4 library binding
ISBN 1-931982-56-2, trade paper
13 DIGIT ISBN 1-931982-55-9 library binding
13 DIGIT ISBN 1-931982-56-6 trade paper

Library of Congress Control Number 2006922852

Printed on acid-free paper.

Printed in the United States of America,
Publishers Graphics

Hardcover binding by: Heckman Bindery

Typesetting and page layout: Angela Brown

Cover design and layout: Jennifer Brown
front cover photo: Richard Day
back cover photo: Angela Brown

Livingston Press is part of University of West Alabama,
and thereby has non-profit status.
Donations are tax-deductible:
brothers and sisters, we need 'em.
www.livingstonpress.uwa.edu

first edition
6 5 4 3 3 2 1

Fountains of Youth

for Oma & Opa

and Harry Alston

Monday

Scores of knowledgeable and faithful readers regard Lester Current as the South's paramount journalist, which is a modest way of saying he's the best in the world. Ever.

Even editors in rival periodicals can't help but laud his brilliance. From the *Pamlico Picayune* to the *Fairhope Enterprise*, the worst anyone's ever had to say about him is a gripe on the fact that he was born into privilege, like he could help that. True, he is a native of Dunes County, and Dunes County is where you find the ocean-view property, and with that you get all the amenities: roller coasters and wacky golf and fishing piers, and boulevards and strips instead of roads and routes. And with these amenities come privileges, if not outright then certainly by default in the sense that a poor man on the beach is always better off than a rich man in a swamp.

Not that the swamp is all bad. But: "If you can't be happy on the beaches of Dunes County, there's no hope for you anywhere in the world." I can vouch for that much because that's a direct quote from the ad that the Dunes County Chamber of Commerce ran in *American Ethic*, the magazine Lester Current writes for. And Lester Current, let me tell you, has been around the world and then some.

And now he's coming here.

Lester Current. Coming to Stillwater County.

Lester Current is coming to Stillwater County.

I can scarcely wrap my mind around the thought of it.

Stillwater County. Here. Lester Current is coming *here*.

My mama said this day would come. I have waited my entire life for this day.

Well, not my *entire* life, but ever since I could read. That's how long I've been waiting.

I have been waiting without knowing exactly when this day would come, and that's the worst kind of waiting. It is worse than waiting for someone to punch you in the gut.

But now I know. See, the new issue of *American Ethic* just came out, with Lester Current stating in no uncertain terms that he is coming here to Stillwater County. See, here it goes right here:

Current Adventures: Demons of Stillwater County
by Lester Current
American Ethic vol. CVI no. 5

WHEN I WAS a boy, on the cusp of manhood, (or well past it, as I then naively believed,) my chums and I boarded the great yellow bus and set out for battle. We were the Badgers. The Dunes County Badgers. And everywhere we went, we let loose our fearsome Badger cry, no doubt inspiring our opponents to soil their tights. Then, in six minutes or less, we laid to waste their egos and reputations and hopes for athletic scholarship.

I offer no apologies. Wrestling is the most brutal of sports, one to which we, the Fightin' Badgers, were particularly well adapted. Gentlemen always were we off the mat, though not entirely estranged from occasional bouts of giddy mischief. However, on the mat, with headgear laced tight and a section of chinstrap tugging on the corners of my mouth like reins on an unbroken steed, I transformed into something animal. I was not alone. I could see it in the eyes of my teammates as well, a malevolent fire that ignited moments prior to the whistle, inextinguishable save for the slam of the official's hand to the mat, an indication of yet another victory.

Ferocious though we were, one opposing school filled our souls with terror. We dreaded the ride to their lair and entered their gymnasium with the ferocity not of badgers, but of bunny rabbits.

They were the Stillwater County Moccasins.

It was said most of their team didn't go to school, but rather had what you might call an Indian's education, if by Indian you mean savage, for we knew Stillwater County as a savage land.

It is an isolated county. The sandy, barren Dearth Hills slump along the southern border. Cottonmouth Lake, named for the vipers that dwell within its opaque black waters, marks its western edge. And to the North and East is Odium Swamp.

Treacherous as these natural barriers may be, we are thankful for them because they confine the four towns of Stillwater from the rest of the world. Pullman, Calloway, Hunters and Odium—to me, they may as well be the names of the Four Horsemen.

Pullman is the smallest, and therefore, likely the safest for any visitors who happen into Stillwater. Yet I wouldn't recommend traveling there in groups of three or less, and couldn't imagine why anyone would want to try.

Calloway is a hornets' nest of witchcraft and ill temper. They've developed a peculiar breed of dog there, one with the ability to foresee an appetizer in every jugular. This situation has lent itself to a rigorous process of natural selection among the townsfolk, a kind of survival of the meanest.

In Hunters, the dead outnumber the living, and an outsider might be hard pressed to distinguish between the two. The living are either dead drunk or mean drunk, while the dead are just mean. Poltergeists lurk in every shed and storm cellar. Specters infest the nights. It's said two haints served on town council for more than a decade each.

Then there's Odium, the county seat. In Odium, they paint their houses with tar. Tar houses, they're called. Fighting is all they have in the way of entertainment there. After the wrestling matches, they go to the cockfights. Once their cocks are killed, they start pitting dogs against one another. Their own dogs. Pet dogs. And when they run out of dogs, it's pigs. Then mules. I've heard of pigs fighting mules. And for a lark at our expense, they pitch in a couple of badgers and pit them against creatures dredged from the swamp. Could be bears. Could be alligators. I'm just telling what I heard back in the day.

On the edge of Odium is Odium Swamp. Bears and alligators do live out there. It's said a band of Gingaskin Indians also lives out there, far beyond the reaches of our kind. Rumor has it that descendents of runaway slaves still live out there, unawares of the Emancipation Proclamation. We feared them and, more so, the Confederate ghosts that continued to hunt them.

Add to that population the territorial trappers and their misplaced steel traps and you begin to get the picture of danger. There's more: Peat fires—at least one per generation, some lasting up to three years. Hard to imagine that a swamp can burn like that, but it will. That much I've seen.

Tributary swamps fingered into our county, and those we wouldn't go near. But once a year, we had to ride that bus along the canal roads into Stillwater County.

The high school itself is in Odium. It had been built as a prison; but due to their general acceptance of lawlessness, the cells remained vacant until they transformed the facility into a county school. That much we could see as our bus rolled into the central compound.

Our coach ordered us to dress out on the bus and leave our belongings there, where they could not be stolen. He warned us not to touch anything in the locker room for fear we may contract an otherwise sexually transmitted disease. And above all, we were not to drink the water, for it flowed straight from the swamp, and its acidic nature might well render us blind, insane or both. Showers would have to wait until we returned to our school.

I grappled the same boy there for four years straight. He looked like a senior my freshman year and a monster by my senior year. He was a hulking brute with braided hair and the face of Sergeant Slaughter. I often wished he would wear a hockey mask or a ski mask or some disguise the pros like to sport, for his face inspired such awe that I swear he could score takedown points on me with his stare alone. I still have nightmares about that face.

He had the touch of a healing evangelist, able to bring me to my knees with a laying of hands. But the real magic in his hands was in their ability to inflict blinding pain. I don't remember his technique or the moves he used, only the resulting discomfort. It never lasted more than two minutes, and neither did I. Nobody on our team survived a first round against a Moccasin.

Our only solace was in the fact that we would not have to face them again in regional tournaments. Their school could not afford to send them on the road. That was the Moccasins' only weakness; they were confined to Stillwater County.

Now I am no coward, as readers of this column can attest. I interviewed a steeplejack as he pasted gold leaf atop a 200-

foot spire. I walked steel girders to lunch with the builders of a cantilever bridge over the Patapsco. I hunted moose from a helicopter in the Yukon, the weapon of choice being concussion grenades. With my bare hands, I held railroad spikes for gandy dancers on the Santa Fe line in rugged Chihuahuan desert. I scalded those same hands assisting sorghum makers on a night that would make penguins shiver.

In my earlier days of journalism, I covered Klan marches, all the while ducking brickbats from both the marchers and protesters. I stomached two dark days and nights on a steamer in the stormy seas off Nova Scotia, my only company a drunken captain with hooks for hands.

I gained exclusive access to the American hostages in Beirut, and I negotiated their release. On the return flight, just ten miles from our final destination, the engine sucked in a Canadian goose and the plane crashed into a grain silo in Amish country. Everyone on board walked away unscathed. But this is the amazing part: We volunteered to delay our homecoming one more day so that we could all pitch in and rebuild the silo. Yes, we rebuilt it in one day, according to custom, and when we were done, the Amish men wept. We all wept.

I have witnessed the worst battles from Nha Trang to Biafra. I held a dying Israeli soldier in my arms while at my feet his mother collapsed in grief.

In short, I have known some troublesome times. But nothing troubles me like Stillwater County. Demons and rumors of demons circulate freely there. Many of them, I am certain, are the product of childhood conjecture, of rural superstition and inter-county rivalries. However, I know of at least one demon that is for real. It is the solitary demon in my past, and I intend to confront it. I can think of no more appropriate means to retire

> *this column than by entering that Godforsaken land and digging my way back through the decades to unearth the one thing in this world that still scares the hell out of me.*

EVER SINCE I could read, my mama put issues of *American Ethic* in front of me, already turned to Lester Current's column, "Current Adventures."

My mama said I was born on the day Lester Current's first article got published. She wouldn't let me read his early work, even if I could read then, because all he wrote about then was the troubles in the world. He wrote the news. But by the time I could read well enough, he'd moved on to better things. His "Current Adventures" column. From that column I learned about what it takes to drive a team of Clydesdale horses and what to do at a Maryland crab boil.

I learned what a key grip does in Hollywood.

I got a pretty good idea on what it feels like when your brother or son comes home from a war. I know the vibrant colors of autumn in Vermont. I can jumpstart a snowmobile in subzero temperatures and flint knap a spear tip better than any caveman. I could operate a windmill if I had to, because I read all about that, too.

I've already read this last column of his seven times now. This one is different. First of all, I've never heard him talk so much about himself. He usually likes to linger in the background and let the wisdom of the moment speak for him.

And never before had I read such harsh words from Lester Current. He's described funerals for babies with more cheerful prose. He made our county sound like the scariest place on earth. He's got me scared to be here and I've been here my whole life. Except—for the first time in my life—Stillwater County sounds like an exciting place to live. You can grow up in a place, think you know it your whole life. Then someone comes along with another story and suddenly it's like you've never been there before. I'd like to know how he did that.

I want a voice like Lester Current's. I want to look like him, too.

I've never seen him, but I bet he looks like what a man should look like. Man needs a tan, the darker the better, and a crewcut that never shows whitewalls around his ears. Man needs a square jaw held high and lines on his face that prove his familiarity with the world. Needs some of that Gregory Peck look in his eyes, too.

I got a tan and a crewcut, and I've nearly outlived Jesus in years on earth, but people still sometimes ask if I'm old enough to drive. I think that's because I haven't filled in yet. I'm still lean and sinewy. Doesn't bother me much, though, because I can be like Lester Current in other ways. The most important thing is the writing.

I've always wanted to know how to write like Lester Current. I practiced interviews on everyone I know. I wrote a story about Amitabh Patil, the Indian guy who owns the motel where I live. I call it: *Amitabh Patel's Story*, so as to avoid confusion. I wrote a story about my mama, G.G. Slant, before she died. That one I call: *My Mama's Story*. Then in stories like *Story of Three Sisters* and *Story of a Blind Man*, I wrote about three sisters and Moses Jefferson (a blind man), respectively. I wrote about a lot of everyday folk, the same kind of people Lester Current writes about.

Lester Current is my idol.

More than that, Lester Current is my father, and I am the demon he's coming to face.

Amitabh Patil's Story
by Cyrus Slant
(1989)

AT THE DIXIE Court Motel in Pullman, the neon still burns bright. Let it burn. This is a story about shining optimism in the face of impossible odds. The optimism belongs to Amitabh Patil, who has spent his whole life, in a sense, to keep a beacon lit for road weary travelers.

Welcoming voyagers with comfortable accommodation is a deep-rooted tradition in Amitabh's family, one that brought them considerable wealth in his home state of Orissa, on the eastern seaboard of the Indian subcontinent.

At age 21, Amitabh was poised to take over the family business. He had been married for nearly six years, and, according to custom, awaited the day when his wife, Mohini, reached the appropriate age to move in with her husband.

That day would be her fifteenth birthday.

That day was rapidly approaching, a fact that would have filled Amitabh with joyous anticipation had it not been for one problem. Nearly six years had passed since the wedding and Mohini's family had not yet paid her dowry in full. They had paid Amitabh's parents the required amounts of gold, silver, brass, stainless steel and vegetables. However, they still owed a rice paddy, a maid, twenty-one sets of dishes and a bedroom suite.

The Patels did not accumulate their considerable wealth by forgiving debts easily. So, according to custom, the men of the extended family—and by extended I mean in the hundreds— launched a massive attack on the bride's family. The attack, being customary, lacked the element of surprise, and a counterattack commenced with the initial assault.

The two families battled for thirty-three days and far exceeded the customary quota of bloodshed. Fearing the feud would not cease until both sides completely eliminated each other, Amitabh gathered up all the gold and silver he could carry, and fled with his wife to America, via Bombay, Kampala and London.

Once in our promised land, Amitabh abandoned his family's ways and refused to speak another word of Oriya. However, finding it impossible to relinquish his religion, he held fast to his faith.

He sought peace through isolation and tolerance for his underage wife. He found both in Stillwater County. But what remained of his wealth by that point was mere pittance. He bet his last gold nugget—scarcely enough to cap a tooth—on a rooster named Shiva the Destroyer and he won. He continued placing bets, and he continued winning. By dawn, he'd won a bb rifle, a mule and the deed to the Dixie Court Motel in Pullman.

Today, Amitabh runs the Dixie Court Motel with the contentment of a man who founded an empire. Sweeping magnolia petals from the walkway, he reflects upon the first time he saw the place he'd won. "It was in ruins. I'm telling you, there was kudzu growing in the lobby and raccoons in every room. But you must be knowing this: Even the Taj Mahal once fell into such disrepair that it was scheduled for demolition. So I restored this to the palace you see before you today. And like Akhbar the Great with the Taj Mahal, I presented it to my wife as a gift."

In return, Mohini provided him with three beautiful daughters: Mina, Arati, and loveliest of all, Sonali.

Amitabh rests on his broom handle and sighs. "Mohini never fully accepted my gift. She did not approve of my winning such things from fights. She said that since we lost everything due to a fight, winnings from a fight only further upset the karmic balance. I reminded her that it was Diwali night, a time when Goddess Parvati sanctions gambling so that we may achieve the blessings of wealth and prosperity in the coming year. Alas, Mohini complained: 'If I stay here, this place truly will be my Taj Mahal. It will be my tomb.'"

And with that, Mohini returned to Orissa, leaving behind her husband and daughters.

But this is a story of hope, of optimism and keeping a dream alive.

"I am dreaming of one day when I can expand my motel into an attraction in itself," Amitabh says. "A structure so

> *splendid that people will be traveling for miles and miles just to stay here."*
>
> *For now, most of his guests are simply folks looking to hide out for a spell and wayward travelers who got lost looking for a shortcut to the beach. Amitabh welcomes them all with his neon sign proudly blazing the colors of old Dixie. Surely without it they would continue to wander aimlessly into the night.*
>
> *Shine on, Amitabh. Shine on.*

MR. PATIL KNOCKS on my door and asks what I'm doing. I tell him I'm writing, because that's what I should be doing, but really what I'm doing is reading over *Amitabh Patel's Story* and trying to decide if I've got what it takes to write like Lester Current.

He says, "Still your pen for a moment and help me with the scooping of snakes. They have made their return to the swimming pool."

Scooping of the snakes. I love that job. Mr. Patil hates it. I'd tell him to leave the snakes be, seeing that the pool looks more like a pond anyway, but catching snakes on a summer morning is just too much fun. And besides, it makes me seem more useful around here. Nothing I'd hate worse than losing my usefulness. Need to earn my keep.

I file my story away under my mattress and click off the rattling window fan. Mr. Patil is waiting outside my door, wearing a white T-shirt, yellow swim trunks and red flip-flops. Pool net in his hands, ice chest at his feet.

I ask him what's the ice chest for.

"Transporting of the snakes. I do not want you catapulting snakes over the back fence anymore. You must show more kindness to the poor creatures."

He's sweating and perturbed about missing his morning swim. I can tell when he's perturbed. He doesn't speak much. Usually, he's more talkative. Folks who don't know him better might think he's uppity, the way he uses big words and talks in complete sentences with that fancy foreign accent of his. He can talk halfway through forever like that.

I think his generosity with words stems from the fact that the essence of his values and philosophy is contained in the great epic, *The Mahabharata*. He used to read it to his daughters. Sometimes I sat in and listened, but it went on too long. I looked it over one time and found it's eight times longer than *The Odyssey* and *The Iliad* put together. Took him months to tell that story to his girls, just as his parents told it to him, and so on for the past 3500 years. I think this is why he's so well rehearsed for lengthy speech. It's in his blood. But now he's just perturbed.

Days that start out this hot can have that effect on people. Make them curse things they'd laugh at in milder climes. It's eight a.m. and sunlight's burning holes in the foliage. Humidity's likely to steam paint off the walls. Parts on the front wall have already flaked off and gathered in the weeds like windblown candy wrappers. Looks like someone ate a whole mess of Charleston Chews and littered all up in front of the motel. I'd better get to that before Mr. Patil has to tell me to.

Mr. Patil knows we need to get this place straight. He knows we're expecting a V.I.P. I told him all about Lester Current coming to Stillwater County. I caught him in the kitchen and made him read Lester Current's latest column.

Odd, he didn't have any comment on it. He just went back to reading his morning paper, the *Stillwater Mercury*, like it had more important news.

Story of Three Sisters
by Cyrus Slant

ONCE UPON A TIME *there were three sisters who lived in a motel. The oldest was Sonali. She was very beautiful and she wanted to be the starlet of Bollywood when she grew up, because the only kind of movies her father watched were funny musicals from Bombay.*

Arati, also beautiful, but not nearly so much as Sonali, wanted to be a scientist. She didn't know yet what sort, but she

---

wanted to invent or discover something to make her father proud.

Then there was the youngest, Mina, who quite often could be a brat and probably would not amount to anything more than that, which is just as well because someone would need to stay at the motel and take care of their father when he got old.

There was also a young man living at the motel. For him, Sonali dressed in exquisite costumes from far away places and danced and sang to his heart's content.

Also, Arati would take him into the forests and swamps of the land, and she would tell him the names of all sorts of plants and animals living there.

And Mina, she would tag along, even when she wasn't invited. But she could fight good. She could take a shiner as good as she could give one. One time she jumped off the roof of the motel just to see if she could do it. She broke her scapula. So she wasn't entirely uncool.

The girls had a golden retriever named Surya because he shined like the sun. He also protected the girls when they played in the forests and swamps. He could find the poisonous snakes in their path. He would pick them up and shake them to death. (The snakes, not the girls.)

The young man did not want Sonali to leave the motel, but knew she must. He often worried about the day when that would happen. Arati told him not to worry so much or he might get a bleeding ulcer before he turned twelve. She taught him how to meditate. It helped his stomach feel better, but not so much his heart.

Mina couldn't wait until they both went away, but she would be sorry when they did, because Sonali would come back for the young man when she got famous and take him away to her movie

> *star mansion, and all Mina would have left was her old dad and*
> *maybe a dog.*

I GOT EIGHT snakes in the ice chest. Mina asks if I need help carrying them around the fence. I tell her I got it, but she takes a handle anyway. She says, "Where'd you disappear to last night?"

"Went to check on Mr. Jefferson."

"That's sweet. How's he doing?"

"Still blind."

"Well, duh he's still blind. Been blind most his life. You think that was gonna change?"

I set the ice chest down at the edge of the thickets. "Just telling you what he said. I asked him how's he doing and he said, 'Still blind.'" Mina squints at me, at the sun coming over my shoulder. "He also wants me to bring him some things today."

"What kind of things?" she asks.

"Sundries, dry goods. The usual."

There's a strange smell wafting out of the thickets. A kind of almond-meets-apple-butter smell. It's not so strange in the sense that it's anything new. Sometimes I can smell it pulling into my room at night. Never figured out what it was.

Mina looks me over and announces: "I'm darker than you now."

"Are not."

"Am too." We push our forearms together. We're about even, but she says, "See? You spend too much time writing in your room when you need to be working on your tan."

She flips the lid off the ice chest. A long fat snake shoots its head up and oscillates its gaze between her and me. Neck spread out, all hooded now, it hisses like a kettle. Mina reaches for its head, but it strikes and retreats before she can take hold.

She's a decade past high school and she still acts this way, like a little girl. I tell her, "Kept his mouth shut, I hope."

She checks her hand for punctures, like she wouldn't already know.

"Yup. What do you suppose a puff adder was hanging out at the pool for?"

"Got me. Better turn him loose before he starts spitting blood out his eyes, though. They get to stinking when they do that."

She kicks over the chest, spilling vipers all at my feet. I dance back, yelling, "Whoa, girl! Got moccasins in there too, now!"

"Sorry," she says. And she drums on the chest to drive them into the thickets.

I head back around the fence, Mina following, ice chest in tow. I ask her how she knew I was gone last night.

"Came by your room."

"What for?"

"I need a reason?"

"You need an invitation," I tell her, and next thing I feel is a chinaberry thwacking me in the back of the head. I spin round and hoist her up in one quick ninja motion. The chest goes tumbling. She's screaming out laughing, her stomach pushing into my shoulder and the rivets in her denim cutoffs poking into my neck. I call her a monkey-face freak and I start wailing on her butt. She reaches down and smacks my hip, screaming for me to put her down. "Stop!" she squeals, "or I won't tell you who checked in last night!"

I drop her down on her feet. "Who?" I know exactly who, but I need to hear it.

"Never mind," she says, skipping away.

No wait, can't be Lester Current. Mr. Patil would've told me first thing.

Maybe Mohini returned. Oh God, I hope not.

Maybe Sonali came home. "It's not Sonali, is it?"

Mina stops in her tracks and huffs. "No, it's not *Sonali*. Why would Sonali come back? And what makes you think would I tell you if she did?"

I don't have time for this.

I bust a sprint to the lobby. Mr. Patil is there disemboweling an old Zenith. Without looking up, he says to me, "If you have come barging in here so harum-scarum to inquire about Mr. Lester Current, I must inform you that he is not on the premises at the moment."

"Why didn't you tell me he checked in?"

He glances up at me, cocks an eyebrow. "First of all, it is not my duty to inform you of the comings and goings of our guests. Secondly, he stayed here no longer than fifteen minutes. I don't know where he rambled all through the night, nor is it my business to know such things. In any case, the fact that he is not here is of little use to you. Therefore, I kept it to myself."

I've got energy coursing through me like I could bounce through the ceiling. "Could you please, if you don't mind—"

"You will be knowing when he is present because he is driving a red Jaguar XJR." He pronounces it *Jah-goo-ar*. He peers though the plate glass window, past the neon. "As you can plainly see, there is no red Jaguar XJR in parking lot of this Dixie Court Motel. Conversely, when he returns, there will most likely be a red Jaguar XJR parked out there. Then you will know. For now, would you kindly remove the paint chips from the motel grounds and dispose of them in the refuse container."

Oh God no please not now. I've got to get sundries and dried goods to Mr. Jefferson in Calloway. I've got to stake out Lester Current's room until he gets back. "How about I get Cal to do it? Cal won't mind picking up paint chips. He loves paint." Cal also loves running into brightly painted things. Sometimes he'll paint something bright just so he can run into it.

Mr. Patil sets down his screwdriver and consults his calendar. He collects calendars, has twenty-eight in all—enough to have two accurate calendars hanging every year. For example, his 1994 calendars are really from 1983 and 1977. The years are off, but the dates match up right. And the pictures are always the same regardless of the year. Same gods, year after year.

I never did get his gods, not the way they look anyway. Take this month's god, Krishna. Wouldn't know if he's a boy or a girl. He's like those glam metal rock stars from the Eighties, like White Snake or Poison or Snatches of Pink. You know they're supposed to be manly, but they're kind of pretty, too. Got all that long hair and jewelry and make-up.

More eye shadow and lipstick and rouge than a birthday clown.

Difference in the gods is they come in an assortment of colors. Shiva's blue, Rama's red, and so on, like a roll of Lifesavers. Mr. Patil has these gods posted all over his room and office. Sure beats looking at a half-naked corpse spiked to dogwood planks and bleeding all over Creation, but I still don't get it. That's why I stick with Jesus. Jesus might not be much fun to look at, all the make-up in the world wouldn't help, but Jesus loves me and that's all I need. He keeps it simple, doesn't need to accessorize. He's kind of like Gandhi that way.

So Mr. Patil examines his recycled calendar, wags his head at Krishna and says, "If Cal comes by today, I will ask him to pick up the paint chips."

"*Dhanyawad.*" I press my palms together and bow back out the door. A moment later, I'm poking my head back in. "Mr. Patil? What's Lester Current look like?"

His head bobbles inscrutably. He frowns and says, "He is shorter than I expected."

Story of a Blind Man
by Cyrus Slant

THEY SAY WHEN *life shuts all the doors in your face, God opens a window somewhere. The same might be true for your eyes. It was in the case of Moses Jefferson. He's blind. But on the day he lost his sight, he became a seer. Two eyes forever shut, a third opened wide.*

This story begins on the banks of Cottonmouth River, which flows from Cottonmouth Lake. The lake is so named because it's shaped in the profile of a cottonmouth snake, with a diamond-shaped island for an eye and a peninsula for open jaws. This peninsula is called Cottonmouth Spit, and it has a pointy inlet that sort of looks like a fang hanging down. What you do here is kick back on the spit with a cane pole and yank catfish out of the inlet until you can't stand it anymore. It's the best place in Stillwater for that. And for the record, no one has ever seen a cottonmouth snake in Cottonmouth Lake.

But this story starts a ways downstream, on the banks of the river that forms the serpentine body of Cottonmouth Lake, and is therefore called Cottonmouth River. Reverend Johnson held his Baptism Jubilee here every Sunday, rain or shine.

Reverend Johnson was the county's most popular preacher ever. He started up his own Apostolic church, called it the Unified House of Prayer for All People of the Church on the Rock of the Apostolic Faith, and he made that church more exciting than cymbal monkeys. People called him Reverend King Daddy Johnson for all the regalia he wore, and some said he was a direct descendent of John the Baptist.

They also said that women, upon first meeting him, often mistook him for a celebrity, though that celebrity could be anyone from Cary Grant to Nat King Cole. All they saw was how handsome he was, and only later came to realize he had a powerful handsome voice to match. Some of those women got baptized up to eight or nine times a year.

Moses Jefferson showed up at the jubilee on a June afternoon. It was overcast and steaming hot that day. His father said he'd have to feed the chickens chipped ice to keep them from laying hardboiled eggs, and Moses believed him because he couldn't have been older than six.

He arrived at the river alone, had gone to dodge the heat, but Reverend Johnson took him in all the same. He held Moses' nose, said his preacher words—in Jesus' name, halleluiah—and eased the boy back under the surface.

Those who saw it offer few variations in their accounts of what happened next. The river churned around Reverend Johnson until he seemed to lose his balance for a moment. Then he yanked his arms out of the water, raised them high above his head, empty handed. He dropped to his knees and scrambled up toward the lake, which everyone else thought odd, since the river flowed from the lake and therefore would carry the boy in the other direction. Those with the wherewithal dived in searching for the boy, some following the current, fewer following Reverend Johnson. None emerged with any success.

Moses saw it differently. He saw the preacher's hand nearing his face, and he kept his eyes open. He saw the sky as he tilted back, and then the water wash it out. Next thing he saw, he says, was a torrent of snakes, like anacondas, swarming around him and pulling him upriver at a speed he hadn't felt since jumping out of a hayloft. The world went bright with dizzying colors, then shut down black.

Some hours later, when the heat of the day hit full steam, two fishermen on Cottonmouth Spit spotted him on the island in Cottonmouth Lake. Flat out on his back and eyes wide open, Moses appeared to be staring at the sun. They mistook him for drowned because of the milky film over his eyes. However, as they approached, he sat up and spoke: "Preacher's son is gonna die tonight."

Now Reverend King Daddy Johnson didn't have but one son. His name was Noah. This troubled Moses because he and Noah were best friends. Yet Moses knew what he'd seen in his mind's eye while laid out on that island: Reverend Johnson in an empty church, his head pressed against a short casket, sobbing to Jesus about why his son was called home so early in life.

So it came with much confusion and relief when Noah

stopped by to visit Moses the next day. Reverend Johnson had sent him to check on his condition, to see if the blindness was holding. It was, and Moses seemed to understand it wasn't about to go away. He told Noah about his vision. Noah assured him he was healthy as ever. Weird thing though, he added, the Hurston boy, Neal, died in his sleep last night.

The second vision came a week later. Hit him at the breakfast table and set him screaming. It was very much like the first, only the preacher cried harder.

The next day his classmate Willie Pete got tore up by Jerimiah dogs.

Visions didn't stop there, either. They plagued Moses throughout the summer, each one the same except for the preacher's level of distress. Folks around Calloway took note of Moses' visions. They also noticed how Reverend Johnson failed to hold Baptism Jubilee for three weeks straight, walked around in shambles instead. And of course no one failed to miss the way boys around Stillwater kept dying.

After Willie Pete, it was Clarkston Hines. Fell out of a tree. Then one of the Mason boys fell under his own mule plow. Then it was the Harrington twins, Harold and Lawrence, one three days after the other. Swarm of hornets and bad ham salad, respectively.

The final vision of death came the day after the dead boys' fathers ran Reverend Johnson out of town. They were furious with him, but others were sad to see him go. The women were particularly affected. Moses could sense their despair and decided to keep it to himself when he saw death coming.

"I might give someone a heads up if they ask," he says now, "but only if it's natural. If it's a son who's about to lose a father, I might say something, but not the other way around."

This is true more often than it isn't. Some people who never asked say he saved their lives with a subtle warning. Some people who begged to know didn't learn when their time was up until it was too late. Moses explains, "If it looks like the hammer of God might strike you down before your iron's hot, there's nothing you can do about it. No point in telling you. Instead, I'll give you the Standard. It's the best thing for you."

The Standard is any vague message about getting right with Jesus. It might be a line out of a book of epigrams. It might sound like a bumper sticker. It tells you about following the straight and narrow road or opening yourself to the Holy Spirit. His favorite is this: "Never race your shadow unless you're running toward The Light." That basically means if you got some darkness in your past, don't follow it around. Put it past you, find forgiveness and run after God. The key word is run, *because if you hear Moses tell you to run, that means you don't have much time left.*

Moses never enjoys telling folks when their time is up. He prefers to find ways to let them live longer, happier lives. If he can, he'd rather advise you on predicaments and the best way to get out of them. He can tell you how to dodge a fight you're about to lose. He can tell you how to bet on a fight and win. He can tell you what to eat or drink to avoid an illness heading your way. He can recoup debts from people you didn't know owed you anything. He'll tell you when's a good time to get married and when to lock up your daughters. He'll warn you of ponds with tainted waters.

"Still, most folk come asking about when they're going to pass. They don't care so much how or why or what happens after that. They just want to know when." He says this while sitting in the darkest corner of his shotgun house. All his lights are

> out, all his curtains drawn. *A ray of sunlight slants through the open door. Moses' door is always open, and when you walk in, first thing you see is a hand-painted sign that reads: When life shuts all the doors in your face, God opens a window somewhere.*
>
> *In Moses Jefferson's case, it was an eye. An eye that sees where God opened a window for you.*

CAL IS STANDING by the railroad tracks that cross the road to Calloway. He's got a bucket of orange paint and he's painting the post of a railroad crossing sign. Painting it orange. I pull over to tell him there's some paint Mr. Patil wants him to pick up. He pauses, mid-brushstroke, nods, then goes on painting.

I'm not comfortable telling him he's got work to do. I don't even like addressing my elders by their first name. But the fact is he's been a dim old man for as long as I can remember and nobody knows what his full name is. I try to be nice and look out for him best I can. When other kids took to throwing rocks at him for fun, I did my best to stop them—even when my mama said I need to stay away from the crazy coot and let kids be kids.

I'd like to get him to paint something that needs painting, like the motel or Moses Jefferson's place, but that seems like too much to ask. Last one to paint Mr. Jefferson's home was a fixit man from Odium. He painted the whole house in tar and told Mr. Jefferson it was sky blue. Mr. Jefferson knew different from the smell. He didn't care. Said it kept the place darker. Said it wouldn't need another coat in his lifetime, either. Besides, if Cal painted the motel or the house, he'd likely spend the next seven days running into the walls.

I once painted a big red eye in a red triangle on the side of Mr. Jefferson's place. I got the design from the All-Seeing Eye on the back of a dollar bill. I thought it would be an appropriate sign for his business and he agreed. Still, for all the mysterious things he knows, he can't tell me why there's an All-Seeing Eye on the back of the dollar bill.

He's smoking a Prince Edward when I walk in his house. It mixes with the tar fumes and the cologne he wears—Jockey Club—and creates a smell that's not entirely unpleasant, if only because this is the way his house has always smelled and I've always enjoyed coming here. I like messing with the trinkets people bring him to make into charms. Engagement rings, fishing lures, harmonicas, cigarette cases, stickpins, chicken feet, postage stamps. People will bring in anything to make it luckier. Mr. Jefferson stores them away in mason jars and, when he gets around to it, he'll say the words that come to him or bury them in holy dirt or whatever it is he needs to do to impart some special power upon them. Sometimes people ask him to put a curse on things, usually eyeglasses and lipstick, but he won't work that way. Says he can, but he won't.

He says to me when I walk in, "Took you so long, boy?"

"Sorry, Mr. Jefferson. We had snakes in the pool again."

He coughs out a laugh. "That time of year already? You know I got something to keep them away. A handy little paste you can spread around the perimeter."

"That's kind of you, Mr. Jefferson, but—"

"But you enjoy the scooping of the snakes." We go through this every year. "How's Mina doing? She helping you out?"

"Yeah, she's good. She asked about you."

"What'd you tell her?"

"That you're still blind."

He's quiet for a moment, then says, "Could've told her better than that."

I shrug, like that's supposed to tell him anything.

He's sitting in an overstuffed chair behind an oak table so big I can't figure out how he got it in the house. It's aged so bad it looks like tarnished silver. Jelly jars and open mail cover the greater part of the surface. And on the end nearest to me, there's a Gideon's Bible. I ask Mr. Jefferson if he stole it from our motel.

He blows smoke in my general direction. He says, "Naw, some fool left it as payment this morning."

I pick it up, examine it closer. Sure does look like one from our motel, except there's a hundred dollar bill marking a passage in Leviticus, somewhere around 21:20. I know better than to read it to Mr. Jefferson. It doesn't seem appropriate, this passage where God tells Moses that no man with crushed testicles or a defect in his sight can offer the bread of God. Instead I ask him, "That all he left?"

"Said that's all he had. Must've been in sorry shape if all he could leave for payment was a stolen Bible."

I tell him, "I wonder if he knew about this hundred dollar bill tucked inside."

Mr. Jefferson leans forward and says, "Hundred dollar? Bring it here."

I do, and he stuffs it in his vest pocket. He says, "Now take a look at this." He holds out a cigar box. "Noah tried to offer me a box of colored pencils as payment for a reading."

Noah never did die. I don't think I mentioned that in my report on Moses Jefferson. He came back to Calloway to run a boneyard. As for his father, Reverend Johnson, no one in Stillwater ever saw him again.

"Noah said they was some really pretty colors. Said they'd brighten the place up, if I ever got to drawing. Told him, 'Much as you owe me, they best be magic pencils, the kind I can draw me some eyes that work.'"

I inspect the pencils. "I don't think these will do the trick."

"Probably all graphite, ain't they."

"No, they're colored pencils all right."

"Good colors?"

"Well, yeah. But the thing is, they're all red pencils, Mr. Jefferson. Nice shade of red, though. Like a raisin box."

"S'marvelous. I'll draw me a red heifer."

"You could do that. Except, well, red heifers aren't really red."

"What?"

"Red heifers. They're generally brown," I tell him. "Sort of reddish brown, I guess."

"For real? Heifers can't be red like stop signs and fire engines?"

"No sir."

"You sure about that?" Now he's just messing with me.

I go along with it. "Could draw them that way if you want. I'll help you."

"Naw, I got a better idea. I want you to draw up a sign for me. I got insights into things some people need to know about. I'll call them out and you write them down in big red letters. You do that for me?"

He tells me to pull a poster from the wall, one that announces the Weaver-Tate heavyweight bout in Knoxville. He has me write on the back: *Things Revealed to You after You Die.*

I ask him, "This a new service you're offering?"

"These are just examples."

His first example: *The location of every buried treasure, dinosaur bone, lost heirloom, gold nugget, and precious stone you almost dug up.*

I ask him, "Someone about to die?"

"You know better than to ask me that." That means there is, and I need to figure out the proper way of asking who, because if he's not telling me, it's someone I know.

The identity of every caller who ever hung up on you, and the nature of every call you missed.

I pull the poster closer to the door so I can see what I'm writing.

The right answers to questions on tests that claimed, "There are no wrong answers."

The mistakes you repeated most frequently.

The outcome of every date you turned down.

"Mr. Jefferson?"

He clears his throat and says, "Now why is it you still address me as Mr. Jefferson? You're a man now, been so for a while."

"You know, I was just thinking about that on my way over here."

"I know you was," he says in that all-knowing tone of his. He shifts on his wooden chair and lowers his tone: "Listen, I think of you as a son. You know that. But it won't hurt to call me Moses. Got that?"

Of course I do, but I still see him as Mr. Jefferson. It's about respect.

I ask him: "Did you know that Lester Current's in town?"

Look on his face tells me he didn't know that. He doesn't answer, just serves up more examples.

Your every unwitting statement that offended someone else.

All the things people said behind your back.

The net value, in real dollars, of everything you took that didn't belong to you.

The net value, in real dollars, of everything others took away from you.

The actual number of hours you spent wasting time.

What you could have done to prove your mettle.

The contests you would have won, had you entered.

A profound knowledge of every species that went extinct in your lifetime.

"How many more of these you got?"

"Endless," he tells me. "But I'm about through for now."

"You're about out of paper, too."

"You write too big."

I tell him, "Hey, I got one. How about, 'The infomercial products that would have dramatically improved your life.'"

He scrunches up his lips and shakes his head.

I try again. "All right. How about, 'The end of every story you didn't have time to finish.' How about that one?"

"Yeah, that's a good one. Write that down. And here's the last one."

He has me write: *All the demons you should've faced when you were alive.*

That last one rattles me. "How did you come up with that?"

He cocks his head and nudges his hat to a rakish angle. He's so good at that. I need to work on that move. He says, "You understand why the Reverend King Daddy Johnson got run out of town?"

I hitch my eyes on his face for a glimpse of what he might be getting at, but it's coming back blank. "That's ancient history."

"Happened in my lifetime. You heard a firsthand account from me. It can't get much clearer than that."

"Well then, sure I understand."

He shakes his head like I don't. "All it takes to be a father is a percolation of the loins, but it takes perseverance and a gut load of patience to raise a child right. You understand that?"

"Sure I do." Though I'm not sure where he's going with this. Maybe it has something to do with Sonali and me.

I REMEMBER ONE time it snowed. It snowed, here in Stillwater. It snowed big.

Sonali woke first and tore all through it without bothering to wake the rest of us. What stirred me up was Mr. Patil yelling for her to put on some clothes. That stirred me up fast. I leapt from my bed to the window and my first sight of the day was that of Sonali in a long red T-shirt. She danced circles around the pool. She threw her head back and her hands in the air like she was receiving the Holy Ghost. And all around her, the snow kept falling. Big white chunky flakes. Grits in a fan.

Wind whipped her hair around, lifted her T-shirt to the top of her thighs. Her father yelled again: "Sonali! Cease your ebullience and come in at once!" He stood in the open door, as though fearing snow, and Sonali's jubilant dance seemed to mock him.

"Sonali! Come inside at once! I forbid your dancing in the snow like some kind of dancing snow monkey!"

It wasn't her usual, graceful Indian dance either. None of those delicate swirls and intricate hand gestures. This was disco. High kicks and suggestive gyrations. Solid Gold dancing. Saturday night fever on a Sunday morning in Stillwater.

Mr. Patil retreated into the motel, suddenly realizing a terrible truth: He had an American teenager for an eldest daughter. Only then did she come in from the cold.

She said, "Good morning, Bapa," and kissed him on the cheek like nothing happened.

I scrambled into a navy turtleneck, maroon velour V-neck, and a pair of green Toughskins. I put on my official Miami Dolphins jacket, turquoise with orange vinyl sleeves. Tube socks to match. I was ten years old and proud that I'd picked all my own clothes from the PTA Thrift Shop in Odium, but mortified when my mama made me wear mittens and a pompom hat.

Mina waited for me outside my door, marching in place like she had to pee. Arati busied herself in the parking lot, searching in vain for two identical snowflakes.

By now the snow was deeper than my hi-top sneakers.

Unsure what to do next, the three of us ran amok in the streets of Pullman. Cal staggered around the post office, looking for something to paint. Couple of older kids—Norman Horton and Jimmy Higgenbothem—chucked snowballs at him. I was tempted to join in, but found Mina a better target. She fired back with deadly accuracy, and with Arati as her backup, chased me all the way to Pal Wiggly's Grill.

That's where Sonali found us. From the wild look in her eyes, I figured she was up for another rousing game of cowboys and Indians. Guess who always got to be an Indian. Me, that's who. Along with Mina. Sonali and Arati always made Mina and me be the Indians.

But Sonali wasn't thinking about cowboys and Indians now. Instead she uttered the most shocking words: "Let's get a Wiggly Burger."

If she had said, Let's steal a car, or Let's smoke drugs, I might've shrugged it off. But she wanted a burger. Beef. Meat from a cow. This was certainly the most forbidden fruit.

Mr. Patil was lenient in many aspects of dietary restrictions, considering what he fed himself. In his perfect world, we'd all be eating lentils and fiddlehead and chard. And curries until our eyes bled. But he didn't force that on us. Sometimes he even grilled chicken for us. Good chicken, too, usually with a mango chutney glaze.

He had to let us eat pig meat. You'd starve to death if you couldn't eat pig products in the cafeterias of Stillwater County schools. It'd be pigs in a blanket one day, barbecue the next, then country ham, followed by smoked sausages. Add to that pork rinds, chitterlings, knuckles and other tasty porcine treats, and you begin to get the picture of the local fare. So he let us eat these things because he knew if we didn't, we'd be regarded as freaks and never get invited to any pig pickins.

But beef. No way. That was understood. He didn't have to tell us not to eat cow meat any more than he had to tell us not to feast on the still-beating heart of a newborn leper.

If a guest wanted to throw some steaks on his barbecue pit, that was fine. But he'd round up his daughters first to protect them from the smell, and he'd have me scrape and soak the rack when the abomination was over. I hated that job. Made me feel unclean, like an Untouchable.

But now this, Sonali's husky whisper: "Let's get a Wiggly Burger." The words filled my stomach with a queasy sense of danger. Worse, she dared me to go into Pal Wiggly's Grill and place the order myself.

"We'll be waiting right out here." She said it like there'd be a reward.

I skulked into Pal Wiggly's Grill and I don't remember much after that, except that the place seemed to list like an old pirate ship. And when I made it back outside, incriminating evidence in a paper bag, the girls were gone.

I was about having a heart attack when I heard: "*Ssst!* Cyrus!" It was Mina, beckoning me from the corner of the building. I followed her around back.

"What was it like?" Sonali asked with morbid curiosity.

I couldn't describe the shame then, but I thought of it seven years later when Mina goaded me into buying beer using Norman Horton's drivers license.

"No big deal," I told her.

The four of us squatted down between the dumpster and the wall. I unwrapped the burger and set it down in the middle. Sonali dared me to take the first bite. I did. It reminded me of the time she made me eat clay. It was a flavor I knew I'd never enjoy.

Mina took the burger next. She closed her eyes and bit right in. Covered her mouth and sucked in air like it was too hot to eat.

Then came Arati's turn. She lifted the bun and sniffed at it. Poked at the pickle. She took a bite. Chewed once. Then again. She filled her mouth with snow to wash it down.

Sonali snatched the burger away from her and took the biggest bite of all. Not only that, she bit over the part where I'd taken a bite. That part of the burger where my mouth had just been. My heart skipped and my head swirled. To me, at that moment there, it was like we'd had our first kiss. I wanted to return the affection, even if it meant taking that nasty burger back and biting over her bite, but Sonali stopped mid chew. She gagged and threw the burger down. She couldn't swallow. She ended up spitting bits of Wiggly Burger all over me. I swatted at it the way I would with yellow jackets. She covered her mouth and a look of horrendous guilt washed over her face like she might cry. She scooped snow over the burger until it was well buried.

With her clean hand, she pushed her hair out of her face. She said, "We did it. Now let's never speak of it again." She made us pinky swear on it. The four of us, huddled around a buried half-eaten burger between a dumpster and a cinderblock wall, our pinkies interlocked. Mine curled around hers, mostly. We had a secret together.

The snow continued to fall, hushing the world and stilling the moment.

It seemed as though life would stay this way forever.

Sonali scrambled to her feet and took off running. I chased her, lobbing snowballs at her as fast as I could scoop them up. Arati and Mina did the same behind me. Sonali's legs, near twice the length of mine, carried her to the motel in half the time it took the rest of us. There she broke down crying. She shattered her solemn oath and blurted her confession to her father. I wasn't there to hear the whole thing. Arati, Mina and I clamored through the door just in time to hear her say, "Bapa! Cyrus bought it for us!"

Mina whispered, "Oh good God, she is such a snitch."

But Mr. Patil turned, looked dead at me and said, "You are not my son."

Well, I knew that. But it still hurt, way he said it.

CAL'S STUMPING THROUGH the tall weeds in the ditch alongside the road. I figure he's heading for the motel. I'd offer him a ride, but he's got orange stripes all up and down his body. Guess he couldn't wait for the paint to dry before he started running into the post.

People hold different ideas on what makes him the way he is. Some say he got struck by lightning six times in one afternoon. Others contend that someone paid Mr. Jefferson to put some wicked mojo on him, but I know that can't be right.

Mr. Patel's got a different story about Cal. He told me this story when I first got my learner's permit. I was driving along in Mr. Patel's Pontiac station wagon, the same one I drive now, because he gave it to me on my sixteenth birthday. He sat in the passenger seat gripping the dashboard and the door handle. We passed Cal stumping along a ditch like he's doing now, only without the orange stripes. I asked Mr. Patil what Cal's deal was. Mr. Patil said he brought it on himself, said he was out carousing one night, probably drunk too, and looking for property to damage.

He said, "From what I am understanding, he was motoring out of Odium like nobody's business. You must be knowing that at the time, I had a series of billboard advertisements along the road that is coming out of Odium in this direction. They were bright yellow signs with big red letters. I painted them myself and installed them along the road like the old Burma Shave signs. The first one said, *Honk your horn.* The next one said, *Ring our bell.* And then, *When you arrive...* And finally, *at Dixie Court Motel!* with a big Dixie flag under the words. I know it is sounding silly now, but at the time it was very clever advertising. Many people said so, but I don't believe our friend Mr. Cal agreed. It is appearing that he took it upon himself and his motor vehicle to remove these signs. First, he crashed through the one that said, *Honk your horn.* Then he proceeded to run down the one that kindly requested, *Ring our bell.* He did not stop there. Oh no. In fact, he accelerated right through the one that stated, *When you arrive* and continued straight for the one saying *at Dixie Court Motel.* Unfortunately for Mr. Cal, this last sign was the cleverest of all, because I painted it on the side of an abandoned house that had been painted entirely with black pitch. At night, it appeared to be a freestanding sign. Mr. Cal must have certainly believed it was, for he plowed through the stars and the bars on the flag of Dixie, and did not stop until the roof caved in on him. However, you cannot fully blame him. After all, he was merely a teenager at the time. Like you, an American teenager. Excepting that you, I can happily say, are not so much the rebel, only that you certainly drive like one."

So I'm not really sure what's wrong with Cal, but I suspect it's something psychological.

There's no red Jaguar XJR in the parking lot at the Dixie Court Motel. There is a pack of teenagers unloading coolers from a pickup truck. Kids from neighboring counties like to come here to party, especially when they're not of legal age. Sometimes they'll come in couples, and the girl will wait in the car while the boy checks in. It's the same for older couples who aren't married to each other. But now we got a truckload of rowdy teens and no sign of Lester Current.

Mr. Patil tells me he hasn't been in all day. He tosses me the room key to see if straightening needs to be done.

I know he's not in, but I knock on the door anyway and call out, "Housekeeping."

No reply.

I turn the key and creak the door open. Can't believe Lester Current made a mess this big in the fifteen minutes he was here without the aid of a depth charge. Bed's unmade, sheets crinkled. Trashcan knocked over, contents spilling out. Box of BC headache powders. Empty. Prescription bottle for Xanax. Empty. Flask of Old Crow. Empty. Crumpled pack of Chesterfields. Left the ashtray half full, though.

He didn't unpack his suitcases. Looks more like they sprung open and spewed out his wardrobe with the force of a catapult. Khakis and Oxfords strewn across the chair and table. Ties and underwear draped on the lampshades. He's a boxer man with a penchant for blue silk.

Wet towel on the floor. Phone off the hook and unplugged. Complimentary items—postcard, notepad, pen—missing. Phonebook and Bible, missing.

I'm checking out the toiletry items he unloaded into the drawer of the nightstand when I hear something like a doorbell chime. I about jump out of my skin before remembering our rooms don't come equipped with doorbells. I crawl across the floor to check the deep pockets of his suitcase for the source of the chime. That's when I see the power cord running from the wall outlet to the mound of clothes on the table.

A quick excavation reveals some kind of computer. Laptops, they're called. Mina's got one. There's a message on the screen. An e-mail message. It says:

LC
2 hrs past ded. Need something from you NOW. Crap out on your final assnmnt and I will crucify you.
-Ed

This is bad. I'm inclined to respond to Ed with a decent explanation, but have none to offer. Maybe I could tell him that Lester Current is out with the mayor of Odium and getting the key to the town. But then, who am I?

Outside, the kids with the pickup truck are throwing bottles in the parking lot and falling over laughing. Some nights that's the best entertainment we got in Pullman. Smashing bottles. It can get old fast.

Mr. Patil is sick to death of it. He never used to allow the likes of them here. Not when we were younger.

A shadow passes by the window. I press up against the wall and peek through the curtain. It's Mina. I hiss at her.

"Cy?" She presses her face to the screen. "What happened in there? What are you doing?"

I explain the crisis at hand. To my complete astonishment, she responds with a solution that will make everything all better. At least for the moment:

Current Adventures: Of Preachers and Creatures
by Lester Current

NOAH JOHNSON WAS born the son of a preacher man, who himself was born the son of a preacher man. By all family accounts, Noah was destined to be a preacher man, too. He accepted the calling early in life and learned to read the Good Book in Greek, Latin and Hebrew by the age of fourteen.

All those years of studying the Word of God, Noah was seized by a divine discontent. He couldn't shake his passion for a place he had grown to love more than heaven.

That place was Jerimiah's Junkyard, an auto salvage lot on the outskirts of Calloway.

He played there as a child, and helped Jerimiah scavenge, search for and sort out car parts in exchange for unlimited access to this Golgotha of automotive graveyards.

"It was a city of the dead for cars," Noah recalls. "But each piece here, see, is waiting for resurrection, for new life. Jesus told us not to put new wine into old bottles, but he didn't say not to put old parts into new cars. That's what Jerimiah always told me."

But Jerimiah passed away when his protégé was merely sixteen, leaving him in sole possession the legacy that was his scrap heap and the dogs that protected it. Noah then knew he had to choose between salvage and salvation.

He didn't hesitate.

"First thing I did," Noah says as he stacks batteries in a corrugated metal shed, "is yank down the old sign and paint up a new one. One that said, 'Noah's Boneyard.'"

Then he got to work on building the thing he'd been constructing in his mind for half his life. He rounded up hubcaps and bumpers, alternators and axles, grilles and pistons. He took a blowtorch to the heap and created his own ark. Noah's Ark, replete with chrome animals. It got to be pretty famous. So famous, in fact, that famous people traveled for miles just to see it.

"Sammy Davis, Jr. was in awe. He wanted to buy a pair of animals and wouldn't leave until I let him go with the ostriches."

Noah has since replaced the ostriches, and added several dozen other species to the menagerie. Currently, he's working on those that face extinction in our lifetime. He'll look at the fender of a Plymouth Satellite and see an Ethiopian wolf. He'll look into the rust-mottled hood of a Corvair and find the coat of an ocelot. And Dodge Dart taillights are good for the eyes of a variety of lemurs.

"I won't live long enough to build them all. It takes more than a lifetime to recreate Creation. But if I did, I'd still have enough materials left over to build and fill a second ark."

He says he's got enough chrome alone to mirror Earth. "That's a good thing, too," he adds. "Everything looks better with chrome on it."

Asked if he ever worries about thieves in the night coming after his precious art, Noah laughs. "That won't happen. Not as long as I've got the Jerimiah dogs."

Jerimiah dogs are a special kind of dog bred by Jerimiah himself. He bred them for two purposes: Killing intruders and killing other dogs. They kept his place secure and made him a small fortune in Stillwater's dogfight circuit.

"They ain't like no other creature on earth. More hateful than a rattlesnake on a red whiskey rage."

Over the years, Noah let the breed die out. He fixed the ones he could afford to fix and kept the rest apart best he could. All that's left now are Ahab and Jezebel, and they're too high in years to produce any pups. "I reckon this is one pair I'll keep off the ark," he says without a hint of remorse. "I'd put them down myself, but can't bring myself to the task. I just hope when these beasts go, they'll take all the hate in the world with them."

For now these wolfish beasts tend to Noah's unusual flock of animals. They'll protect it well until they're gone. As for Noah, when he's gone, he expects that kudzu will flood in and drown his project.

"Then maybe my boneyard will provide a hospitable environment for God's true creatures," Noah says.

And so the son of a preacher man, (who himself was born the son of a preacher man,) finds redemption not so much in rehashing the Word of God, but in recycling the metal of men, and in the end makes the world a more beautiful place.

I'VE CORRALLED THE pickup-truck kids back into their room and left them with a stern warning. Told them to knock it off and pipe down is what I did. Maybe that was too harsh.

I've also hung up Lester Current's clothes and stowed his suitcases. I replaced the towels, phonebook and Bible, made the bed, emptied the ashtray, and took out the trash. Place looks decent now. I'm satisfied with it.

Mina's finished typing out my manuscript. She asks if I want to proof it once more. I tell her no, just send it. She does. With the push of a button, my manuscript on Noah's boneyard, previously rotting in a notebook under my mattress, has crossed cyberspace, as they call it, and is now in view of the chief editor of *American Ethic*. Only now it's got Lester Current's name on it.

This was Mina's idea. I liked it at first, but now I'm not so sure.

We sit. We wait. Nothing comes back.

I ask her, "Now what?"

"I suppose you ought to go out and find Lester." We both turn to the nightstand to check the time on the clock, but that's missing, too. Hadn't noticed that. Doesn't matter. It's already dark out. Bats cartwheel through the air and the tree frogs sound like kittens in distress.

Mina says, "Best wait until morning, though."

"But what if Lester Current comes back tonight and finds out what we've done?"

"How's he gonna know it was us?"

"What, he'll think kind little journalistic gnomes broke in here and wrote a column for him?"

"If he does find out it was us, he should thank us. It's good writing." Seeing a proud smirk cracking at the corner of my lips, she adds, "Better than his usual drivel anyway."

"But what if Ed hates it?" I ask. Mina rolls her eyes, heads for the door. I grab her wrist. "Sit tight," I tell her. "We need to wait for some feedback."

She pulls her arm free. "Don't talk to me like that. You ain't my daddy." Then she's pushing me toward the door. She's telling me, "If Lester doesn't come back tonight, look for him in the morning. I'll even help you. Heck, we can get Surya in here to sniff his clothes and hunt him down."

"Like that'll work." Surya's grown into a mat dog in that he's scarcely distinguishable from an oversized welcome mat. "He couldn't sniff out pork butt in a pig pen."

She shoves me out the door, locks it behind us. A breeze pushes the smell of almonds and apple butter around the motel. Got some beer stink in it, too, but otherwise it's a mighty fine breeze. It wraps her hair around her head, covering one eye. She leaves it that way and says, "Get some sleep, Cy. I'll be by in the morning."

IT'S LATE. I can't sleep.

My eyes keep darting around my room, at the love notes pulsing between two fireflies crawling up my window screen, at the moonlight reflecting off the pool and wiggling across my ceiling, at the face of Jesus lacquered onto a sanded piece of driftwood, at the glow-in-the-dark planets that came out of a box of Quisp cereal. I collected all nine and built the mobile with Mr. Patel's help. It was his idea to use the ceiling light fixture at the sun.

In my private solar system, the sun is a frosted square with etched-out designs that look like corn on the cob.

As much as I love my radiant planets, my eyes keep returning to a photograph on my nightstand. It shows Mr. Patil, my mama, Sonali, Arati, Mina, Surya and me. We're all standing in front of a backstop on the playground at Ephesus Elementary.

I remember when we had this picture made. It was the day Mr. Patil tried to teach us how to play this game called cricket.

He got out his willow bat with the cane handle. It looked like the paddle that the principal at Ephesus Elementary liked to display in his office. Then he stuck some stakes in the ground behind home and second base, all the while rattling off about a hundred laws of cricket. He told my mama to take the position as wicketkeeper. Mina was supposed to be the silly mid-off, Arati the slip, and Sonali got to take the deep fine leg, whatever that was.

He told me he was going to *bowl* the ball at me. He didn't. He chucked it right at my belly. Good thing it was a tennis ball or I'd have lost a rib.

After a few more throws like that, we turned mutinous and launched a baseball revolution. Five in the field with Surya as catcher against a rotating batter and three ghost-men. Rules are much easier in ghost-man baseball, even when your equipment is limited to a cricket bat and a slobbery tennis ball.

Sonali, of course, was beating us bad, with twenty runs to my twelve to Mina's ten to mama's six to Arati's five to Mr. Patel's zip. Still, I believed I could catch up with Sonali on my third up. But then wouldn't you know, with two outs and the bases loaded, Mina dived for a grounder and fired it to Surya to tag out my ghost-man heading home.

You can't tag out ghost-men. That's so basic a rule I shouldn't even have to say it, much less argue over it. But I did, and no one listened because the game had to be called off on account of Surya came up with his own game of chase-me.

In the picture, Surya still has the ball. Looks like he's gnawing on a naval orange. Mina's thrusting out her elbow to show off the strawberry she got while diving for that grounder. Arati's staring at her own feet, or maybe at some buttercups growing up between them, just like she did in left field all through the game. My mama's squeezing my shoulders like she's trying to hold me still.

Sonali liked to tease me about this picture. She said I looked like Chachi with a crewcut. I didn't mind that. Chachi was older than me back then, about the same age as Sonali, and he wasn't all bad looking. Joanie liked him well enough. Matter of fact, turned out she loved him, as the title of their own show would indicate. But Joanie never looked half as fine as Sonali. I know that now as well as I knew it then. You can tell by the way I'm looking at her in the picture. You'd think she was made out of candy, way I'm looking at her. But she's holding hands with her father, got her eyes cast up at him. I can see why and it still makes me jealous.

Mr. Patil is handsome in a rough-hewn way. He's structured like a timber-frame house, so pronounced are his skeletal features. His jaw, his forehead, his eye sockets—every bone appears to be held in place with solid joists. And his muscles, while not bulky, are just as evident. He stands tall and rigid like a flag post that could bear the weight of every banner in the world.

In the picture, his hair is styled like a Kennedy's. I've never known him to get a haircut, but not a strand on his head has changed since.

He always smells of mentholated shaving cream.

Put him in a suit and a city and he could pass for a hit man or a secret agent. I'm sure he could play either one, or maybe even an astronaut. I think that's why Sonali sometimes looked at him like he was some kind of movie star.

Sometime my mama looked at him that way.

My mama and Mr. Patil used to stay up late and talk about what they could do with the motel. I could hear them out by the pool, their voices scarcely a murmur over the sitar jangling from Mr. Patel's cassette player.

My mama leaned toward building an Indian-themed mini golf course around the motel. She was thinking Jungle Book characters throughout and a fiberglass Taj Mahal on the eighteenth green. She thought maybe we should all wear white turbans and carry scimitars. I liked her ideas, but every time she mentioned them, Mr. Patel's face turned like he was holding back a burp.

Mr. Patil envisioned what he called a holistic retreat. He'd start with opening the diner. He wanted it to look like a real American diner, but he would serve healthy Indian food. The diner sits on the sunny side of the parking lot, but it's too big a mess to think about restoring now. Mr. Patil should've got to that right after he chased the raccoons out of the rooms, but instead he got sidetracked raising kids.

He also talked of spa treatments. Turkish baths and massage parlors. My mama warned him against that, said it would bring in the wrong clientele. She never said why. I'm still not sure what a holistic retreat is, either, but I liked the idea better than my mama's.

Sometimes Mr. Patil would moan on about how much he missed his wife. My mama would tell him it was for the best, her leaving. She'd say Mohini didn't deserve a man like him.

But my mama wouldn't say much about the loves of her past. Didn't hardly mention Lester Current unless I begged her to. Turns out it wasn't much of a relationship, really. She was involved with another boy at the time.

His name was Quiet Bear, and he was a renegade.

It's said that he was the last of the Gingaskin Indians, the only one to escape the Great Peat Fire of 1963-65. He never attended classes in Stillwater County schools, just showed up on game days. And they let him play because Stillwater never lost when Quiet Bear was on the court, mat, field or track.

My mama said he lived up to his name, mainly the quiet part, but he was also strong like a bear and fiercely attractive. My mama said, "He was handsome in a way that girls find wild ponies handsome and go begging for one every Christmas."

My mama would watch him at every game, meet and match. That's when she noticed Lester Current, at his senior wrestling match. My mama was just a sophomore then, but she felt sorry for him all the same because Quiet Bear brutalized the poor boy. Put a hurting on him but good. She saw Lester Current on the verge of tears as he ran from the gym.

She followed him outside. She found him kneeling in the parking lot, sweat streaming down his face and neck, steam billowing from his spiky black hair. He looked like a Greek statue, she said. A sweaty Greek statue with spiky black hair. My mama, on the other hand, was what you might call a ravishing blonde with Audrey Hepburn eyes. I don't like to describe my own mother that way, but that's what folks would tell me.

So they hit it off pretty much right away. My mama never went into many details about it. They stole away into the night and the next morning she was certain of my presence. That's about all the detail I need.

She said he called her often, and she would tell him all about me. About when she could feel me kicking in her stomach and what my first words were and how I looked more like him every day. He promised to come visit us and take us on assignments with him. But the more successful he got, the less she heard from him. By the time I was old enough to hold a phone, the only way we'd know he was still alive was from the columns he wrote.

As for Quiet Bear, he just wasn't the same after her night with Lester Current. She no longer wanted anything to do with him. So he just kind of faded away.

But then, all the charm of Stillwater kind of faded away for my mama. She had to get out for a while, see the world. So at the tender age of three, I escorted my mama on a fantastic journey:

My Mama's Story
by Cyrus Slant

GLORIA GRACE SLANT *walked out of Hunters with a red suitcase in her hand and her son on her back. She was nineteen, closer to twenty, and had seen every movie ever made that featured Audrey Hepburn in Paris.*

So Gloria Grace was going to Paris. She would get there even if she had to swim the whole way with her son on her back.

The morning they left Hunters was a cold one. Cold enough for a sweater and maybe a hat. She walked on the sunny side of the canal road, but as she crossed the Stillwater County line clouds piled in low and the road darkened. What's worse, she noticed, was that a man had been following her ever since she stepped out of her yard.

He seemed a familiar figure, and yet a menacing one. He trailed closer, close enough to telegraph his ill intent with a slight gurgling growl. She turned to face the man. All she could make out was his terrible teeth and his yellowing eyes.

Above him, tree limbs extended clumps of Spanish moss, dangling them like the shaggy heads of slain pirates. Gloria Grace quickened her steps. A cold wind fingered her collar and, at once, the clouds split open and rain fell in fat gobs. Mist thickened along the swamp's tree line on the far side of the canal.

The man closed in, his footsteps out of synch with the raindrops.

Gloria Grace worked up a trot, but the suitcase and her son weighed her down. She feared looking back, certain she was now within the man's reach. She cut left, attempting to hurdle the canal. Instead, her heels slid down the muddy banks. She fell back on her son, and the both of them slipped away into the murky water. Immediately, she released her suitcase, twisted round and pushed her boy above the surface. She did not emerge until she reached the opposite bank.

Her suitcase floated away, back toward Stillwater. And the man, he crouched down, as though ready to pounce across the canal. Gloria

Grace scooped up her son and dashed into the mist and muck of Odium Swamp.

She sloshed and slogged her way to nightfall. When impossible darkness swallowed the trees, she followed the greenish lights of incandescent swamp gas. Quicker and dimmer than heat lightning, the ghostly flashes coaxed her to higher ground. She collapsed on a turtleback mound, on dry earth that smelled of burnt hair. She curled herself around her son and crashed headlong into sleep.

Daylight and hunger woke her son crying. His face took on a purplish bloom because of the cold.

She looked up. A black canopy blotted out the sky. She looked round. Found herself surrounded by six black pillars, all mossy on the north side. She realized then where they were. Underneath a swamp shack, the kind trappers use.

She gathered her son on her back and climbed the cypress boards nailed to the front post. She unlatched the door and crawled inside. It smelled of pitch and paraffin. A hammock stretched between the north and west walls. She set her son there. An ammo crate underneath was stocked with shotgun shells, can opener, mosquito netting, sewing kit, gauze bandages, rope, compass, skinning knife, tackle box, wool blanket, harmonica and waterproof matches.

Steel traps in a variety of bite sizes hung on the walls, along with hip waders and last year's calendar. Pinup girls falling out of their dresses to climb on shiny cars. Gloria Grace tore it down, rolled it up and stuffed it in a potbelly stove the size of a beach ball.

Breakfast that morning came from rusted cans without labels. She figured it for potted meat and strained squash. Could've just as well been honey-cured ham and pumpkin pie, hungry as she was. Her son, however, couldn't hold it down.

For the next hundred days—give or take, hard to tell since she burned the calendar—Gloria Grace labored every waking minute in the capture and cooking of animals. She trapped squirrel, muskrat, *swamp rat, fox, rabbit, coon, mink and otter. The son learned to skin the animals with expert precision, but he preferred fishing for black crappie and catfish. Sometimes he hooked bream. Bass when he was lucky. Most of all, he enjoyed foraging naked through the great wilderness morass for blackberries and chive grass.*

In those rare moments of idleness, sitting on an ammo box with her son in her lap, Gloria Grace believed she had everything she needed right here. This was better than Paris, she decided. She was happy. Her son was happy. Acted feral at times, but happy. And so they stayed for another hundred days, give or take.

She wore mink. He caught crawdads. It seemed the world would stay this way forever.

On a late summer night, when swamp gas flashed with volcanic intensity, the trapper returned to his swamp shack. He found his walls and floors coated in pelts. He found mother and son sleeping in his hammock. Without a word, he raised his shotgun and drove them out into the night.

She fled with her son at her side and a mink stole under her shirt, wrapped around her belly.

The two of them held hands as they trounced through the dark swamp. They followed the greenish lights, as she had done two hundred days earlier. Sunlight assisted their ascent out of a muddy ditch alongside the canal road. There she knelt, catching her breath at the edge of steaming asphalt.

A shadow fell over them.

Gloria Grace looked up. The sun scorched a dark silhouette from the lone figure. She couldn't make out his face, but she recognized his teeth and eyes.

She bowed her head, exhausted. The shadow receded. When she looked up again, all she saw was a red suitcase.

She told her son to climb up on her back. He obeyed. She picked up the suitcase and walked back into Stillwater.

THAT'S THE WAY my mama would tell it, so many nights as she tucked me into bed. I often asked her to take me back to that shack. She often said she would. Then one night I made her promise me. She did. But the next day, she died.

Tuesday

I WAKE, CLEAR in body and mind, to that smell, that sweet flavorful aroma gushing out of the thickets. It's powerful this morning. Smells like almond the way stinkbugs can smell like almond. Bitter almond, really, but the smell this morning has an apple cider tinge to it as well. Strong enough to make you a little queasy, like you ate your fill at a county fair and you can still smell sugar burning in the taffy pull.

I open my door to a stinging hot morning. Biting insects buzz, steam rolls off the blacktop. It rained last night. Rained hard, but I must've slept all through it. Difficult to imagine how, what with branches down and downspouts still gurgling.

Sky above is white hot, but clear on the horizon. Sunlight slants through the trees and hangs a halo over every leaf. Smells carry better in morning haze, and mixed in with the almond and apple is Mr. Patel's cooking. Curried eggs, I'm guessing. And cloves hint at strong hot tea. It chases off the sweet queasiness and restores my appetite.

I love days that start off this way.

Mina's waiting for me on the swing under a beech tree. Letters cut into the bark abbreviate a hundred love affairs. She's reading through my notebook. I ask her if she's checked Lester Current's e-mail yet. She has. Nothing but spam, mostly invitations to view pictures of lesbians. That's what she tells me. That and Lester Current's car still isn't here.

I ask her, "Where you reckon we ought to look for him?"

She shrugs. "How about we try Hunters? Could be he's gone there to look for your mother."

I get a cold shudder through my chest. "We go to Hunters and I'll have to go by Mrs. Harrington's, see if her water's getting high."

Mina's anticipated that. I know from her response. "All right by me. I wouldn't mind seeing that."

Doesn't happen that often, but no, it's not anything anybody should want to see any more than an open-casket funeral.

Mrs. Harrington is the mother of Harold and Lawrence, or Harry and Larry, as she calls them, the twins who died after Mr. Jefferson's vision. He couldn't have been older than six then. You'd think Mrs. Harrington would be shriveling into old age by now. She isn't.

Mrs. Harrington's hair is full and dark and healthy. She parts it down the middle and keeps it in a bun, like a librarian, but she dresses like a spy. All in black. Black beret. Black trousers. Black turtlenecks. Long black coats. Anything black, she'll wear, even in the summertime. She has skin like a brand new candle, the scented kind, and the posture of a giraffe. You wouldn't think she was half done with her forties.

Mina dials through the radio as we head for Hunters. She picks up a rockabilly tune from the college radio station in Dunes County. She cranks it up, beats on the dashboard like my car ain't beat up enough already. She's swinging her hair round like a wild woman out of control and singing along to words she doesn't know, singing about her broken heart drowning in a sea of flames.

She's got me tapping the wheel and driving a little faster than I should.

We pass the Hunters water tower, where graffiti from the class of '79 still shows through chalky blue paint. Turn left at Troll's Tavern, on past the ABC store to The Deer Hunters Bar and Grill. Once we reach Bub's Pub, it's a straight shot to Bluestone Road.

Mrs. Harrington is out in her yard when we turn onto Bluestone Road, and she sees us first, like she's been waiting for us all day. She runs in front of my station wagon, going, "Cyrus, honey! Oh, thank God you're here!"

I mash the brakes to keep from running her over. "Mrs. Harrington. How are you? You're looking younger every day." It's almost true, but I'm just telling her this to calm her down.

"Why thank you, Cyrus." She smiles. Teeth all bright, all there. But she's still trembling.

"You've been taking in the waters again, haven't you?"

She shrugs and looks away like she doesn't know what I'm talking about.

I tell her, "Government people haven't determined if it's safe. I've told you that before."

"Pshaw," she says. "I've been taking in the waters for sixty years. Can't hurt now to take in more."

"But they're getting high now, aren't they?"

She nods.

"And how's your bottle tree holding up?"

"Fine, except a couple broke off."

"You mend it?"

She shakes her head.

I feel a frown pulling at my jaw and sweat on my temple. Heat's building up in the idling car. Through the shimmering vapors over the hood, her house appears to be hopping and wiggling. Air's stock still, but her screen door is banging away. I tell her, "Let me go have a look."

She bows away as I park the car. The homes are nice on this block, better than any in Pullman. Lawns are mowed and shaded. Windows got screens. Not like they need them, because everyone keeps their windows shut. Central air units buzz from every backyard.

One house stands out, though. Shingles falling off the roof. Each wall a different hue of yellow. I see why right off. Cal's out front painting the picket fence a horrendous shade of cat pee.

I ask Mrs. Harrington who lives there.

She squints at me and says, "Nobody's lived there since your grandparents died."

"My grandparents?"

She takes my hand and squeezes my fingers. "You never met your grandparents, did you? Oh, they were an ornery couple."

"I don't really remember much about them on account of I was so young when my mama and I left Hunters."

"Yes, you were young," she tells me, releasing my fingers. "So young you were just starting to dent out your mama's belly."

"No, actually, I was three when we left. My mama told me so."

She shakes her head. "Three months inside the womb, maybe four. I remember clear as day. She walked out with her red suitcase and didn't look back. Her parents left the day after, let their house fall into ruins. Didn't want nothing else to do with Stillwater."

Mina butts in asking, "Why didn't they sell the house?"

"Couldn't. Not with that man there, showing up every week to paint it ugly yellow."

I gnaw on my thumb knuckle, not knowing what to think.

Mina's getting impatient. She wants to know how she can help with the task at hand.

I dig two milk bottles out the back of my car, give them to her, telling her, "Go ask Cal for some paint. Ask him if he'll fill up your bottles and tell him you'll pour it right back into his can."

She weighs the bottles in her hands and huffs. "You letting me go in with you?"

I gaze up at Mrs. Harrington's house. Screen door flapping. Curtains inside rustling. "You best let me have a look first."

Mina skips off as I approach the house.

Mrs. Harrington warns me: "They're full of spite today."

I take a moment to lean against a mulberry tree and collect myself. Branches above me seem to growl. Mrs. Harrington's cats are stuck up there.

The house looks different up close. It shows its age with warped slats on the porch and moss poking from cracks in the cement. I hesitate at the screen door, wait for it to slow down and let me in. It does, and both doors slam shut behind me.

A stillness sets over the house. They know me by now, know what I'm coming for. Three times already I've lured them out. They'll be more careful this time.

Last time I threatened them with Mr. Jefferson's mojo, told them it would put them away for good. They must've figured by now that Mr. Jefferson would never work that kind of mojo.

But they are being careful. They've opened the china cabinet, but didn't break anything this time. Most of the mess is in the kitchen. Looks like they tried to build a sandcastle out of sugar and lard. And they left a trail of flour from the stovetop to the back stoop. I reach in the pantry for a broom. That's when they decide to shove me inside, shut the door and bang pots and pans on it.

I sit down on a footstool, munch on Nilla Wafers til they're done messing around.

So they got me once. Big deal. I'll get them back.

I hate this job. This favor for Mrs. Harrington. I feel sorry for her, having to put up with these kids for so long. She can't handle it anymore. Not sure I can. It's like working stink out of a motel room after ten kids been in there partying all night. Generally, I like kids. But Harry and Larry? They're such brats and they'll never grow up. Sometimes I think if Mrs. Harrington would let herself grow old, her kids might too.

A hush falls over the house again. I poke my head out of the pantry, ready to duck anything that might fly my way. I call out, "Harold! Lawrence! Y'all about done messing with me?"

Chairs clatter to the floor in the dining room.

The kitchen window darkens. I pull the curtain aside and peek out. Mina's out back with the milk bottles, now painted yellow on the inside. She's gawking at the bottle tree like she's never seen one before. It's just a cedar, stripped of its green, but it's got about fifty bottles on it, all different colors. Way the sun shines through it sometimes, it could pass for a church window.

"Boys! Listen up! I brought a friend this time. And she's a pretty one." I can't believe I just said that about Mina.

They shove me aside. The curtains bluster apart.

Mina turns one bottle upside down and slips it over an upward-pointing branch on the bottle tree.

They stomp footprints in the flour and bust out the back door. I can see them, sort of, warping the air like heat vapors as they rush towards Mina. She's stretched up on tiptoes, trying to place the second bottle.

I shout at her. "Mina! Get back!" She can't hear me through the lead glass window.

She gets the bottle in place on its branch, but she takes the hit like a wide receiver reaching for a high pass. It flattens her to the grass. She pushes herself up and crabwalks away from the tree.

A breeze kicks up, and all the bottles begin to moan. This frightens her more, but it's a good thing. It gets their attention, draws them away from her and into their new bottles. I know it's worked when I see the yellow bottles rattling on their branches. They're stuck in there. For a while, anyway.

I trot out to Mina, help her up. "You all right?"

"Yeah. That was them?"

I nod.

"Wow," she says. She lifts her shirt to expose her side. A welt puffs up across her ribs.

"That'll bruise."

She runs her fingers along it and says, "Neat." She stagger-steps back. I catch her around the waist and hold on. We walk like that round to the front yard.

Mrs. Harrington clasps her hands to her bosom. "You got my boys put away?"

"I believe so."

"Anybody get hurt?"

Mina says, "We're all good."

Mrs. Harrington sighs in relief. "What'd they go and tear up this time?"

"Made a mess of your kitchen is about all. Were you baking something?"

"I don't bake." She sounds insulted. "I got help for that."

"Smells like almond cookies and apple pie, is all."

She looks at me like I'm dim. "Whole damn town smells like almond and apple. That's what happens when the waters rise. Got that almond and apple odor, and it smells up everything."

"Well now I know." I turn Mina loose. She pats the tree trunk, kissing at the cats up there. "Learning all kinds of things about your neighborhood today," I tell Mrs. Harrington.

She crosses her arms, cocks her head back. "You hardly come by. I'm surprised you remember where I live. How'd you even know to come out here today?"

"Didn't. I'm looking for someone else. His name's Lester Current and he drives a red Jaguar XJR. Seen anyone like that lately?"

"What's a Jaguar XJR?"

Mina answers: "Fancy sports car for rich folk who don't like sports."

A look of recognition passes across Mrs. Harrington's face. "Matter of fact, Daphne Betts said there was a fancy red sports car prowling around Hunters yesterday morning. Tooling around, back and forth, up and down between Troll's and Bub's."

Daphne Betts said no such thing. Daphne Betts suffered a stroke some years back. She can't talk now, uses a notepad instead. She can't hardly walk, either. I can't imagine the sight of her shuffling around town at that early hour, with her hollow haunted face. Hasn't seen more than an hour of sunshine since the stroke. And when she is out during daylight hours, she's wearing a hooded purple cloak. Hate to sound mean, but she looks a little bit like Skeletor, the arch-villain from the *He-Man and the Masters of the Universe* cartoon show.

Mrs. Harrington tells me, "Daphne figured the driver for lost. She caught him at a stop sign, went to his window to see if she could help out. She said he looked a terrible fright, like he could use a drink. And you know, Daphne always carries that silver flask with her, won't leave home without her mash."

I did not know that, but it explains a lot about Daphne. The waters don't seem to help much if you mix them with another vice.

"She said he didn't take kindly to her offer. Nope. Instead, he tore off toward Odium."

The cats finally shuffle headfirst down the tree, pounce into Mina's arms. She passes them over to Mrs. Harrington and tells me we need to go to Odium.

This is true, but I've got other things to tend to first.

MR. PATIL IS on his knees scrubbing puke from the bathroom floor in the room where the kids held their party last night. He's doing my job. Or maybe it was Mina's turn. Either way, he's doing it because we took off for Hunters.

"How about I finish that," I tell him.

"No, not at all. Already there is precious little to keep me occupied today. Not a human soul has paid a visit since ten-thirty this morning."

I smooth out the bedspread, brushing my hand over its maple-leaf pattern. "Hope you didn't get too lonely here."

He laughs. "Not at all. The gods are always keeping me company. Yes, Krishna was here just now to remind me of his struggles." And he starts up on one of Krishna's epic battle scenes. It's always the battle scenes with me, and Mr. Patil tends to exaggerate Krishna's bravado. The girls hear about his love scenes, and here Mr. Patil tends to omit many details on Krishna's renowned exploits with shepherdesses. I notice this more and more every time I leaf through *The Mahabharata*. Krishna was not the Sergeant Rock that Mr. Patil makes him out to be, but he had a way—his way—with the ladies.

So I sit on the corner of the bed and hear all about how his blue god defeated an entire platoon of demons armed to the teeth with death rays and RPGs.

He has strange ways of explaining his religion. That's because he rarely talks about it in terms that he learned from his family. Instead, he's adopted aspects he picked up from Hindus elsewhere. He grew up in his father's hotel and learned the regional customs of their guests, who hailed from all over India and parts of Uganda, London and Mississippi. And stories can get mixed up when they spread that far and wide.

Then sometimes when he thinks I'm bored, he embellishes, like he's doing now with SuperKrishna.

When he's done, I ask him about the shepherdesses.

"Some stories must wait until after one's wedding night," he says, voice cracking with embarrassment. "Even then, one should not presume to take on the role of a god. Now kindly change this topic of conversation."

"Sure, what can you tell me about my mama?"

"Your mama?" He stands, drops the scrub brush in the bucket. Washes his hands like he preparing for surgery. "What is it you are wanting to know about your mama that she did not already tell you herself?"

"Tell me about the day when we first arrived at your motel."

So he tells me. He tells me while he puts away his cleaning supplies, tells me while sweeping the pool deck. In his long, roundabout way of explaining anything, he tells me everything about the day my mama and I showed up at his motel.

In short, this is what he tells me: My mama walked into Pullman with a red suitcase in her hand and her son in her swollen belly. She was twenty and had not yet seen the ocean.

The morning she arrived at the Dixie Court Motel was a hot one, too hot to go barefoot. But she was. Her tennis shoe laces were tied to the suitcase handle, socks rolled and stuffed in the toes. She wore a blue button-down blouse and tan clam diggers, both dirty and soaking as though she'd crawled out of the bog.

"Mohini saw her first," Mr. Patil says. "She noticed at once the poor girl's condition. It would have been difficult to miss. However, she recognized also the haze of family rejection that clouded her eyes. More than anything, she understood her inability to continue wandering. She invited the girl into our motel, assuring her that although it was not the Taj Mahal, it would afford adequate comfort."

My mama retrieved a mink stole from her suitcase and offered it as payment. She said, "I trapped it myself, but my son did the skinning."

Mohini asked her where her son was now.

My mama pressed her hands against the small of her back. "Right here, of course." And she thrust out her belly.

Mohini declined the mink, said they could work out payments later.

Mr. Patil cracks a sheepish grin. "I must confess here that I lacked her enthusiasm for taking in this bloated waif. I might have suggested that our motel had no vacancies at present and recommended a stable down the road, as I was accustomed to doing in such situations. You must be knowing I could not allow my young daughters to see an unwed woman in such a state, and I was further afraid of the prospect of her rapscallion bastard running amok in their presence. However, Mohini insisted that we care for them."

Mohini checked her into room 24, the honeymoon suite. Actually, half the rooms at the Dixie Court Motel are honeymoon suites, with such amenities as a king bed, kitchenette, whirlpool bath with complimentary bubbles, extra ice bucket, and free tokens for the *Tron* video game in the lobby.

Mr. Patil replaced the king bed with a double to make room for a crib. Then when I got older, he replaced the crib with another double. That's the way room 24 remains now. Except now, it's mine. Technically still a honeymoon suite, but with two doubles instead of a king. And I had to give up one of the ice buckets. Plus the video game no longer works, so the free tokens are pretty much for show.

Anyway, Mr. Patil is telling me I was born in room 24, not Hunters.

To be sure, I ask him, "So my mama and I didn't live in a swamp shack outside Stillwater for two hundred days when I was three?"

And he says, "No, Cyrus, that would be impossible. Many strange and incredible things happened in the year when you turned three. Mina joined our family. Mohini returned to India. But nobody I know traipsed away into the swamplands outside of Stillwater. Furthermore, I know for fact that your mama never left Stillwater except—"

Except the day she decided she had to see the ocean.

That's what she told us that day. She had to see the ocean.

She up and hitched a ride to Dunes County. Then rode the bus from Orson to Whitehead Beach. Caught the ferry to Picket Isle. Walked across to the far shore for a view of enormous and unobstructed ocean. She saw the ocean.

Apparently, that wasn't good enough. She had to get *in* the ocean, see it from a fish's point of view. Or maybe, I sometimes think, she tried to swim to Paris. Maybe she thought she'd be happier there, though I can't imagine how. If you can't be happy on the beaches of Dunes County, there's no hope for you anywhere in the world.

"—except that most sorrowful day for us." Mr. Patil's steeled up the nerve to say it. "The day the angels called her to a better home."

Problem was, the Dunes County sheriff said, the ocean kept pulling her in directions she didn't want to go. It was in turmoil that day, he said, whipping up whitecaps that looked like frothy milk.

My mama died fighting a rip tide, was what the Dunes County sheriff told me, and I pictured her submerging in a sea of milk.

Mr. Patil reminds me this is the time of year for the brooming of the bats. I figured as much, since this time of year always falls the day after the scooping of the snakes.

As the sun slides on down over Cottonmouth Lake and saturates the sky with a Technicolor wash, bats flutter through the air like big clunky butterflies. Brooming the bats is easiest at this time of day because most of them have already left the attic space. But there are always a few late risers who linger well past dark. My job is to prod them out into the evening with the soft end of a broom. Or, if they're hiding in the baffle, they get the pokey end. Either way, Mr. Patil calls this brooming the bats. It's a fun job.

The hard part is making repairs so that they can't get back in, which first requires me to figure out how they got in to begin with. Either there's a broken soffit vent or a torn screen in a roof vent somewhere. I got to get all over the roof inside and out to inspect each and every vent. Doesn't take more than an hour to replace the damaged ones. Thing I can't figure out is why the bats don't use the bat houses I installed up in the beech tree.

So I broom all the bats out. Inspect all the soffit vents, replace two of them. Only one of the roof vents needs replacing. I'm on it, with a flashlight in my mouth and a hammer in my hand and nails behind my ears. I pull up the old vent and I see, staring dead at me, the biggest bat in the whole world. Well, I can only suppose about that, but it's at least as big as my head. It gnashes its teeth at me and shoots out of its hiding place. As I somersault backward, I catch a glimpse of its wingspan, wider than any turkey vulture I've ever seen, and it occurs to me at this point that I'm falling off the roof, and that Mina broke her scapula once upon a time pulling a similar stunt. Difference is, Mina was kind of graceful and cool when she dropped, while I, I feel like quite the fool.

You'd think the impact I take on my back would knock that foolish feeling right out of me. It doesn't. Matter of fact, it seems to pound it in deeper. I lie there for a long moment, checking for feeling in all my fingers and toes, hoping that nobody saw me fall. Surely they'd come running by now, or I'd have at least heard their laughter, but Surya is the only witness. He trots over, sighs, then curls up next to me like a cat. When everything seems as though I can pretend it never happened, I climb back up the ladder and finish my job.

At least I didn't break my scapula. That's got to count for something.

MINA HISSES AT me from Lester Current's room as I'm passing by. "Cy! In here," she whispers through the window screen. Its shadow on her face looks like the kind of veil that sultry villainous women wear in Bombay musicals. Even her eyes look dark and villainous. And maybe even a little bit sultry.

"Where the heck you been?" she asks once I slip into the room.

"Your bapa got to talking." She knows what I mean, knows how he can ramble on forever. "What's up?"

"There's a new message." She points to the computer screen.

LC

· Nice start. A bit short, but nice. You had me worried there, big fellah. I'm glad to see you're taking a shine to Stillwater. I was afraid you really were going to speak your mind for once and trash the joint. Well, a change of heart is always good, especially for your corroded old ticker. ;-) Now get out there and bring me the rest of the story.

-Ed

Mina asks me: "Do you think Lester really has it in mind to badmouth Stillwater?"

"What? Naw. He would never do such a thing."

"That's not what I got from his last column."

I get what she's telling me. I felt it, too. But I dismissed it as some sort of literary device. He was just, I don't know, adding a little drama. Like when he covered the soapbox derby in Wichita. Those kid racers could've just as well been careening down an alpine crevasse in derailed rocket sleds, way he described it. He always likes to make it sound like he's getting himself into exciting and dangerous situations. Problem is, Stillwater completely lacks that. Danger, I mean.

I ask Mina what we should do now. She slides my notebook over the table and opens it to a dog-eared page. "I think you should send this one." She's talking about one I wrote on Mrs. Harrington and her boys some ten years ago. I tell her no way. I wasn't half literate when I wrote that one.

She says, "But it's good enough we can fix it up."

"Don't want nobody reading it. Who'd believe it anyway?"

"That's true. I didn't really believe it until I saw it." She turns to another page. "How about this one?" It's basically a journal of endangered species that live in the Odium Swamp. Mink, fox, otter. Anything with nice fur. I wrote it after Arati took me on one of her nature hikes. Lots of plants are dying out, too. Swamp is getting low on the ones used for conjuring.

"Lester Current wouldn't ever write anything like that," I tell her. "Too newsy."

We debate a few more pages. She keeps coming back to Mrs. Harrington. So finally we agree to combine it with another piece and settle the matter.

Current Adventures: Miraculous Waters of Hunters
by Lester Current

NOBODY KNOWS FOR *sure where the waters begin. Nobody can explain what's in the waters or why they behave the way they do. All that's certain is these are no ordinary waters. These waters have powers.*

Near as anyone can figure, the waters begin in Odium Swamp as regular swamp waters. Nothing too special about them, except part of the waters turns colder than the rest. This causes them to sink deep down into a spring that runs under the swamp.

The spring carries the waters westward, where they filter through the sandy soils under the Dearth Hills. It's still all normal water at this point, but then it crooks back in a northerly direction and something strange happens.

Just north of the Dearth Hills are the Calypso Fields. Story goes, this was where the Gingaskin Indians buried their dead. For thousands of years they planted bodies here. All kinds of dead. Baby dead, war dead, elderly dead. Those who died in hunting accidents or drowned or just dropped dead. Gingaskin Indians had a habit of dying early and often, which helps explain why none are around today.

The ground got so full of death it couldn't take any more and started rejecting the dead. That happened right before the Gingaskins decided to move away, deep in the swamp. But it was too late by then. The ground had had more than its fill of death, and more dead were on their way.

The Calypso Fields today are little more than crumbly stretches of dirt that looks and feels like red clay. Only it's not red clay. Its color and substance is said to be the result of tremendous bloodshed during the Civil War.

Now, any educated historian will tell you that no part of any war, Civil or otherwise, ever took place in Stillwater County. There are no records of any battles here, no letters or journals or orders to send troops here from either side. Yet this dirt that looks like red clay has yielded buttons and badges, swords and bone dice, and enough cannons, rifles, buck and balls to shoot your way through to the Pope.

Every so often, the dirt turns up something new, which is why Civil War fans come out here to scavenge for Civil War souvenirs. They know good and well no government official will stop them because, officially, the armies were never here.

But no doubt about it: A fierce and furious battle went down. It stands to reason that the armies raced at each other like lightning from all seventeen quarters of the heavens and ripped into one another before anyone had a chance to write an account of it. People died here fast and hard.

That's what the old ones say, anyway. Strange thing is, for all the buttons and bullets and whatnot, the soil has yet to yield a single bone. Old ones say the ground gave the skeletons enough strength to up and walk away to find hallowed ground for a proper burial. And they say whatever was in the ground rejecting mortality, it got in the waters.

So in the bloodied soil of the missing dead, the waters pick up momentum and flow toward Hunters. They usually stay deep enough underground to keep from disturbing the dead there, but every so often the waters rise. They seep into Mount Calvary, which isn't really a mountain, but rather a valley that holds Stillwater's biggest cemetery. The waters get in there and stir up the souls of the dead. And then there's trouble in town. You got agitated souls running around and bumping into things like they're in the funny pages.

Nobody knows the trouble better than Tookie Harrington. Her twin boys have been dead for decades, but they keep coming back. Every time the waters rise, they set to smashing things around her house, scaring her cats and chasing Tookie out into her yard. That's what Tookie will tell you, anyway. That's how she'll explain what she's doing when she's standing in her front yard at six in the morning, wearing nothing but black pajamas.

Like most folks in Hunters, Tookie has a bottle tree to trap wayward spirits. They're drawn to the colorful bottles like tourists to neon, and then they get trapped inside. But the bottles don't always hold, especially when the waters rise.

"The waters, they're not all bad," Tookie says. "I figured that out years ago. I figured anything with enough power to raise souls from the dead could be applied to useful purposes."

Tookie claims that the rejuvenating powers of the waters have preserved her health and restored her youth. That much is evident in her looks. She says she also uses the waters for her garden. The result: Okra the size of bananas. Tomatoes like softballs. Peaches nearly as big as your head. Best of all, she's never had to replant a crop the following season. They just keep coming back.

"Protects against pestilence and frostbite, too," she claims.

That's not all. You can pour a bucket of the waters on your car to get rid of rust and restore its factory shine.

"Put a few drops in your gas tank," she says. "It'll triple your mileage."

It'll remove gum from hair and upholstery. It'll mend torn trousers and broken hearts alike. It'll soothe aching muscles, strip your floors, lift your spirits, improve your memory, and keep collectors from your door.

Of course, you'd have to possess enormous quantities of superstition and gullibility to believe any of this. If you've been raised in Hunters, you'll swear by every word of it. You believe in ghosts and miracle cures and the rest of that nonsense. You believe that an overabundance of death contributed to the waters' rejuvenating powers. It's just nature's way of striking a balance, as they say here.

So, do you believe?

Are you certain?

Because truth is, nobody knows for sure where the waters begin, and nobody can explain what's in the waters or why they behave the way they do.

MRS. HARRINGTON ONCE told me you can't always trust a thing that goes on forever. She was talking about her light bulbs, ones her parents bought some ninety-odd years ago. They're Shelby Electric Light Bulbs, hand-crafted with thick carbon filaments. Mrs. Harrington can't remember a day when she hasn't relied on at least three of them. And today, some ninety-odd years since they first lit up the house, they still burn bright.

"You might think this has something to do with the waters," she told me, "but you'd be wrong."

It has to do with the way the Shelby Electric Company made light bulbs. Made them to last. Did their job right. Their bulbs never burned out. So nobody saw reason to order new ones. The Shelby Electric Company soon went broke.

I think about her light bulb story every time I turn out the lights for bed. I used to worry that I might not be able to turn them back on if I needed to. Now it doesn't bother me so much. Since hearing Mrs. Harrington's light bulb story, I figure a burned out bulb in the middle of the night isn't necessarily a bad thing.

I lie here alone in the dark and think about the day. Thing that stands out, besides Mrs. Harrington, is what Mr. Patil told me. About being born here, in this room. You can grow up in a place, think you know it your whole life. Then someone comes along with another story and suddenly it's like you've never been there before.

My mama's bedtime story is shot now. I can't tell myself I spent two hundred days in the swamp anymore. There's no comfort in it, now that I know it's not true.

And yet I can still hear my mama's voice sometimes when I lie still like this. I can hear her telling me that story. I can hear her out by the pool exchanging visions of the motel's future with Mr. Patil. But sometimes I hear her say things I don't like.

One time they invited Mr. Jefferson over for dinner. Mr. Patil grilled up some chicken with a mango chutney glaze while my mama went to pick up Mr. Jefferson. Mr. Patil enjoyed Mr. Jefferson's company, trusted him on everything. When Mr. Patil first arrived in this town near broke, it was Mr. Jefferson who advised him to bet on the cockfights, said he'd know exactly which one to go with once he heard the name. Shiva the Destroyer.

That night, however, Mr. Patil and my mama sought different advice from the old seer.

Mr. Jefferson heard out their lament and came up with an arrangement. A sinister, unspeakable arrangement. I was supposed to be sleeping at that point. Wasn't supposed to hear any of it. Still wish I hadn't. Shocked me to hear him devise something so horrible when so many times he's said he doesn't work bad spells. But I heard it, every detail. And I know it will all come to pass when Mohini returns to Pullman, because that's how Mr. Jefferson said it would happen.

About the only hope I got going is that Mohini will never return to Pullman. And just in case she does, I've been particularly kind to Mr. Jefferson in the hopes that he'll reverse the spell and call off the arrangement.

Tears me up inside thinking about it now, as if I don't have enough to worry about filling in for Lester Current while he's gone missing. Whole thing's giving me a bellyache. Reminds me of Arati when she said I'd get bleeding ulcers if I didn't learn to meditate.

I realize I need to do this more. Meditate. So I meditate upon Arati, try to picture her meditating, because this is how I learned. But Arati is hundreds of miles away now. She's a research assistant at a pharmaceutical company in Colorado. Coloco, it's called. I'm not clear on what she actually does because she hardly writes anymore.

If I meditate on Sonali, I get a better picture. She's not as far away. Last I heard, she got a job handing out prizes at the Wilmington Motor Speedway and she gets her picture taken with the winners. Sometimes with their cars.

I meditate on that.

I get an image of Sonali in her long red T-shirt. She's leaning back upon the hood of a black stockcar, one bare foot propped up on the bumper. I'm focused on her shirt, the way it's hiked high on her thigh. The contrast between her sienna skin and the red fabric. Stop sign red, no… fire engine red. Yeah. Red-hot Sonali.

But then something weird happens. My vision of her shrinks, pulls away. Freezes in a photograph. She's a calendar girl tacked to the wall in a motor shop. And I see all these mechanics gawking at her, making crude remarks.

One grunts, "Fine young heifer!"

The other goes, "Finest red heifer ever I did see!" I recognize the voice. It belongs to Mr. Jefferson.

And then there's a third voice whispering my name. It's Mina's.

Sonali's calendar image flutters away and I see Mina there in her place. She's chucking snowballs at me. She's spilling vipers all at my feet.

She's freaking me out.

Now she's waiting for me on the swing under the beech tree and the sun is cutting a halo in the haze around her. And she's in the grass under the bottle tree, reaching for me to help her up. She looks like she wants to kiss me.

There's something profoundly wrong with this picture, and I'm thinking this meditation deal is about to hand me a nervous breakdown.

I tell myself: Must focus on nothingness.

I hear her voice again, more urgent this time. "Cyrus!"

I sit bolt upright and yank the chain on the bedside lamp. It fires off like an old flashbulb—blinding for an instant, then darkness filled with bluish spots. I press my palms to my eyes and whisper back. "Mina? What are you doing in my room?"

"I'm scared."

I huff, claw through the drawer of the nightstand for a flashlight. "Scared of what?"

"I don't know." She says it like she knows, but is too embarrassed to tell me. This isn't the first time we've been through this. Few months ago, she came in here seeking refuge from a late-night televangelist preaching damnation and hellfire at non-Christians. Before that, it was something in the news about India. Floods or earthquakes, maybe both. And on at least three separate occasions, it was some old movie, the same movie all three times. Something about a psycho with a switchblade trying to kill a blind woman in her own apartment.

I ask Mina, "What were you watching this time?"

She skulks over to the bed next to mine. "Wasn't nothing on TV tonight. It's what happened today."

I give up looking for the flashlight, lie back down. "You scared Ed won't like our piece on Hunters? Was it that bad? I thought you liked it."

"Not that. I'm talking about what happened *in* Hunters." Sheets rustle as she burrows under the covers. "You know, out by the bottle tree."

"You scared of ghosts?" I'm about to bust out laughing at her and she can tell. She's not answering me. "You scared of Harry and Larry? They're just boys."

"But they're supposed to be dead."

"They are."

"They ain't exactly resting in peace."

"We got them put away."

"But was that the right thing to do? Trick them into bottles?"

I think a moment, try to make sure I'm not missing something. "Of course. It's what their mama wanted. Boys gotta do their mama's bidding. Long as they do that, they'll be fine."

She exhales a long breath of relief and release, much in the way Arati instructed me at the end of a meditation. I turn one loose as well, then wait for her to say something more. Her breaths slow into tranquil little puffs, like she's blowing bubbles. In a strange way, this relaxes me. Doesn't take my mind off my dilemmas so much as make them seem more bearable.

Wednesday

I DON'T REMEMBER the day Mohini left, but I can imagine. I picture her the way she appears in the photo Mr. Patil keeps by his bed. It's the only photo he has of her, and in it, she's standing in front of the Dixie Court Motel when it was still in ruins. Her hair is braided and her slender body is bound in a maroon and gold sari. It's kind of ragged, like it was stitched from old Seminole football uniforms. She has one hand on her shoulder, the other touching her lower lip. Her face is beautiful and round, but her eyes are weary and distant.

This is the expression I see when I picture her telling her husband that she simply cannot stay here anymore, that this motel will be the death of her. I hear her saying that. In a singsong accent, she says, "If I stay here, this place truly will be my Taj Mahal. It will be my tomb." And I see her setting out on foot, beginning her walk out of Stillwater, suitcase in her hand, sandals on her feet, arguing with herself the whole way. And yet somehow, she gets out of the county, gets past the swamp and crosses the ocean without hindrance.

My mama quickly assumed her responsibilities at the motel and as a mother, affording Mr. Patil the time to grieve her absence. She told me he didn't handle the loss in an entirely healthy manner. He retreated to his room for three days. Every time my mama brought him something to eat, she'd find him stretched out on the floor, face up, head pointing south. He'd set the table lamp next to his face and kept it lit, day and night. He'd tied a cloth around his head as though he had a toothache. He'd also tied his big toes together and, somehow, his thumbs as well. All his pictures of Shiva and Krishna and the rest of the pantheon, they'd all been turned to face the walls. He'd used towels to cover all the mirrors. And he never ate what my mama brought him. Just acted like he was dead to the world, was what she said.

When Sonali left, he didn't break down in sadness right off. She went to answer a casting call in Wilmington. Some movie about hoodlum girls on motorcycles. *Chopper Chicks* was the working title. She was nervous, so he worked himself into a cheerful state because he wanted to send her fearless into the world. His enthusiastic front faded by nightfall on the day she left. Next morning, he didn't come out of his room. My mama went to check on him around lunchtime. She came right back out and described a scene identical to the time before: Tied up on the floor, mirrors covered, gods facing the walls.

Sonali got the part, though. Cast as "third rumble casualty" in what counted as a speaking role, even though all she did was scream. I'm sure she gave a stellar performance, but they never finished making the movie. The leading actor, Jan Michael Vincent, threw a tantrum after a local critic described him as a "drive-in has-been." He stormed out of Wilmington halfway through shooting and never returned. Likewise, Sonali never returned to Stillwater.

When Arati left for the University of Colorado, Mr. Patil turned morose and cut straight to his breakdown. Couldn't wait for her to get off the premises, couldn't make it to his room. Soon as she stepped out of the lobby, he dropped into that state my mama had described twice before. Dead to the world. Made it hard to check in guests. He didn't take up much floor space, but his vacant, rheumy eyes and ghostly pallor sometimes upset them, and they failed to grasp the significance of the covered mirrors, turned around pictures, self-bondage—and why such a display had to take place in a motel lobby. Neither my mama nor I were in any position to explain any of it beyond, "It's what his people do, customarily." And yet my gut feeling told me that wasn't entirely true.

None of his mourning behavior made any sense to me until the day my mama died. That's when I covered my own mirrors, turned a picture of Jesus to face the wall, sprawled out on the floor. I tied up my head, toes and thumbs. Stayed like that for three days. It helped with the misery. Matter of fact, it helped a lot. Being dead to the world made me feel like I was by her side, walking her out of Stillwater and halfway to heaven. We said goodbye on the third day, and I returned to my normal state, heavy of heart but not as broken up as you might expect.

Mr. Patil, on the other hand, had neglected his standard grieving procedures in order to arrange a memorial service. Then his business mind calculated the troubles her absence would cause, the responsibilities he'd have to assume. He trained Mina and me to assume some of his responsibilities before he took on the ones my mama left behind. Mina, scarcely thirteen, would have to learn how to check guests in and out, verify their credit cards, understand the difference between a honeymoon suite and a super-deluxe suite, while I would have to master skills such as the scooping of the snakes and the brooming of the bats and a host of other standard motel maintenance procedures. It's a great deal harder than you might imagine.

For instance, let's say a guest kicks down a door. That happens on occasion. A guest gets to twirling nunchakus in the parking lot and I guarantee he'll karate kick down a door before the night's through. Then I have to replace it. Might sound easy, but doors are a pain to hang. It's not like they come with any instructions. A window fan with nothing more than an on/off switch comes with a whole booklet of instructions in several languages. Pack of gum spells out how to open the pack and how to dispose of the gum. But you buy a door and all you get is a slab of door, hole for a doorknob if you're lucky. I ain't never seen a door that came with any hints on how to get it on rusty hinges in warped frames. That was a skill Mr. Patil had to teach me.

We would have to learn all these skills so that he could attend PTA meetings, frost a hundred cupcakes for the library's bake sale, tend to our skinned knees and elbows. Stuff like that. And during this period of great transition, that's when Mr. Patil began to talk to his gods. Or rather, that's when they began talking back to him. Neither Mina nor I wanted to tell him he'd finally snapped. We figured he'd get along well enough as long as he didn't know. Besides, we knew there was a fathomless deep melancholy within him, and nothing we had to say would change that.

The sadness still shows through some days. We know it's welling up not so much by how much he talks or remains silent, but by his possessive nature. Clingy is what you might call it. On bad days, he won't let Mina nor me set foot off the premises. Today it's just Mina.

I need to go to Odium today. He knows that, and he'll let me go. Mina's dying to go with me, but Mr. Patil is in one of his clingy moods and won't let her leave his sight. She's screaming how unfair it is and demanding an explanation and reminding him that she's a grown woman now. He won't hear any of it.

He says to Mina, "I will not have you stray so far away from this motel for no good reason. You will be staying near to me until I give you further notice."

Mina looks to me for help, but I can't argue with him. He's lost so many women he could sing stone country.

So I shrug it off and let Surya ride along instead. Surya's better company than Mina any day. "Yes you are," I assure him in Mina's presence. "You're much more fun than Mina, aren't you boy?" He groans and hobbles over to my car. "And prettier, too, aren't you boy?" I shove him up into the passenger seat and shoot a wink at Mina.

ODIUM ISN'T SO far away in distance as it is in time. Mina graduated from Stillwater County High years ago, and neither she nor her father nor I have found any cause to return to Odium since.

Following that old school bus route, tar joints in the road thumping a familiar rhythm, I think about the past, about Arati helping me finish my homework along the way. She was in all the AP classes, while I tended more toward remedial levels. So she could do my homework without much effort, leaving me time to stare out the window and wonder who would come back home first: Sonali or her mother.

Things are different now in Odium. The five-and-dime with the pet store is gone, burned down, not there to sell you baby red-eared slider turtles. Weeds in the lot fall over from growing too tall.

The Stardust Drive-In is now home to a weekend flea market. Weeds never took root here on account of the oyster shells they put down. Full-time gun shop takes up the concession stand, and the movie screen looks to function as a target.

The PTA Thrift Shop is still going strong, but I don't shop there anymore.

Jake's Café, the parent of Pal Wiggly's Grill in Pullman, is now a Hardee's. You can smell their charbroiled burgers six blocks away. Mr. Patil would like to die if he came back here, way things are now.

But then I see the high school and it takes me back. Makes me wonder why I was in such a hurry to finish. Makes me wish I could go back and start over and live half my life over again, just like it was. Except the second time around I might spend less time worrying about Sonali. I don't know what makes me think that. Maybe it's the bleachers over yonder, where I hid away on a hundred afternoons to watch her run in circles on a dirt track. Maybe it's the track itself, where I later spent another hundred afternoons trying to break her school records.

I could spend the rest of the week here wondering about those days, but I've got more important business. I ask Surya, "Where you reckon I ought to look now?"

He whines, bereft of the vigor and moxie that drove his more youthful days. He's pushing twenty or so. That's a hundred and forty to you and me. I'd say he's not doing all bad.

I hang a left on the canal road that leads out of Stillwater on toward Dunes County. Tar joints along here are thick enough to rattle parts off my car. Feels like running over a parade of little animals, squirrels and such, and Surya is shaking miserably. Otherwise the road is about as straight and flat as a runway. So it's weird to see a pair of skid marks laid out on the asphalt up ahead. Why would anyone need to slam on the brakes out here? If something got in the road, you'd see it a mile away. And it's not like anything could just jump out in front of you here, not with canals on either side. There's a bridge, sure, but that was a good fifty yards back.

I haven't been down this road too many times, but I don't ever remember seeing that bridge before.

I pull a six-point turn—the canals don't leave much room for error— and head back for that bridge. It puts me on a dirt road that runs along a river leading to deep swamp, where boats can get in and out without worry of hitting mud or getting hung up on cypress stumps.

Lot of folks made a living out here not too long ago. Not only in the fur trade, but in oysters, lumber, peat and pitch. Their homes and stores, now abandoned, remain propped up on stilts over the black waters. Sign on a dock offers boat repairs. Beyond that is an oyster-shucking house, its banks gleaming with mother-of-pearl, its dock reduced to rotting pilings with moss caps.

I keep driving, don't know why, down the sloshy, rutted road. Another mile or so—seems much farther when you don't know where you're going—and all the while the trees close in on me. Junipers scratch at my windows. Spanish moss presses down on my windshield like those big brushes in a drive-thru car wash. Sunlight mottles the hood in brief, bright splashes. And then, up ahead in the heavy shadows of tree limbs, I spy something red.

"What we got here?" I ask Surya.

He peeks up over the dash, scans over where the river fades into open swamp, across the road, to a slough where a shiny red car has come to a rest. The problem is clear: The road disappears under grapevines and blackberry briars and jewelweed the color of tangerines. The driver tried a three-point turn. Earth gave way under the wheels and the car slid back into unforgiving muck. Front tires are about a foot off the ground.

I cruise up a little closer in my Pontiac station wagon, the only car I've ever driven. I've never even seen a Jaguar XJR. But I tell you what, I'm pretty sure I'm looking at one now.

I cut the ignition and stare for a while. The engine ticks away its heat. Catbirds and loons start a shouting match over the waters. Surya pricks up his ears then scrambles out the window. He trots over to the car, sniffs around the front bumper then piddles on it.

"Surya! No!" I charge him, stomping my feet. He's not afraid of me. "What's wrong with you, boy? Don't you know whose car this is?"

He paws at the door. His ragged nails, never been clipped, raking the red enamel. I snatch up his scruff and yank him back. Still he's determined to claw open the door.

"What's got into you?" I cup my hands around my face, press up to the tinted windows. Can't see nothing but my own eyes staring back.

Surya squats heel to haunch, like he's ready to pounce as soon as I open the door. I stuff my hands in my pockets, casually glance back up the road and over the water and into the thick green tangles. Coast is clear. I try the handle. Door pops open a crack. I step back, double-checking my surrounding, pulling the door open as I do. I've got my gaze fixed back up the road when Surya crouches back and snarls at the ground beneath my feet. I turn to see a snake there, slithering out the car and aiming for my ankle. Its head is bluish black and about the size of a Popsicle. Surya darts low and seizes it by the neck. He whips it round, all six or seven feet of it, until it's kinked up like a string of Christmas lights.

"What's got into you, dog? You gone senile?"

He drops the snake at my feet, wags his tail and waits for a treat.

"No call for killing black racers. They can't do no harm." That's not exactly true. While they've never brought me harm, they've left nasty bites on kids I know weren't careful.

To worsen the situation, Surya, with her muddied paws and bloodied jaws, clamors into the Jaguar. At this point, I might be inclined to put the dog down for all the damage he's causing. However, one look into the car and I see he can't possibly trash it out worse. Lester Current apparently holds in lower regard the appearance of his vehicle than his motel room. I mean, he's got clothes strewn all over like in his room, but these here sorely need laundering. And he's got crumpled cigarette packs and Moon Pie wrappers and Corn Nuts all over. I wouldn't be surprised to find rats in here if that big old black racer hadn't just crawled out.

Surya loves the mess. He's tugging at the deflated airbag that sags out of the steering wheel. He's pressing his jowls all into the sweat stains on the button downs, rubbing his nose into the nacho cheese crusted into the upholstery. I yank him out of there to keep him from catching something incurable, and he—as if he hasn't been acting out enough—he books off into the thickets.

So here I am now, booking along after him, briar and nettles scratching and stinging my arms and shins to all get out. I'm sloshing through the shallows and choking on the stink. Stinks like rotten collards when you stir up the shallows out here. Attracts deer flies, too. Got them biting my neck and I'm inhaling clouds of gnats. I'm sweating like a mule and about ready to curse. This goes on for, what, a good fifteen minutes when suddenly I feel a thump against my head. The whole world lights up like a flashbulb and turns all catawampus before going completely black.

BACK IN HIGH SCHOOL, toward the end of my junior year, Mina wanted to see this double feature horror show at the drive-in. Couple of those Jason flicks, you know, where the guy in the hockey mask just won't die. All told, I think there are ten in the franchise. Ten and counting. Thing is, I'd never seen one before, didn't know much about them. Mina knew, and she was dying to witness the spectacle for herself. Problem was, these movies are rated R. She wasn't old enough to go by herself. She needed an adult to accompany her. So she asked me to take her. That kind of threw me, being considered an adult all of the sudden like that. And though my first responsibility as an adult was to consider if the movie's content might be unsuitable for young Mina, I never thought past the part of her—and the MPAA—seeing me as an adult.

So in a way, *Friday the 13th*, Parts 3 and 4, are my coming of age story, my gateway into manhood. As I drove Mina to the Stardust Drive-In in Odium, in my car, I felt like an adult for the first time—for a moment, anyway. Mina had to go and ruin that wondrous newfound feeling of maturity by asking me to buy her some beer. I couldn't do that. Many months would need to pass before I could purchase beer and wine, or even vote and register for the selective service. Add another three years before I was man enough to buy liquor. I told that to Mina.

She said, "Don't let the government challenge your manhood. Get me some beer."

"Yeah? And how do you suppose I do that?"

"Use someone else's license." She scanned the cars lining up to the drive-in. Then, pointing to a red Camero, she said, "Go get one from Jimmy Higgenbothem."

"That wouldn't fool a blind man. In case you haven't noticed, Jimmy's *black*."

She chewed her thumbnail and leaned forward, squinting. "Who's in the car with him? Norman Horton? Get his."

"Norman Horton? His dad's the sheriff."

"So?"

"So I don't look a thing like him. He's got blond hair and an impish grin."

"You'll pass," she huffed.

She was right. And despite the shame I felt in illegally purchasing beer, that sensation of manhood returned to my heart and inflated my head. And so we sat in my car, front and center of the drive-in lot, sharing a six pack of Mickey's Big Mouths.

Mina tuned my radio in to the station that provided sound for the movie. I cracked the windows, hoping for a breeze on the stifling hot night. The sun had not yet set when the previews began. I'd complained about that to the manager once before. He snapped back at me, telling me to write my congressman and demand a repeal of daylight savings time. Nothing contributed more to the demise of the American drive-in, he told me.

So I was going to let it slide this time, squinting against twilight to make out the coming attractions. I felt pretty good. Near done with my first beer ever, I felt larger than life and twice as handsome. Mina wasn't looking all bad, either. She explained at length the first two *Friday the 13th* stories for me so I wouldn't get lost in Part 3, which was supposed to be the best one, she said, because it's the one where Jason first gets his hockey mask and it's in 3D.

As dim as the previews appeared, they got my heart palpitating and my stomach aflutter. Few things of God's green earth excite me more than anticipating the feature presentation. I love movies. Always have. I get hooked into anything, whether they're the hokey musicals Mr. Patil special ordered from Bombay, or the old-timey tearjerkers shown in the Little Calloway Theater. I'd have to say my all-time favorite movie is *Gunga Din*. After sitting riveted through two hours of its drop-jaw action, I believed India was the most exciting place on earth. Mr. Patil tried to tell me otherwise, but I'm still not convinced it isn't.

While my head swam giddily and my grip tightened on the steering wheel, twilight shrank away and the first feature began. Mina and I slid on our 3D glasses and scooched a little closer to each other. But then, dear Lord Jesus have mercy, that movie dived straight into Hell. I mean, there were eyeballs popping out and innards on pitchforks and all kinds of unholy slaughter flying off the screen. I looked over at Mina and she was grinning at it all. Sure she scrunched down in her seat till she was barely peeping over the dashboard, but she definitely had a smile on her face.

I said, "God in Heaven, Mina. What *is* this mess?"

"Isn't it great?"

I had to look back at the carnage again to make sure we were focused on the same show. "It's nothing but the senseless murder of innocent kids. It's sad trash. No, worse: This is pure evil!"

She waved me off. "Don't look at it like that. Consider it the mythology of our time. That guy with the mask? Jason? He's no different from Grendel or the Minotaur."

I folded up my 3D glasses and took a good hard look at her. She saw it askance.

She said, "If it bothers you that much, we don't have to watch." She set down her beer, her third one—we were both near done with our thirds at this point—and gazed at me through tinted lenses in zebra-pattern, cardboard frames. I was about to ask what she had in mind when she launched herself at me and planted a huge kiss. On my mouth. Open mouth. About cracked my front teeth, too. Hints of watermelon flavored lip-gloss and warm beer snaked over my tongue. I shoved her away, rubbed my bare forearm across my lips. "Oh Mina. For shame."

"What's your problem?" she said with a sneer.

I waved both hands up at the screen as though she hadn't noticed it yet. "Kids are getting killed up there. Tortured. Impaled. Hacked to pieces. And you want to kiss while that's going on?" It so happened at that moment two of those kids were kissing hard and getting ready to make bad decisions.

"They seem fine to me now," Mina said.

"That doesn't count. You know they're about get snuffed."

"So what? They're just acting!"

"Yeah? And what if that was Sonali acting up there? What if that was Sonali with a machete sticking out her head? Would you think it was funny then?"

You'd think I called her a fat heifer, way she looked at me then. She slammed down the rest of her beer, backwash and all, and snarled, "I'd think it was pretty damn hilarious." And she popped the door open.

I grabbed her wrist and told her to stay put. She spun round and socked me on the jaw. People had to see that, what with the interior light on. She got out, slammed the door. And then she stomped off, crunching her way over broken oyster shells.

I took off after her, ducking and hissing for her to come back. By the time I caught up with her, she was leaning through the passenger side window of Jimmy's red Camero, trying to bum a cigarette from Norman.

Norman offered her a plug of chaw instead. She reached for it, but I grabbed her in time. Pulled her wrist round, hiked it up behind her back and wheeled her over toward my car. She spat off a string of cuss words and tried to twist away, but managed little more than stretching out the neck of her T-shirt until her bra strap showed. Strange how her 3D glasses stayed on, though. People flashed their headlights at us, honked their horns and hollered. That got the attention of the manager, same fat old man who snapped at me about daylight savings time.

He caught me with Mina in a hammer lock, her ankles clamped up in my armpit and her face down in her seat. I didn't see it coming, but he threw me in a head lock, made me drop her, sent her crashing into the sack of empties on the floorboard. That's when he about burst the veins in his forehead when he saw the empty Mickey's bottles in my car. He threatened to call the police on me and Mina's parents on her. That set her bawling. She begged him please, for the love of God, don't call her father. We'd be good, she promised. We'd keep quiet and just watch the movies. We'd leave right now if he wanted us to.

I don't think he expected such a dramatic reaction. He kind of shuffled back and stuffed his hands in his pockets. He said, "No, don't leave. Stay and enjoy the shows. Can't have you driving off now, not after you've been drinking. But if I *ever* catch you acting up here again—" He wagged a finger at the both of us in a way that didn't require him to spell out the consequences.

Mina sniveled and sobbed out apologies through the rest of the movie, fell asleep before the second one started. I flipped through the radio stations so I wouldn't have to hear all the screaming and killing and the predaceous soundtrack that whispered: *chh-chh-chh, kuh-kuh-kuh, ah-ah-ah.*

81

I found a station playing Johnny Cash in concert. That settled me down some, enough to watch the movie and try to figure it out, why it was so horrible. Mina's theory didn't fly with me. Only reason she brought up mythology was to remind me that she was breezing through lit class as a freshman, whereas I near failed it as a sophomore. No, I saw this movie not so much as a myth but an allegory.

See, it's like this: A long time ago, when Jason was just a kid himself, he drowned in a lake. Crystal Lake, it's called, and it's in the middle of a summer camp called Camp Crystal Lake. So his mama, Mrs. Vorhees, spent the next couple of decades plotting and avenging his death. Only it turns out he wasn't really dead. The waters in Crystal Lake kept him alive and young for years and years. Kind of like the waters in Hunters. Only when he left the lake did he grow up into a big hulking brute and go on to do his mama's bidding, which was the continuous slaughter of otherwise happy teenagers.

Bad enough his mama went and killed the *Footloose* kid in the first episode. Now he was after poor Mr. McFly from *Back to the Future* and one of the Corey kids from *The Goonies*. I got to thinking, God Almighty, who's he going to kill next? Ralph Macchio? It made no sense.

Stranger yet was how Johnny Cash's music seemed to go along with the movie, especially when he sang about shooting up cocaine and shooting down his woman. He sang that in "Cocaine Blues" and the audience cheered, just like they did at the drive-in when Jason killed girls. Then he—Johnny Cash—sang about shooting a man in Reno just to watch him die. And in his song about Delia, the woman he wanted to marry, he sang about tying her to a chair and shooting her with a machine gun.

I don't know who's the bigger psychopath, Jason Vorhees or Johnny Cash.

Anyway, I figured Jason wasn't really killing these kids. It didn't make sense. I figured his ritual murders were a kind of drastic symbolism. They merely represented the American teenager's rite of passage into adulthood. Jason was just trying to tell these frisky, playful teens that it was time to grow up. Problem was, Jason never could talk, so he had to find other ways to express himself, a way of saying: *Sure, growing up is painful. Hurts like hell, don't it? But it's time to leave summer camp and move on.*

But then, for all I knew he was a subliminal warning about the possibilities of a Canadian invasion. I needed an explanation, any explanation more plausible than the simple story of an immortal serial killer stalking the young and the beautiful, because these movies were scaring the bejeebers out of me. I had nightmares about them for months. They were like my private Vietnam, way I'd wake up screaming and sweating over the flashbacks I was having. I couldn't walk alone in the woods. I couldn't even listen to Johnny Cash without coming down with the heebie-jeebies.

Seems ridiculous now, but Jason Vorhees became my solitary demon, the one thing in this world that scared the hell out me, and I had to confront it.

So here's what I did: I rented *Friday the 13th*, Parts 5 through 7, and I invited Mina to my room to watch them. We got hopped up on Mountain Dew and Charleston Chews, turned out the lights, and watched the carnage with pillows tented over our heads.

I didn't tell her why I was doing it, but I did share with her my theory on the symbolic slaughter of adolescence. She said that was the dumbest thing she'd ever heard me say.

I asked her, "So you think that the killings are just that? Murder? Death?"

And she said, "Yup."

"But it's so pointless. It's unreal."

"That's what makes it so funny." She flopped over on her back, scooped up the remote and shut down Jason mid-rampage. The only light in my room now was a red and blue flicker from the neon outside. She whispered: "You want to see something really scary?"

I didn't, but nodded anyway.

"All right. I dare you to do this." Her voice affected a grim tone. "Go into the bathroom, but don't turn on the lights. Just stare directly into the mirror."

I cut her off right there. "This sounds imbecilic."

She whomped me with a pillow, saying, "Shush up and listen." Then, in her ghost-story voice, she said, "Stare into the mirror and say 'Bloody Mary, I got your baby.' Say that five times, real slow. You do that and she'll come. You'll see her in the mirror. And boy I tell you what, you'll regret summoning her."

I asked her where she got that from.

"Two weeks back at Dee Durham's slumber party? She told us about it. Holly didn't believe a word of it and went off to try it."

"Holly Danneger?"

"God no. Nobody in her right mind would invite that stuck-up bitch to a slumber party."

I should've known that, both Mina and I having hosted more than our share of slumber parties and sleepovers. Our friends thought living in a motel was cool as beans, and they jumped at the chance to stay in ours. We had to be particular with how we handed out invitations, but Mina's strategy often crossed into plain snobbery. I never figured it out completely, but I knew it came straight out of Sonali's playbook, the one she designed for her Hollywood soirees.

Mina said, "I'm talking about Holly Plyler. She went off alone into the bathroom. Two minutes later, we heard glass shattering and she came tearing out. She was so scared she could hardly breathe. Stood there sucking air like she'd been drowning." Mina bit off a wad of candy and washed it down. "Took us till dawn to calm her down, and still all she would say was, 'I saw her!' And, 'Blood! So much blood!'"

I wasn't sure how much of Mina's story I believed. Wasn't hard to accept most of it at that late hour in the night, the room dark, and four-odd hours of horror shows fresh in my head. I asked her, "So did you try it?"

"What? Hell no. Not after what happened to Holly Plyler. But I dare you to."

"I will if you will."

She agreed. "Fine. But you have to go first."

So I did. I stood in my bathroom, in the dark, and faced the mirror. Mina's shadow broke the crack of light under the door as she pressed her ear against it.

I stared into the mirror until I thought I could make out the outline of my head. I said, "Bloody Mary, I got your baby." Said it four times, real slow. I gripped the edges of the sink and breathed out the fifth one. Soon as I did, I heard Mina scuttle out of the room and slam the door behind her.

I stayed put and I waited.

I didn't see Bloody Mary. Still not sure who she is. But as soon as I was done telling her for the fifth time that I got her baby, something turned inside me. It twisted round till it snapped. The spell was broken. The man in the hockey mask no longer lurked in the recesses of my mind. He was gone, and to tell the truth, I was a little sad about that, sad in the way you feel you've lost something when you realize your favorite song has gone stale or your best joke is no longer funny.

On the plus side, I slept well at night. Slept the carefree sleep of children, with dreams of my mama tucking me in with bedtime stories. Of Sonali dancing for me. Of throwing snowballs at Mina. And after I dreamt of Arati walking me through the woods, naming all the endangered plants for me, I realized I'd no longer have a fear of walking alone in the woods. But I'd have done well to keep that aversion, because that's where I am now. Alone, deep in a swampy forest, knocked out cold.

Doesn't take me long to figure out the light glaring in my eyes is shining off Surya. He's lolled out in the only patch of sunshine available for miles. What I can't figure out right off is what I'm doing flat out, cheek pressed on mossy ground with vague memories of my first three beers. A Johnny Cash tune is stuck in my head and my skull is reverberating like his guitar—the red 1958 Gibson J-200 with heavy-gauge strings and his name inlaid in the neck. For some reason, that one comes to mind.

I also got this pain in my ribs, like someone's poking me with a pointed stick. I roll over onto my good side and that's exactly what I see: Someone poking me with a pointed stick. He's crouched in a defensive stance. His shoes are muddied, as are his trousers up to the knees. His shirt's torn and blackened as though burnt. It's tucked in front, but its tails are loose. Sleeves are rolled down and fastened at the wrist with gold cufflinks. His wristwatch is gold, too, but it's coming unhinged.

I push myself up to one knee, keep a close eye on him. He steps back, weighing his stick in both hands.

He's thick in the midsection and has a coffee can of a neck. He bares his teeth like a Jerimiah dog, but they're all ground down and yellowish brown. His face is half black with oily smudges, half red with bites and hives. He's got troll eyebrows and both eyes are near swollen shut. His hair is plain brown and thinning, about gone, but brown stains on his scalp give it a thicker appearance.

He says to me, in a kind of grunt, he says, "You speak English?" When I hesitate to answer, he asks again, louder and slower: "Speak English?"

I tell him, "Yes sir. Yes sir, I do speak English." I shove myself up to both knees and try to stand. My head won't allow it yet. I sit back on some wet rocks. "Where do you think you are?"

He lowers the stick, stands up straight. "I'm not so sure anymore." He offers me a hand up. "You got a cigarette?"

"Can't help you there," I say, wobbling to my feet. A cool breeze pushes through the branches and about knocks me over. I glance over at Surya. His patch of sunshine is fading fast.

The man sizes me up. I'm a good four inches taller than him. He asks, "Well, son, what are you doing way out here in this Godforsaken swamp?"

I pull together my recollections best I can. They aren't coming easy. "One of our guests has gone missing. I'm out looking for him."

"Guests? You in the hospitality business?"

"Yes sir. I work over at the Dixie Court Motel in Pullman." I thumb the direction over my shoulder. It feels like the right way.

"That seems like a lot of trouble to put yourself through." He narrows his swollen eyes at me. "You offer this service to all your guests?"

I shrug. "Never had one go missing before." I press my hands to my tailbone and lean back to work out some kinks. "Thing is, this one's a celebrity. Our first one. I'd hate for us to lose our first celebrity guest."

He drops his stick and hugs his arms around his belly. I can see a chuckle working its way up from there. "I'll be damned. I didn't reckon on anyone seeing me as a celebrity. Certainly not in these parts."

The wind blows cool again and the first drops of a heavy shower anoint my head. He's smiling big now, and I can see the man emerging from his savage veneer. "You aren't— I mean, are you? Are you really

Lester Current?"

He thrusts his hand out. "The one and only." As he's got my hand locked in a handshake, he tilts his head back as though uncertain where the rain is falling from. He says, "This looks like it might go from bad to worse. Come on. I know a shelter not too far from here."

I follow him along a deer track. That's when I notice his curious smell. It's pine-fresh, but wholly unnatural to an overpowering degree, like the toilet cleanser we use at the motel.

Surya plods along behind me. At one point, Lester Current warns us about a tripwire camouflaged under pine needles. I step over it, but Surya plows right through. A cut sapling springs over the path, too high up to hit the dog, but just right for smacking me upside the head were I standing three feet back.

Lester Current grins and says, "The one that caught you had a knot on it as thick as your elbow." When he sees I'm not smiling back, he adds, "Sorry about that, but a man can't be too careful. Bears and alligators do live out here. It's said that a band of Gingaskin Indians also lives out here."

He's quoting himself straight out of his last column, but I'm not so sure he's got it right. I've never seen signs of bears nor gators out here. As for Gingaskins, the last one is supposed to be my mom's old boyfriend, Quiet Bear, the rest having perished in the Great Peat Fire of 1963-65. I can't see how Lester Current doesn't know that.

We soon arrive at a shelter perched atop six black posts. Lester Current huffs his way up the boards nailed in the front one. I tell Surya to stay put. He finds dry ground directly beneath the shack and turns circles before settling down. Before climbing up, I ask him if he'll be good there. He rubs his face into the dirt and licks up a wood beetle. Couldn't be happier.

Inside the shack smells of a wet-wood fire and boiled crawdads, with a pile of red shells in the far corner giving the crawdad stink the upper hand. Lester Current's pine-fresh smell lingers behind it. He kicks off his muddy shoes, eases into a hammock and shoves a toothpick in his mouth. I sit Indian style on the floor, gaping up at him. A million questions swarm my mind.

First one to come out is this: "What are you doing here?"

He stares at the ceiling, at the sound of rain rattling down. He says, "Now there's a story."

So I sit quiet and let him tell it. He starts off with, "When I was a boy, on the cusp of manhood…" And I realize then he's reciting his column, "Demons of Stillwater County." The whole thing. I don't interrupt him because I'm amazed at how much he sounds like he writes.

When he's done telling me what I already know, I'm left in awe and wonderment all over again, over all the incredible things he's done in his lifetime.

I ask him, "Did you really hold railroad spikes for gandy dancers? I mean, with your bare hands?"

"Indeed I did."

"Wow. And hunted moose from a helicopter in the Yukon? Using concussion grenades?"

His gaze drifts off to somewhere between here and the Last Frontier. "Well, yes. But that was a long time ago. Nothing to be proud of in these times."

"Yeah, but still. You've really done it all."

He squirms in his hammock. "Don't get too swept away, sonny. I may have exaggerated truths in my time."

"What do you mean?"

"Applied my poetic license. Took some liberties with Madam Hyperbole."

An aching queasiness pushes down in the pit of my stomach. I'm not sure I want to hear any more talk like this from him, but I need to know. "For example?"

"I don't know, just a few details here and there." He squeezes his temples and rubs his hand down his face. "They sure add up fast over a lifetime."

"Did you really hold a dying Israeli soldier in your arms while his mother collapsed in grief at your feet?"

He says, "No, that was Cronkite. But I was there." He rolls over to face the wall, adding, "I was there when it happened, and he said I could have the story."

His words are punching the air out of me, and all I can say is, "Oh for the love of Pete." This does not adequately express the betrayal I feel right now. Just yesterday I learned my mama wasn't being truthful with my favorite bedtime story. I still haven't got over that. Now I'm finding my father is prone to gussy up the truth as well. Am I the child of two liars? What does that make me?

He can sense I'm shook up. He says, "Listen here, sonny boy. I don't know why you're so rattled, but you need to know something about life. You learn it in the newsroom your first day. It's a saying we have. It goes: If your mother tells you she loves you, check it out."

"What's that supposed to mean?"

"Don't trust anybody's word."

I hold out for one last shred of hope. I ask him, "Did you at least help rebuild the silo?"

"What?"

"The Amish silo. After your plane crashed into it?"

"Didn't hit the silo. Near miss. Landed in a cornfield."

"But that was your best story!" I loved that story. I first read it when I was in sixth grade, and I marveled on it then—as I did throughout the rest of my life until this point. So many different people with all kinds of problems, problems incomprehensible to one another, and yet they managed to come together and accomplish this amazing feat. Rebuilding a silo. Restoring livelihoods. In one day. That's what I loved most about it: That so much could happen in one day when none of it was planned. I believed that could happen. I believed it could happen to me, so much so that I sometimes wished a jet plane might one day crash into our motel. Now I can barely withhold my outrage. I blurt out, "How could you fib about that?"

"Amish don't read my column."

"So you just go and make stuff up?" I glare holes in the back of his head. If he could see the look I'm giving him now, he'd take one of the bear traps off the wall, set it on the floor and stick his head in it just to change the expression on my face. "Is that all you've been doing since you came back to Stillwater? Squatting in this shack and making stuff up?"

He swings his legs out of the hammock and plants his bare feet on the floor. "Listen here, boy. That's not what happened." But then he stops like there's nothing left to say.

So I ask him, "What happened once you got back to Stillwater? I mean, where have you been all this time? How did you end up in this shack?"

"You don't like the shack?" He snorts in the stench of it. "Beats the Dixie Court, if you ask me."

"What do you mean by that?"

"You ought to call it the Stinky Court Motel." He thinks that's hilarious, the 'Stinky' part. He also suggests Skunky, Lumpy, Dumpy, Weedy, Frowzy and Crap.

"It's an old motel, I'll give you that," I tell him. "But Mr. Patil has plans to fix it up real nice one day, make it an attraction in itself."

He grunts out a belch. "Try as you might, boy, but you can't shine a fart." When he sees I'm not amused, he sighs and scratches his belly. "You want to know what I'm doing in this pitiful shack? Well, boy, not much of a story there, I'm afraid."

But there is. I know there is. It's not the kind of story he would ever write for his Current Adventures column, but it is a story. Getting it out of him is like pulling teeth from a piranha. I dog him with half the questions that clutter my mind. I warn him repeatedly he best not fib to me anymore.

He answers repeatedly, "Truth from now on, so help me God."

And as the rain falls, I put the pieces together in my head for writing down later.

Lester Current's Story:
The Return to Stillwater County
by Cyrus Slant

Monday

The second hand swept past midnight and set off a brand

---

new day the very moment Lester Current redlined his Jaguar XJR across the county line. He followed the canal roads from Dunes to Stillwater. He'd traveled the same roads as a boy, staring out of a school bus window into the impossibly black swamp. He watched for ghost fires then and often saw them, the phosphorescent green lights crackling over the waters.

And now he could watch for them again, except he'd have to stare dead into the swamp to really see them and he needed to keep his eyes on the road ahead. His headlights lit up the narrow dark road like a muzzle flash in the barrel of a rifle. That's how he felt returning to Stillwater, as though he were staring down the wrong end of the barrel.

A muzzle flash can last forever when you're staring down the wrong end of the barrel. He knew that much from experience. A bad experience, to be sure, but no more dreadful than his drive back to Stillwater, for he was returning here to face the solitary demon in his past.

And the ghost fires, he couldn't see those, but he knew they were there.

In search of welcoming lights, he gunned through Odium and didn't slow down until he reached Pullman. There he spied a warm beacon, the amiable neon that spells out Dixie Court Motel. And, better yet: Vacancy.

He secured one of its fine luxurious rooms, but took little time to enjoy its many amenities, such as complimentary pens, soap and ice buckets. Unfortunately, he soon discovered that a minibar was not among the amenities. Disregarding the sparkling cleanliness, (standard in all rooms at the Dixie Court Motel,) he tore through his luggage in search of drink. He scattered his belongings over the floor and furnishings, but could not amass a sufficient amount to slake his thirst. He set up his laptop computer and searched the Internet for courier services, but none guaranteed a fast enough delivery. And so, armed with a handful of complimentary items, as well as a copy of the telephone directory and a Gideon's Bible for good luck, he lit back out into the night.

Now, Lester Current, being a native of this great state, knew the laws well enough to understand that the sort of drink he sought could not be purchased legally after midnight on a Sunday gone into Monday. People need to start off their workweek clear in body and mind is the reason behind that. He also understood how to always get what he wanted. He'd just need to find a fight first, so he sped back to Odium looking for one.

Old Lester, he's got a nose for finding fights. He could find action in a can of soup.

What he found in Odium was a Weckerling's Service Station, with a long line of cars and trucks that needed servicing at this odd hour. A mechanic sat out front in a metal folding chair and busied herself by rubbing a red rag over a tire iron. She was a boulder of a gal in a clean pressed shirt with the name Lucinda stitched over the pocket. Lester pulled out a fat roll of Hamiltons and asked, "How much for an oil change, Lucinda?"

Lucinda said she'd do it free of charge, but there was a two quart minimum. Lester tossed over his keys. She rose from her chair and lumbered into the office. She reached over the desk, finding there a hubcap that doubled as a key ring. A brass key opened the door between the air freshener display and the Lancet cracker snacks. Beyond the door was a dark passage. Lester entered alone, following the stink of cigarettes and sawdust and live poultry.

The door at the end of the hall opened to a garage. Shouting and barking and rooster squabble echoed from the center bay. There on the rack was the skeleton of a pickup chassis, four utility lights hooked up under its struts. Feathers flew up from the well below.

Lester used a crisp Hamilton to befriend a Filipino cocktail waitress, told her to keep the bourbon coming as he elbowed his way into the gambling fray.

The bourbon kept coming. The roosters scrapped on. Feathers flew. Then fur, maybe. Details got hazy.

Six hundred dollars later, give or take, he emerged into a full-blast sunrise. Lucinda handed him his keys and asked him if there might be any more services his car might require.

Lester replied, "Nope. I just need to steer it straight to the nearest watering hole. Anything open at this hour?"

She checked her watch. "Might be, but they're probably just setting up for breakfast." She leaned over and flared her nostrils, adding, "And you realize you stink like a petting zoo."

He raised his arm. Sniffed. "Anything you can do about that?"

Lucinda spritzed him down with air freshener, the kind that'd make a cattle truck smell like an alpine forest. She said, "If a bar's open at this hour, it'll be in Hunters."

LESTER CRUISED HUNTERS. Up and down, back and forth, between Troll's Tavern, Bub's Pub, the ABC store and The Deer Hunters Bar and Grill. They were all dark. The sun was too bright. The bourbon in him was losing its hold and turning him somnolent. He flipped down the visor and rolled down the windows.

His car drifted to a stop at the intersection of Bluestone and Helms. Not a soul on either street. He glanced at himself in the mirror. Black satchels swelled under his bloodshot eyes. He pressed his trembling hands to his face.

That's when the ghost woman appeared, the silent ghoul in the purple hood, at his window, speechlessly imploring him for a piece of his soul. That's what he figured, anyway. She wanted him dead, at least. He knew when her bony hand parted her cloak to reveal the silver grip. He didn't wait for the rest of the gun.

He screeched off. The woman disappeared in a white cloud of tire smoke.

He figured her for a hallucination. Slapped himself.

Then he realized he was headed back to Odium. Slapped himself again, harder.

But he'd have punched himself in the head had he learned that his phantom assassin was Daphne Betts, an old lady with a purple robe and a silver flask, a frail old woman who happened to resemble Skeletor, but came to him bearing mash. At this point, however, Lester wasn't thinking about the He-Man cartoon show. He'd never even heard of it. Too old for that. Instead, he was thinking about where he was supposed to go now. He didn't want to go back to Odium, wasn't ready to bed down in the cozy bliss that is the Dixie Court Motel in Pullman.

That left Calloway.

Lester banged a U-turn and shot off toward Calloway. He was half conscious from his all-night bender, and yet still half-crazed with fear. His state of mind helps explain why he thought he saw God on the side of a shotgun tar house in Calloway. This time he couldn't write it off as a hallucination of his own creation. He stomped his brakes and stared into the eye of God for a good ten minutes, maybe twenty. It was a big eye, wide as his windshield and encased in a triangle of furious red. He was sore afraid, but knew well enough not to run from it, for it was an All-Seeing Eye, and therefore would see him no matter where he ran off to.

Because God's eye was on the house, he assumed it was a house of God. Not a church, mind you, but a house that belonged to God, a place where He kept some of His stuff, like His eye, for example.

Lester clutched the Gideon's Bible to his chest and peered through the screen door. The darkness within revealed nothing to him, but a voice inside told him to come on in.

Lester wiped his feet before entering the house. His eyes strained to adjust to the dark. First thing he saw was a hand-painted sign that read: When life shuts all the doors in your face, God opens a window somewhere. *He wished God would just open a curtain so he could see what he was walking into.*

Voice asked what he wanted.

Lester stood in the doorway, kept the sun on his back. He said, "I don't know, really." He hitched his gaze on the floor, on the stretch of his own shadow. Darkness inside cut it off at the neck. He said, "I think I'm lost."

Voice confirmed that with, "Mmm-hm." And then, "You sound tired, like you been running around in a hurry for a long time. Running in all directions. Back and forth. Up and down."

Lester took a step closer to the voice and said, "Yup, that about sums up my life."

"You believe I can help you with that?"

And Lester, without hesitation, answered, "Yes, I believe you can."

A match lit up the room, revealing a dark man in dark glasses. He ignited a cigar, then a black candle. Things around him seemed to glow on their own, with their shadows turned all upside down. He said, "Come on over here, give me your hand."

Lester edged around the table, tucked the Bible in his armpit and placed his hand into the blind old seer's hand. A strange energy coursed between them. It made the old man shudder. He said, "All I can tell you is this: Never race your shadow unless you're running toward The Light."

"That's it?" Lester didn't know whether to be more afraid or relieved. "I could swear you saw more than that."

"That's all I got for you."

Lester suddenly felt taken for a fool. Heat pricked the back of his neck. Sweat welled on his brow. He asked, "How much do I owe you for your chacanery?"

"Whatever you think is fair."

Lester said, "Man of so few words could stand to pick up a few more." He slid the Good Book on the table. Before backing out the room, however, he slipped a Benjamin between the pages with no thought on the passage it marked.

When Lester creaked open the screen door, the old man spoke again. He said: "You be careful about the lights you choose to follow. Ones that seem the most familiar might get you lost, but getting lost isn't always a bad thing."

Lester sighed and rubbed his eyes. "I don't mean any disrespect, but can you drop the these crypticisms? Talk to me like I'm a child."

And the old man said: "Somebody out there is about to hurt you bad. Not out of any ill intent. He's just childlike and don't know any better. But that's not to say you don't deserve it for how you done him wrong."

Both men faced each other through the candlelight, one regretting his answer as much as the other for asking.

IT'S LIKE WHEN *you find a raccoon in the trashcan, so you slam the lid shut, and the poor creature trapped inside goes completely spastic trying to smash it open. It'll slam its furry little head and feet all against the insides, topple the can and set it spinning in the parking lot, all the while banging furiously for a way out. That's what Lester felt in his chest as he drove out of Calloway. That frantic pounding. That inescapable panic. He raked the contents out of his glove box, spilling crackers and Pepto bottles and maps, but he couldn't find his medications, the pills to keep him calm. He dug under the seat and throughout the console, turning up newspapers and money and dirty laundry, but no pills.*

He blasted through stop signs and ran a tractor off the road. Much like the raccoon in the trashcan, he demonstrated little control over his vehicle. Nor did he care. This was about escape. Escape from Stillwater County and his mistake in returning here.

He spotted the county line, that point in the canal road where the tar joints end and the asphalt turns smooth. But before he could cross it, a man appeared in the road before him.

Lester mashed the brakes. He laid on the horn and laid down a skid. Man didn't move til he disappeared under the hood. Car stopped on a heavy thump. Engine died.

Lester gripped the wheel. His eyes shifted from the horizon in the road ahead to the one in his rearview. Except for the man under his car, he was alone on the road. He pushed the door open, stepped out. His shoes crunched on loose gravel as he approached the front end of his car. No damage there.

He dropped to one knee, then the other. Pressed his palms to the hot asphalt, his left cheek, too. He found nothing there.

He struggled back to his feet and spun round full circle. He checked the canals on both sides of the road. An egret waded through the shallows on the far side. He packed himself back into the drivers seat, keeping an eye on the horizons, starting with the one in front of him. He checked the rearview. That's when he saw the man again, sitting there in the back seat. Sunlight shining through the rear window hid most of his features. All Lester could make out was his terrible teeth and yellowing eyes.

Man spoke with a gurgle: "Turn this car around."

Lester obeyed. The man then directed him off the canal road, over a bridge and down a dirt road. Roots and ruts bumped and scraped up into the undercarriage of his low-clearance sports car. Sounded like a tool belt in the dryer, but Lester didn't so much as flinch. They passed a ghost town of river shacks over black water. Lester watched only the road as it disintegrated under ferns and vines.

When they reached the end and the car could go no farther, the man thumped his palms on the back of the headrests. He seemed equally frustrated and disappointed, as though he'd expected the road to continue through the swamp. He sighed heavily and said, still gurgling, "Just— I don't know, turn around and go back."

Lester tried a three-point turn, but earth gave way under the wheels and the car slid back into unforgiving muck. He started to open his door when the world exploded in a solid white cloud and knocked him out cold.

Tuesday

IT'S LIKE WHEN *you wake up at a slumber party and you don't know exactly where you are. Your eyes are open, but all you see is white. Something doesn't smell right. You hear laughter in familiar voices. You begin to understand that your friends have bagged your head in the fat kid's briefs, but your mind is still too dazed in sleep to fully appreciate the gravity of the situation.*

That was the level of disorientation Lester experienced when he woke in his car with a deflated airbag wrapped halfway around his head. The important details didn't occur to him, such as why the airbag had deployed. His first concern revolved around the passage of time. He wondered how long he'd been out. An hour? A day? His personal pass-out record stood at forty-four hours, following a binge on shoe polish and toast with the brave Soviet soldiers who guarded Russia from the Finns.

Ah, but that's another story.

His watch indicated the time at 3:15 am on a Tuesday. This information was useless to him, he soon realized, because he had no idea where he was or how he got there. He hoped he was in Denmark, weathering a long winter night through unbridled consumption of absinthe.

Ah, absinthe. He closed his eyes and conjured up images of the wormwood beverage, the way it trickled over sugar cubes, through the perforated spoon, into cool water, where as if by some enchantment, it louched into emerald opalescence. There the Green Goddess came alive. He fell in love with her all over again, La Feé Verte.

Eyes open now, he scanned for signposts of his present location. With car's interior lit and the darkness outside, he saw nothing in the windows but his own reflection. The mirror image shocked to mind the man in the back seat, and he twisted round in a panic only to find him gone. He shut the door, cutting the light, but the world outside remained impossibly black, as though someone had tarred over each window.

He would stay here until daylight, maybe longer. Nothing in the world could lure him out of the car on a night like this. He reached under the seat for a weapon. Found a square-bottom bottle, empty. He clutched it by the neck and weighed it in his hands. It did not offer the security he craved, not like a full one would.

Worse now, the images of his day returned to his mind. He remembered the All-Seeing Eye and the old seer's warnings. He recalled the silent phantom in the purple cloak. He pulled his feet up on the edge of his seat, tucked his chin to his shoulder and stared out the passenger side window.

That's when he saw her.

She appeared for a shimmering moment, then vanished. He held his breath and waited.

She returned, closer this time. Her image bled into form, at once cloudy and focused. He recognized her at once, her wispy arms, her fluid motion, her lovely green tint.

And then she was gone.

He shoved his door open and scrambled out screaming: "La Feé Verte!" He sunk in muck and crawled through mud. He tore through tangles of thickets and nettles and blackberry briars. He sloshed through waters and slipped on slime all for chasing this apparition in the night.

As the sun rose, she vanished for good, left him hugging a tarred post.

It was so like her to leave him like that again.

The love emptied from his heart and the fear returned. It raced in his chest and pounded against his ribs like the raccoon in the trashcan. He climbed the post and found an empty hunter's shack. He rifled through the ammo crates, but found nothing to eat. Worse, nothing to drink.

He had no idea where he'd left his car.

He scouted the paths and perimeter around the shack. Signs of other humans were not in evidence, though he did find willow saplings freshly chewed down by beavers. He used them to set traps similar to the bamboo whips he'd seen in Vietnam. He set the tripwires, but lacked the energy to whittle and fasten the requisite spikes. He turned his attention to gathering food instead. Despite the steel traps and tackle in the hunter's shack, he couldn't catch anything bigger than a crawdad.

Fearing the return of silent purple phantoms, elusive green fairies, strange gurgling men, or any other creatures that might bring him harm, he bedded down before dark and kept his eyes shut throughout the night. He listened for the traps he'd set.

Mosquitoes feasted on half his face, the half not smeared with pitch.

He slept, he believed, not more than fifteen minutes.

Wednesday

THE NEW DAY *promised nothing until it was half done.*

A golden retriever found him poking a stick under rocks in a shallow creek. The dog was old, graying in the face, but fresh blood stained its jaws. Lester recalled something he'd heard about the ferocity of dogs in this county, and raised the stick in defense. That's when he heard one of his willow whips snap and a body drop to the ground with the thud of a carcass. He followed the sound and found …me.

Thursday

I KNOW WHAT kind of horseplay goes on in the world. I get a pretty good idea from the things I find while cleaning out motel rooms. People check into a motel room and behave like they're out over international waters. That's what Mr. Patil says. I'm not exactly clear on what he means by that, but it has something to do with their general sense of lawlessness.

I'm not just talking about piling up empty beer cans and liquor bottles neither. I have found drug paraphernalia. Those leather strips with colorful feathers you see hanging from people's rearview mirrors? That's what you call a "roach clip," and it's used to smoke "joints."

Guests have peeled wallpaper off the wall to roll joints. Or they'll smush up perfectly good soap and model it into a pipe. Or unroll all the toilet paper and use the cardboard tube.

That's not all. People leave all kinds of kinky mess behind. Handcuffs and whipped cream. Crisco and rosaries. Bale wire and catheters. Worst thing was raw ground chuck smeared in the sheets. I had to burn them, the mattress, too. Scariest part is it happens more often than you'd guess. People can get pretty weird outside the privacy of their own homes. But I think I've already said too much on that subject.

Point is, I was not so shocked, really, to hear what sort of mischief Lester likes to pull. Sure I was somewhat put off by the fact that he's family, that his wild blood runs through my veins. But then again, it does make some sense. After all, it was me who bought beer before I was of legal age. I think I mentioned that already. And don't forget it was me who bought the Wiggly Burger and took the first bite. Not that I find any pride in that. I'm just saying it sort of makes sense now, why I sometimes get out of control like that.

Like one time, a few years after I graduated from high school and Mina was a senior, she told me to get her out of class so we could go crabbing. We ordered a dozen barbecue wings from Jake's Café and took off for Dunes County. Found an empty pier on the Arapaho Inlet. Ate five wings each there, tied the remaining two to kite string. Crabs can't resist Jake's wings. You can pull them clear up to the cooler, drop them on ice and they still won't let go.

Mr. Patil busted us both when we came home with a cooler full of blue crabs and smelling of Jake's barbecue sauce. And even though it was Mina's idea and Mina who skipped classes, I got the worse scolding for being old enough to know better. I was a troublemaker, he said. A rapscallion. A hellcat. If we'd been back in India, he'd have beaten me with a rattan switch.

But for all the vices a man might have, it's far more disturbing to watch him suffer through the night without them. It was creepy staying the night in a shack with Lester, knowing how prone to panic he can be. He slept the sleep of the tormented, grinding his teeth and yelling about gunfire and green fairies. He wheeled one leg round and round like a dog having a nightmare. My mama would die again if she knew what he's turned into.

I wished we'd gone back to the motel, but the rain didn't let up all night, so we had to stay put till dawn. Took him half that long just to tell his story, the one he said wasn't worth telling.

I've got it fixed in my head now, the whole thing. Word for word, the way it needs to be told. Took me hours to get it right, way it needs to be written down.

I need to go home and write it down.

Rays of sun bolt through the swamp canopy. Day's getting ready to steam like an oyster roast. I wake Lester and tell him we need to get the show on the road. We scuttle down the cypress post and find ourselves halfway to our knees in water that wasn't there the night before. Surya, still on high ground, is only up to his ankles.

I ask him, "Surya? You still good?"

He noses around in the water and chomps down a tadpole. Couldn't be happier.

I tell him to show us back to the car. He knows what I'm saying, knows the way too, but he has to run us in concentric circles for a good half hour before taking us in the right direction. He's embarrassing me near to death, acting out like that. I try best I can to chat up Lester along the way, hoping to distract him from the fact that my dog's out to make buffoons of us. Lester doesn't notice as long as I talk about him and his work.

I say, "So, this demon you got going on here, the one you come to face, what's he like?"

He slogs through the muck behind me and grunts something about I wouldn't understand.

"Sure I would. Try me. Take me back to that night. The night of your last wrestling match." He doesn't answer, so I try again. "You need to fess up to me sooner or later."

He growls out, "Look, sonny. I'm tired. I'm wet. I'm hungry. Just get me out of this swamp and I'll tell you whatever you want to know."

A soaked layer of rotting leaves squishes and foams under our feet. It's a good sign. We're reaching higher ground.

"We're about there, right?" Lester asks.

Then, a little later, he says, "We must be getting close, don't you think?"

I can no longer picture him ever doing his job on his own.

Surya finds the cars the way we left them. Lester's Jaguar backed into a slough. Mine in the middle of a road I can't make out anymore. Lester winces at both of them, his for the vivid reminder of how it ended up that way, mine for the unstylish discomfort he'll soon be riding in.

He'll like my car better once we plow our way out of the swamp.

I EXPECTED A return to civilization would cheer up old Lester, but the look on his face as we approach Odium goes beyond disappointment. It's disdainful. He scowls at the bullet-ridden movie screen at the Stardust, bristles at the weedy lot where the pet store once stood. Only thing that seems to make him happy is the smell of burgers burning in Hardee's. He tells me to carry him there, says, "But first let's stop for a pack of smokes."

No way I'm stopping for anything right now. He's got too many questions to answer, and I'm gonna get those answers if I have to starve them out of him.

I flip on the radio to help me think. It's still on the college station Mina found, and it's playing that same rockabilly tune. I picture her swinging her hair and singing along. I see her drumming on my dashboard until Lester turns the dial to some adult contemporary station. Light piano and synthesized violins and a drum machine set on rumba. I recognize the tune, sounds a lot like The Rolling Stone's classic, "Paint It Black."

Boy, that takes me back. I probably wasn't even born yet when it first came out, but I was, like, seven when Sonali bought the single, "It's All Over Now" with "Paint It Black" on the flip side. She played it on her little blue record player all the time, dancing like mad. Mr. Patil appreciated the fact that she still enjoyed dancing to sitar music.

And later, when I was in high school, the longhaired boys used to play it every day. They liked to sit there in the parking lot, smoking cigarettes and playing it over and over. Can't say I ever liked The Rolling Stones, but then I never realized what a catchy tune this was until now. It's pretty nice music once you take out the drums and vocals. Makes me want to go back to high school and hang out in the parking lot.

So that's exactly what I set out to do.

Lester stares at the radio dial and says, "I recognize this tune. It's probably well before your time."

"Yup."

"Well, let me tell you. It's called 'Paint It Black.' A Rolling Stones classic. Only if it was the original version, you'd hear Brian Jones playing the sitar." I glance over and catch him grinning. "Boy, that takes me back. I was still in high school when this song first came out."

I tell him, "I'm glad you feel that way because guess what? We're going back to high school." And I whip my car into the Stillwater County High parking lot.

Lester grabs hold of the dashboard. He sees the gym looming before him like prison walls, the Mighty Moccasin painted up high and ready to strike.

"Holy Mother of Christ!" Lester yelps. He tucks his chin to his chest and shuts his eyes like I might drive right up the stoop and crash into the locker rooms. "Why are you bringing me here?"

I slam on the brakes. I say, "Tell me about your Moccasin opponent."

He's still digging his nails into the cracked vinyl. Won't say nothing.

"He was a bear, wasn't he?"

He raises his jaw, gazes up at the ten-foot snake on the Sanford brick wall and says, "He was a hulking brute with braided hair and the face of Sergeant Slaughter."

"So I've heard."

He realizes I've read that line before and he's told me the same since, so he adds this: "His name was Kyle Barr, and it's said that he was the first great FEAR driver."

No. That's not right. His name was Quiet Bear, and it's said that he was the last of the Gingaskin Indians, the only one to escape the Great Peat Fire of 1963-65. Lester better get his lies straight, because I'm not going to warn him but once more. "Don't be fibbing at me," I tell him.

He gives me this stern look and tells me he got his facts in line now, tells me how Kyle Barr put Figure Eight Auto Racing on the map. "He came from a family of stockcar racers. Everyone in the Barr family had a stockcar," he says. "I mean everyone. Uncles, daughters, brothers, cousins. They all raced. None of them any good. I'd say just about the entire Barr family perished in fiery auto wrecks in a series of races between 1949 and 1968."

He reflects on the strangeness of their family curse, says it was lesser known but more tragic than the infamous Curse of Talladega. "First to go was his mother, Mary Barr. She raced up until she was eight months pregnant. That was her last race, and it was legendary."

I know what race he's talking about. That was the night a car jumped the wall at the Dunes County Speedway and crashed through the bleachers. I heard Tookie Harrington talking about it on occasion. She was there to see it happen.

Back in her day, drivers would flock to Dunes from across the state and beyond. The half-mile dirt track drew in drivers like Red Vogt and

Rusty Hatch, Cannonball Baker and Fireball Roberts. You name it. Because why? Because the track was a challenge. Windblown sand could strip the paint off a car. Pit crews used chicken wire and masking tape to protect front surfaces. What's worse, the sand could turn a dry track slick as snow.

Last time Mary Barr raced there was at the end of a long summer drought.

I don't recall Mrs. Harrington ever giving the driver's name, only the kind of car. She said it was a 1941 Ford coupe with modified flathead V8s—kind of car favored by moon-shiners, complete with quick-release bumpers and a rear-mounted radiator.

Lester seems to think it was a '46 Packard with overhead-valve V8s. I'm siding with Mrs. Harrington on this one.

Lester says, "Her driving style was best described as rampant. Her car seemed to go sideways more than forward, the rear tires scrambling for traction and throwing rooter tails as she fought the wheel for control. Crazy as she drove, she had everyone beat, if not lapped.

"But then, out of her dust came Smokey Cleary in a '41 Ford coupe with modified flathead V8s. A moon-shining car if ever there was one, and Smokey was hanging it all out for a pass after the white flag." Lester's hands are flat out, palms down to illustrate the position of the cars. "He tugged for the lead down the backstretch, got a run in her draft and pulled out for the pass in turn three while Mary went wide and to the side. She floored up on his tail in the final stretch. And that's when the boy jumped out of the stands."

Mrs. Harrington says it was a girl. A tomboy is what she said, but a girl all the same. For reasons still unknown—caught up in the excitement and vying for a better view, perhaps—she leapt out on the track and cheered the cars on.

She was cheering for Mary, no doubt. Little girls never had many women drivers to cheer for on the racing circuits. Problem was, she jumped out in front of Smokey Cleary's car.

"Cleary slammed on his brakes, threw up a cloud of dust and dirt and sand. Mary braked too. Then she veered right, high toward the wall to keep from hitting him. At that point, the boy saw Cleary's car was about to run him down, so he scampered back toward the stands. Scampered into the path of Mary's car is what he did. When he saw her barreling down on him, he froze up right there.

"Now Mary had but two choices: She could run him down, and in doing so pass Smokey Cleary and guarantee herself a victory. Or she could brake harder and squeeze in behind Cleary, where she would likely bump him across the finish line.

"Though it is uncharacteristic for a Barr to forfeit a win under any circumstances, Mary Barr pulled back behind Smokey Cleary. Unfortunately, she underestimated his rate of deceleration. His car all but came to a stop right in front of her. Her car kept going. It climbed up the back of Smokey's coupe and went airborne. It looked as though she just might leapfrog over Smokey and take the win anyway, had she maintained her trajectory.

"Alas, she did not.

"Her Packcard rolled right and screamed over the wall. It sailed over the first three rows and nailed the benches in the fourth and fifth. By the grace of God, they were the only empty benches in the stands at that moment. Seconds earlier, the family sitting there had got up to fetch some fried chicken before concessions closed."

Mrs. Harrington said it was a family of fifteen who had got up to take the young'uns to the facilities before the lines got long.

Lester says, "The Packard ended up nose down in the dirt under the bleachers. Mary crashed through the windshield, ended up nose down in the dirt as well. And damn if she wasn't a worse mangled wreck than her car. Nearby spectators reported her as screaming, 'Where's my baby? Where's my baby?' Doctors had to choose between saving her and saving the baby, but she was so tore up it wasn't much of a decision."

Mrs. Harrington reported her as decapitated. Her body was still strapped in the seat. Only her head went through the windshield. Mrs. Harrington says they found the baby on the floorboards.

Lester says, "They delivered the baby under the stands at the Dunes County Speedway. And that's how Kyle Barr was born."

Lester checks his reflection in the side view mirror, satisfied with his story. I remain quiet, waiting for his trademark footnotes. "Mary may have lost the race, her life as well. But she was posthumously awarded

Carnegie Medal of Heroism for her deeds that night. That's right."

He leans in, says in a confidential voice, "I'll tell you something else about her, too. It's said that you can conjure her spirit by staring into a mirror in a dark room and saying, 'Bloody Mary, I have your baby.' Say it eight times and she'll appear." He nods at me like he's just taught me the trick for turning water into wine. "She'll appear the way they found her under the stands. Bloodied to all get out and screaming for her baby. And then you'll wish you'd left her alone."

He glances once more at the mirror on his side, then abruptly pushes the door open. Steps out, stretches his limbs. "The family, they went on racing. They raced what was called Barr Cars, the meanest supercharged stockcars you ever saw. They were fitted with every outlawed add-on you could think of and painted colors you thought you'd only see in Hell."

Which was just as well, he suggests, because they raced like demons. "But Kyle now, he had to one-up all his brothers and cousins and uncles. Oval tracks weren't exciting enough for him. He had to take his business on a figure-eight track."

He tells me that unregulated intersections tend to add a few thrills to breakneck speeding, says Kyle learned that in Stillwater County, where the first traffic light didn't appear until 1975.

"Can you imagine? Charging through an intersection twice to finish one lap? Kyle Barr raced like that. He wasn't afraid of anything."

"He was something else," I say. I'm struggling to get this story heading back to the part where my mama meets Lester, but the best I can come up with is this: "And he really kicked your rear end time and again, didn't he?"

Lester ducks his face away from the sun and nods.

"But you won out in the end, didn't you now? You showed him who's the daddy."

He kneels to the crumbling asphalt, picks at white stones in an oil stain. Sweat streams down his face and neck. His scalp glistens. "Why are you doing this to me? If you know what happened that night, why don't you go ahead and state your accusation?"

Makes me nervous, because I'm not about to get into the details about what he did that night with Kyle Barr/Quiet Bear's girlfriend, who would henceforth become known as my mama. I tell him, "Nuh-uh. No sireebob.

I am not going there. You got a confession, I will hear it out, but don't expect me to say it for you."

He stands up straight and tall. "You're right. I came back here to come clean. To stop lying and stop hiding my past. So I'll tell you." He limps over to the stoop leading out of the locker room, grabs hold of a handrail and eases himself down on the top step. Reaches into his shirt pockets for cigarettes. Finds dirt.

He says, "The fourth and final time Kyle Barr pinned me to the mat, I felt such fury that you would not believe. I punched out every mirror in the locker room and kicked open the door here." He shrugs back to the one behind him. "I paced around in this parking lot, smoking one Chesterfield after another. All I could think was how much I wanted that boy—that monster—to die. I thought of waiting for him out here with a tire iron warm in my hands. I thought of guns and switchblade knives and bicycle chains. But I always arrived at the same conclusion: That no matter how well armed I was, he'd still beat me senseless. And then I saw, in that corner of the parking lot—" He points to a torn up section of asphalt near a batting cage. "I saw his car parked there. I saw his Barr Car, and I knew what I had to do."

He says she was a '63 notchback Ford Galaxie fitted with a FoMoCo 427 wedge engine and dual 4-barrel carburetors. I'll take his word on that. "We're talking a single overhead cam monster that could produce 650 bhp on the dyno. Can you believe?"

What he's saying is the boxy, notchback roofline was not what you would call a slippery design, not very aerodynamic. To throw such an advanced engine into this primitive model was akin to fixing propellers to a covered wagon.

"Oh, but she was a beauty and a beast, with a shiny duotone finish. Orange and yellow. Orange like fire. And yellow. Yellow like brimstone. Yeah, I wanted her bad. I couldn't stand the way he treated her, running her down double-looped tracks reserved for jalopies and demolition cars. What a show off! It was his way of saying no one else could touch his car, not even in a crazy race like the figure eight.

"Well, I touched his car. I slid right under her and reached all up under her bonnet. I popped open her hood and caressed her engine." His hands relive the motions before me, and a sinister smirk spreads between his jowls. "Then I reached for her brake line and gave it a little pull, just a flirty little tug, just enough to get her juices flowing. And I left her like that. Dripping."

His dirty little grin fades from his face. His hands rest in his lap. "I regretted it as soon as I shut the hood. I took a knee on the sidewalk there and I prayed. I prayed for guidance. I got an answer, too. The Voice said, 'Go back and undo that which you have just done.' I was about to obey, too. But then I saw one of the Stillwater students coming around the corner of the gym. She stopped there. Lights behind her kept me from seeing her face, though I certainly made out her figure." He whistles like she was something foxy. "I knew she was staring at me. I didn't move." He rubs his hand over his thinning scalp. "I stayed on my knee and kept my head down. I didn't want anyone seeing me cry, you know. That's the worst thing in the world, crying in front of strangers, in front of anyone. So when I thought I could no longer fight back the tears, I got up and ran back into the locker room."

"Whoa, hold up there." I pause for a moment, searching for a delicate way to ask. "You didn't get with her?"

"*Get* with her?"

I clarify, cautiously: "You see this fine-looking woman alone and watching you. Don't you go over to her, talk all sweet, steal away into the night and, you know, *get* with her?"

The imagery dawns on him with a display of flu-like symptoms. Shudders. Queasiness. He spits and says,. "Hell no. What makes you think I would get with a girl from Stillwater High? Nobody from Dunes County would even dream of getting with Stillwater swamp trash. That's more like a nightmare. We'd been warned about the girls here, how they got more diseases between their legs than most clinics can name, how they breed like swamp rats and all their children run around wondering who their father might be. I don't care how fine she is, no way I'm touching that filth."

I mull that over, then check back with him. "So you're saying you didn't *get* with her."

"That's what I'm saying. I ran back into the locker room and I had my cry there and I returned to the gym. Heavyweight match was about over by then. Moccasins made short work of our team. Didn't seem like anyone missed me."

He crosses his arm. Sweat drips over the tar smudged on his face. "But the problem remained: That which I had done could no longer be undone. I never told anyone about it until today. Had I learned of the consequences, well then maybe I would've stepped forth to take responsibility. Maybe there were no consequences. Maybe Kyle caught it in time. I checked the race reports. He was listed as a no-show every week until his name dropped from the rankings."

He's quiet for a long while. His hands tremble in his lap. He clenches his teeth, shuts his eyes as tight as they can go, but it's no use. He starts bawling. Bawling like a fragile boy fallen down. He sobs, "You satisfied now?"

I've got nothing to say to that.

He says, "Hey, I'm talking to you, sonny boy."

Then he says, "All right, that's it." Indignant now, he wipes his sleeve across his face, smearing new swampy pigments across his eyes like war paint. "Take me back to the motel this instant!"

"Don't talk to me like that," I tell him. "You ain't my daddy."

He looks at me queer. "Well, I knew that," he snips. But I can tell it still hurt him, way I said it.

ON THE RIDE back to the motel, I ask Lester about a hundred questions, all some variation of "That's it? That's your demon? A wrestling racecar driver named Kyle?" and "Are you sure?" and most of all: "Are you telling me the truth?"

He's long through with crying. He's just fatigued now, fighting his own accumulation of dirt and rank and swamp stains and guilt. He says, in a voice that affects the weight of thought: "Sometimes you have to tell lies just to hear what they sound like. If they sound good, you hold on to them for a while. But whether you're telling lies or hiding the truth, it all accumulates fast over a lifetime. Some folks say a lie, no matter how small, will come back to bite you in the ass. That's not true. Not for me. Lies made me famous. But I look back now and see I built a career, an empire, on telling lies and hiding truths. And it's tearing me up inside, it really is."

That's when I see his demon in full form. It's not about me or my mama. It's not even what he did to Kyle Barr's car. It only started with that, that secret act of sabotage, here in Stillwater. That was the genesis of his nemesis and it grew into a monstrous demon from there. Only thing I can't see now is how coming back here is going to undo that which he spent a lifetime creating. He can't even figure out the truth about whatever happened to Kyle Barr.

Lester sniffs at his collar and says, "Saddest thing is, the truth I hid most often was about what a horrible place the world really is. You have to understand I thought I was doing my readers a favor. They got so tired of hearing about war and famine and disease. You know, 'the news.'" He makes the quotation marks with his fingers. "I wanted to make them believe that the world was a beautiful place full of folksy characters hard at work on preserving life as it was in better days. I got good at telling stories like that, and my readers loved it.

"The kicker is it was all a load of crapola. There never were better days. Anyone who believes there were is deluded, and I'm ashamed of myself for contributing so much to that delusion, what with the stories on the steeplejacks and the gandy dancers and the sorghum makers. Those people weren't happy. They were old and bitter and pissed off that the world around them was changing and they couldn't stop it no matter how hard they worked. But I, I had to tell the world how quaint and charming they were. Well, I'm telling you now: Bull hockey."

Lester's got veins bulging in his neck and scalp. He's starting to scare me. He says, "I'm ready to retire that column, but I'm not going out like that. From now on, it's the truth, the whole truth and nothing but the ugly truth."

It occurs to me that Lester thinks Sillwater County is ugly. He thinks our motel is stinky. He thinks it's Skunky, Lumpy, Dumpy, Weedy, Frowzy and Crap. Don't get me wrong. I'm tickled that Lester has seen the light and resolved to tell nothing but the truth as he sees it. I just wish he didn't choose to start his crusade here.

"Truth from now on," he says, "so help me God."

YOU CAN GROW up in a place, think you know it your whole life. Then someone comes along with another story and suddenly it's like you've never been there before. I've accepted that. But I had no idea the same rules could apply to people as well.

I always figured I had a father. I believed my father was a famous writer and I believed he cared about me. I grew up with those two assurances, took them for granted. True, my father was never around, but I believed he cared enough to phone in and check on my mama and me. And then even when he got too busy to call, he thought of us when he wrote. I believed, in a way, he wrote all his columns thinking of us.

I believed he cared, he loved, he wondered, he worried.

I believed I could make him proud one day.

Now all that's gone, and I don't even want to think about who my daddy might be, because the only possibility left is my mama's high school sweetheart. I guess I wouldn't mind so much being the only son of the last Gingaskin. Matter of fact, that might be pretty neat. But now I believe there was no Quiet Bear, only Kyle Barr, and I believe I'd be mighty disappointed to learn that I'm the only son of a dead stockcar driver, especially one crazy enough to race in figure eights.

Like I said, I don't want to think about it. All I want to do now is lock myself in my room. I don't know. Maybe I'm just crabby from lack of sleep, but if Lester wants to write about Stillwater as though it doesn't warrant the space it takes on God's green earth, let him. I don't care if he scares the world away from here. I don't want to see the world anyway.

I don't want to see Mina, and I don't want to see Mr. Patil. They're about to drive me up a wall, way they've been acting. They're so worked up you'd think I'd been off to war and missing in action. Both look like they got less sleep than I did, which almost amounts to none. Mina tried to hug me and kiss me and smack me upside the head when I walked in. Mr. Patil didn't know whether to thank his gods or scold me to death. He ended up doing both and I didn't think he'd ever hush up.

Strange of him, worrying about my whereabouts. It's not like he can't run this place without me. Sure there'd be more work for him if I sank in quicksand or dropped off the planet, but he always pulls through. I don't think he'd even take off the three days to turn his gods around and tie up his toes. The Dixie Court Motel means too much to him, and he'd find a way to keep in going on. It's his life.

Lester best not call it stinky in front of Mr. Patil. And he best not write anything bad about it. He can paint the rest of Stillwater any ugly color he wants, but I'll tell you what: He'll get his chops busted if he badmouths the Dixie Court Motel.

I GOT LESTER'S story written down. I got out a fresh notebook and newly sharpened pencils and wrote down everything he told me up to the willow whip snapping and him finding me on the ground like a carcass. I wrote it the way it needs to be written down.

I would've liked to write it in the same notebook with all my other good stories, but I can't seem to find it. Mina must still have it.

Would've liked to write more, namely about how I'm still sore at him, but he's out there banging on my door and screaming for me. He's screaming, "Sonny! Sonny!" He still doesn't know my name. "You in there, boy?" He sounds like he's been drinking or having a stroke or both.

I don't know what he thinks his problem is. I done told him his car is getting fixed. Lucinda sent a wrecker to fetch it from the swamp and carry it back to Weckerling's Service Station. She said she'd drive it over here day after tomorrow, said Lester won't owe her a cent on account of the eight-hundred-some dollars he dropped in the well the other night.

So I don't appreciate him out there banging on my door and using salty language. No sir, I don't. I have a good mind to tell him that.

Minute I step outside, he grabs me by the wrist and drags me back to his room. He's not saying a word now. We pass Mina on the walkway. Because she knows better than to open her mouth in the presence of Lester's fury, her eyes ask what's me going on. Mine reply with bewilderment. She follows along.

Lester shoves open his door, demands the meaning of this.

This. This what? This mess he's made? I assure him I tidied up his room spic-and-span and now look at it. Looks like the Legion of Doom tore through here with the wrath of vengeance. Sheets are rumpled, trashcan's full, cigarette smoke hangs blue in the air. Khakis and Oxfords strewn across the floor. Wet towel on the bed. And water bugs now. I see two water bugs scurrying for cover. We've had some awful slobs here in the past, but none has ever attracted water bugs into the room.

I tell Lester: "If you have complaints about the condition of your room, take them to your mama. Now I say good day, sir." And I try to pull myself free.

"Cyrus!" Mina gasps "You can't talk to him like that!"

She's right. Mr. Patil has warned me plenty: never invoke a guest's mama, even if it is her fault for raising such a slob.

Lester yanks me over to the table, to his laptop computer. He's got his e-mail open and there's a new message from Ed.

It says:

LC

I don't know how you sniff out nuts like Tookie, but keep em coming. She's a gem! I'd like to put your last two pieces on hold, but it's up to you. Would you rather retire on a few short columns or a cover story?

-Ed

It's like when you pump up a Daisy bb rifle and take aim at a cardinal, track her flight in your sights and shoot her right out of the air. Your sense of accomplishment is as immediate as it is gratifying. An instant later, however, you realize you're going to Hell. That's how I feel right now. I am overcome with pride and fear.

"Call it my journalist's instinct," Lester snarls, "but I believe you must be responsible for this."

Mina blurts: "Hey, I helped."

I roger that. "Yeah, it was all her idea," I tell him. "But I can explain. See Tookie is—"

"I know who Tookie is. I read the messages in the outbox." He clicks up the outbox to show us the messages we sent. I have to confess I never saw that coming. I didn't know we could send a message and keep it at the same time. "What I need to know now is why you knuckleheads decided to take on my job." He takes a belt of Old Crow from a hip nip bottle. "What kind of monkeyshine motel is this?"

"It's, um, one of the many fine services enjoyed by guests of the Dixie Court Motel," I explain. And, as an afterthought, I hold out my hand for a tip.

"Dixie Court," he grumbles, and the sigh that follows smells like ethanol. "This dump's gone too far south for that name."

"What's that supposed to mean?" Mina asks.

"Means I've seen more class in a Tijuana flop house." He leers at her, adding, *"Qué putada."*

That's when I snap. I get in his face and tell him in a low, steady voice: "Badmouth our hotel one more time and see if I don't punt your monkey ass back out in the swamp where I found you."

"Cyrus Slant!" Mina scolds. And that's when it occurs to me: She's not worried about my disregard for her father's rules of hospitality. No, she's aghast because she thinks I'm disrespecting my own father. She still thinks this lout—this drunken lie-monger—is my father.

I need to clear that up with her, but now is not a good time. I'm busy staring him down, close enough to breathe in his fumes, and I'm sick with fear until he says, "All right now, mister. Just back off."

He didn't call me *boy* or *son* or *sonny*. He called me *mister*. I haven't felt this big since I took Mina to an R-rated movie.

I step back, stand down. I tell him, "I apologize, Lester." That's the first time I called him Lester to his face. I'm so adult now. "Let's deal with this like rational adults. Maybe it was wrong for us to handle your assignments. But hey, Ed seems happy. he extended the deadline, offered a cover story. Now you can tell him what happened, that it was all a hilarious misunderstanding." I snap my fingers in revelation and lay out the headlines in the air: *"Confessions of a Drunken Lie-Monger.* That could be your big story!"

He stands there reeling on his feet and squinting at me. To be fair, Mina's squinting at me, too, as though trying to figure out what possessed me to talk this way. "Your editor, Ed, he was livid over your missed deadlines," she explains. "I deleted those messages."

Maybe now was not the best time to tell him we deleted his mail. Good thing I'm quick to think of a compensating offer: "But hey, as long as he's extending a new deadline for a cover story, why don't you tell him what happened, that it was all a cruel hoax, and then write up your own story?"

"Or you're welcome to use ours," Mina adds, smiling and nodding. "We won't tell."

"That would be dishonest," I warn her. "Lester here wouldn't dare misrepresent himself to his readers. Right Lester?"

He's staring down at the computer screen and squeezing the back of his neck. "Huh? No." He clears his throat, confirms with a brusque "Certainly not." He slumps down in the chairs and pokes furiously at the keyboard.

Mina and I are still staring at him. No, I'm more like gawking. I know he's not the man I thought he was. He's not been all true in his words. And I can forget about him being my father. He never fed me that lie, isn't aware it exists.

Besides, all it takes to be a father is a percolation of the loins.

So he's not my daddy. I can let that go. But he's been my hero for as long as I could read, and that's not so easy to shake.

His hands pause over the keys. He shifts his glare to Mina and me. He says, "You mind getting the hell out of my room? I'm working here."

As we back toward the door, I catch a glimpse of what he's written: *Stinky, Skunky, Lumpy, Dumpy, Weedy, Frowzy, Crap.*

Once outside I whisper to Mina: "Remind me later to break his face." She looks at me like she doesn't know who I am.

MY MAMA MISINFORMED me about a lot of things. I figured that out a long time ago. She used to stare at the clouds and make up things about them. Once she told me that she saw Paris in a cloud. She said, "Sometimes clouds get so high up in the air that you can see them from thousands of miles away. If you stand on a sand dune and see clouds on the far eastern horizon, you can bet it's somewhere over Europe. And if you look through binoculars, look at the right moment when the bottom of the cloud is shining with rain, you'll see the reflection of what's beneath that cloud. That's how I saw Paris."

I never saw any distant clouds while standing on a sand dune. I don't get to the beach that often. But I'm fairly certain you'll never see a city in a rain cloud. I think maybe what she saw was the Kingdom of Heaven and mistook it for Paris. At least that helps explain why she was so determined to get there.

She also told me that starlings were pernicious birds bent on stealing the homes, food and songs from other birds. "Shooting a bird is a sin," she warned me, "unless it's a starling. To kill a starling is an act of heroism for other birds."

When you're ten years old and you have a Daisy bb rifle, a lot of birds start to look like starlings. You can convince yourself that a sparrow is a starling. Same goes for barn swallows, blue jays and mockingbirds. But once you shoot a cardinal, there's no way of pretending you saw it as anything else. You'll never shoot another bird again, even though you know you're already going to Hell.

Now sometimes I like to stand on the roof of the motel with a pair of binoculars and watch for cardinals. I look through the wrong end to make them seem far away. Sometimes this makes me forget how close everything really is, and then I walk straight over the edge.

Still never broke anything. Never had no stitches, either. Might say I've lived a sheltered life. That's not entirely a good thing. I'm not adequately prepared for the hurt I'm feeling now.

I wish I could spend the day's waning hours in search of bright red birds and cities in clouds. Can't though. I almost wish I could take a nap. I'm so tired my head is buzzing and my joints feel loose like they might fall off. But there's no time for napping. More important things need tending to. Lester Current's fixing to trash the Dixie Court Motel before the whole world and I can't let that happen. Pains me to think about what that could do to Mr. Patil.

I can forgive my mama for misleading me into thinking that Lester Current's my father. I've already let that go. I only wish she'd warned me about what a heinous jerk he is, but I guess now she didn't know about that.

I don't know how to even begin dealing with him anymore. I need professional help. That's why I'm on my way to see Mr. Jefferson. He'll have the answers for me, I can rest assured of that. But something about this visit is vexing me. He's got no lights on to make his house stand out against the darkling sky. I feel my way up his front porch, creak open the screen door. I call out for him, too loud, as if my voice won't carry as well in the dark.

His comes back closer than I expected. "I'm right here, Cyrus." He lights a match, about burns my nose as he raises it to his cigar. The shadow it casts on the wall behind him doesn't look like a shadow at all, but a chalk outline.

"I need your help, Mr. Jefferson."

"About time you asked."

"I'm falling apart."

"We'll see about that." He touches his match to a black candle, finds his chair on the far side of the table. He says, "Stick your thumb in your mouth."

"What for?"

"See how bad you're falling apart, that's what for."

I insert it as instructed. Feel like a baby standing here with my fist to my lips and sucking my thumb. But then I find it, something solid wiggling in my mouth. Back molar coming loose. It's like those weird dreams I have sometimes where my teeth start falling out of my head.

Mr. Jefferson reaches out and says, "Hand it here."

I rock that tooth back and forth between my thumb and my tongue. I feel it cracking at the root and breaking free. It stings a little, but in a good way, and only the slightest coppery taste slides over my gum.

Mr. Jefferson's getting impatient. "Whatever it is, spit it out and hand it here."

I twist it round and yank it out. Wipe it dry and press it in his open palm. His fingers close around it, squeeze it tight. He goes, "Mmm." And then, "Mmm-hmm."

And finally the verdict: "You're falling apart, all right. You got troubles."

"For crying out loud." My lower eyelid twitches right before I really lose it. "Damn straight I got troubles, Moses! Now what am I supposed to do about them?"

He chuckles low and deep. "Best get a hold of your temper first. Then we can talk about calling in your debts."

Moses can recoup debts from people you didn't know owed you anything. I think I said that already. Thing is, you don't go calling them in willy-nilly. You call in debts you didn't know you had, and soon somebody will turn up on your doorstep to ask you for a favor you didn't know you owed. I don't think I mentioned that part. Shouldn't have to. It's just common sense.

I tell him, "Maybe I don't want to call my debts in just yet. Maybe I was saving them for something bigger."

"Bigger than this?" he asks, showing me the tooth. "What troubles could be bigger than this?"

I don't want to say it, but he asked. "Troubles I'll be facing when Mohini returns." And from the look on his face, I can say, "Ha! Yeah, see? You don't know everything. You had no idea I knew about that."

No sir, I don't like talking about it at all. But now that he knows that I know, it might as well get spelled out here. See, Moses is a man of many talents and strange powers. He can conjure and he can heal. I'm pretty sure he can even talk to animals. I mean so they'll understand. He can see into the future, often sees problems and predicaments, sometimes death. But he also knows a lot about love, and matchmaking is one of his finer skills, one he enjoys most.

So one night, when I was still very young, my mama and Mr. Patil invited him over for dinner to consult him on the subject of love and matchmaking. In Mr. Patel's culture, matchmaking and arranging marriages is commonplace. I don't know why my mama got involved. In any case, by the evening's end, all agreed that I should marry Mina. Not Sonali, as is my lifelong dream, but *Mina*.

It gets worse. There's the whole issue of the dowry. It's too much. I can't accept it.

"You need to call off the arranged marriage, Moses. I can't marry Mina."

His dumbfounded look disintegrates into laughter. "You don't have enough debts to call in to get out of that arrangement."

"But I've long since promised myself to Sonali."

"Sonali? Well, now I see. That's a serious matter." His laughter stops, but he bites his lip to contain it. "Tell you what. You call in your debts on what's important now, and I'll make you a deal."

Shoot, I don't know. Last time I struck a deal with Moses, I lost my best cat's eye and ended up applying salve to the soles of his feet. That was back when I was about eleven, and I've been wise enough to avoid making deals with him since. But then, what choice do I have?

He says, "If Sonali comes back for you first, you go on and marry her. If that's what you want. But if Mohini returns first, you stick to the arrangement."

Last I heard, Sonali was in Wilmington. Meanwhile, Mohini's way off on the far side of India, and I can't see how she'd find the nerve to come back after all these years. Doesn't take me long to figure I've got the odds on my side in this wager.

I tell Moses, "Deal." We spit in our hands and shake on it.

"We can do better than that," he says. "Let's drink on it." He hustles into the kitchen, rambles through the fridge and returns with two bottles of ginger ale. We both kick back and take long sips. He asks who spilled the beans on the arranged marriage, guessing it was Mr. Patil. He's surprised to learn that I overheard it all that night, that I've known all along. Surprised, but more so, amused.

With the bottles near empty and sleep pressing down on me, I summon the strength to ask him what debts I'm calling in. I ask him who owes me a damn thing and what they can do for me now. I hear him giving an answer, but it makes no sense. It's like when you have those dreams where you're trying to read something important. You can see the print, even though your eyes are closed in sleep, but you can't make out the words.

His words float around me like ether, comforting to the point of stupefaction. The candle burns itself out and all I can see is a chalk outline, the kind police draw around dead folk. Weird thing is, it's on the table now, close to me.

Friday

Bacon in Stillwater
by Cyrus Slant

THE STILLWATER COUNTY *Center for Homemaking,
Vocational Training and Fine Arts has many high-tech
classrooms. One comes equipped with a fake sink and toilet.
Students who aspire to be plumbers practice their plumbing here.
One comes with typewriters and alarm clocks so that would-be
reporters can practice news writing under deadline pressures.
Another comes with real ovens so that people can practice cooking
for their families. They always cook bacon. Another comes with
cash registers full of bacon. I don't know what they do in there,
but they are fools.*

*"The human mind? Easily fooled." Bacon was always saying
things like that. Asking questions that weren't always real
questions and answering them himself, even if the students raised
their hands first. "We recognize what? Only the facts that confirm
our beliefs."*

*Teachers grumbled to themselves, murmured begrudgingly
about Bacon's undeniable brilliance.*

He told them not to call him Bacon.

So some people called him wuss-boy, others frou-frou and francis.

He said no, call me Kevin. He wanted to seem amiable. He visited the classroom where they stitched together strips of red cotton into fishing nets. He spoke knowingly with the students of Prowess and Divinity. All had won scholarships in various potato-stamp contests, and he commended them for that.

At last, Kevin called an assembly. Students and teachers gathered round him in the garage, where he unveiled his paintings. Portraits of priests and friars whose faces appeared as if made of raw bacon.

The students were disgusted, the teachers repulsed. They threw things at him. They threw wrenches and ink ribbons and frying pans. Someone threw a cat's eye. It hit Kevin smack dab in the middle of his forehead and became lodged there. He didn't seem to notice.

People stopped throwing things and stared at this large glass marble in his forehead. They wanted to tell him about it, but worried about embarrassing him. Some tried to warn him with subtle signals, wiping and scratching at their own foreheads. He didn't catch on.

Instead he torched his paintings and dispensed more wisdom.

He said: "Never race your shadow unless you're running toward The Light."

He said: "You have ghosts on your shoulders where angels and devils should be."

He said: "If I have to go up in front of the whole town, you're going to learn to dance."

He said: "Cryptic messages from your ancestors are often mistaken for a calling back to your roots when in fact they are directions to your destiny."

Finally, he said: "Ameliorate. Resonance. Fiasco."

The students scoured their dictionaries. When they understood

> *what he'd said, they became so full of wisdom that they burst*
> *into tears. They wept so hard that when their tears dried, they*
> *turned into pillars of salt. And Kevin, he climbed high atop a*
> *ladder to look down upon this, the dawn of Vesuvius, and saw*
> *they all had cat's eyes embedded in their foreheads.*
>
> *I saw it too, and all I wanted to know was which one was*
> *mine, because I wanted it back.*

NONE OF THAT actually happened. I didn't even dream it happened. All I dreamt was that I was writing, and that's what I wrote in my dream. I dreamt I was writing it for the "Life in These United States" department of *Reader's Digest*, but now I don't think it's appropriate for that because they only take true stories and, like I said, it was just a dream. When the dream began, I can't be sure. With all the dreams and fibs of late, I sometimes need to pause to figure out what's true.

I woke in Mr. Jefferson's house this morning, woke curled up on a Persian carpet I didn't know he had. Sat up and smacked my head on the underside of his table. I miss my bed so bad it hurts. My teeth feel soft and sugary from not brushing after drinking the ginger ale, but the strange thing is they're all there. I'm not missing a one.

I crawl out from under the table and call out for Moses. No reply, but the clock says I slept half the day away. I shuffle out into the glare of a hazy afternoon. Air is thick with buzzing and prayers for rain. Whole earth seems to be wilting away in the heat.

The tan vinyl wraps on my steering wheel are too hot to hold. I've got to protect my hands with a comic book. Turns out, it's the one where Casper meets Hot Stuff the Little Devil, and we learn that ghosts are indeed flammable.

Roadside weeds don't mind the weather. Honeysuckle vines thrive on it, look like they're having a party, falling over fences, climbing poles and running off in seventeen different directions. Must be the most cheerful vegetation I've ever seen. That's what gives me the idea to plant some around the motel. Got all this free honeysuckle growing wild out here that would look great covering the cracks and flaking paint on the Dixie Court.

So I pull over, take a shovel and rake out, rummage through the tangles for the roots. It's tough work. Takes me over an hour just to fill half a station wagon, but once I get them in the ground at the motel, I'll never have to tend to them again. They got this big without anybody's help. That's probably due to the dirt. Nice dirt. Near black with nutrients. Bet I could grow sweet peas in dirt like this. So I load up on extra scoops of that, too.

What's more is I'm uncovering a treasure trove of useful things. Somebody lost a bathroom sink along the side of the road and I don't think they're coming back to claim it. Looks like it's been here for years, way it's buried under so much vine.

We could use a sink like this in room 6.

After I load up the sink, I turn up a perfectly good fan motor. There's an electric oven, too, but I can't lift it on my own, so I'll leave that. There are shotgun shells—red, yellow, blue—which must be good for something. Capping rebar, maybe. Or you could string them together for festive patio lights. I wade out farther into the wildflowers and find every kind of hubcap you could desire. Some pretty enough to decorate a fence.

About the time I'm heaving all that and a fine bale of chicken wire into the back of my wagon, Norman's dad pulls up behind me, calls me over. I say, "Hey, Sheriff Horton! You heard from Norman lately?" I still get a little nervous around him on account of it was Norman's license I used that time I bought beer. I swear one day he'll find out and lock me up.

"Doing fine, Cyrus," he says, grinning large. His window's rolled down but a crack. Cool air spills out like he's storing ice cream in there. "But you look like you're about to drop from heat stroke. Why don't you set in here a spell?"

I trot round to the passenger side, slide on in. He tells me to get a salt pill from the glove box, just to stay on the safe side. He says, "I got a photograph from Norman last week. Looka here, they stationed him in Tegucigalpa."

Sure enough, Norman's standing at attention in his Marine uniform, in front of the U.S. Embassy in Honduras. His expression is as mean as he can make it, but he's still got a glimmer of impish mischief in his eyes. I don't know if Sheriff Horton can see it. Way he holds that picture, you'd think it was of Jesus. He's about to burst into tears, he's so proud of his boy.

"Hoo-yeah, that's my Norman. Gunnery Sergeant Norman Horton. He outranks his old man now." A 10-73 squawks over the radio. A 10-73 is a mental subject. Norman taught me the tencode long ago.

Sheriff Horton radios back: "What's Cal doing now?"

I don't know why they still say 10-73 when Cal is much shorter and easier to remember. There's a long pause, then the dispatcher changes the call to 10-82, animal carcass, then a 10-96, mealtime, before issuing a series of frantic 10-22s, disregard all previous tencodes.

Sheriff Horton switches his radio off. "Norman gave us a call the night before last, said he was on his way to meet the U.S. ambassador to Honduras. Can you believe that? An ambassador. I am so glad they got him out of the Gulf and into a real war. The War on Drugs."

Way he says that, I swear he's alluding to Mickey's Big Mouths. He just wants to see me squirm before he busts me, so I try to play it cool. "Don't that beat all." I admire the picture, proud to know Norman. He's the closest living thing to war hero ever to come out of Stillwater, him and Jimmy Higgenbotham.

"Staff Sergeant Jimmy Higgenbotham," Sheriff Horton tells me. "He snapped the photo." Sheriff Horton tucks the photo in his breast pocket. His shirt's so tight I can't see how he fits a photo in there. Got a brown tie cinching his neck, mirrored glasses denting in his temples, razor burn from his ears to his gullet, and still he's grinning bigger than a game show host.

He turns his attention to my car, with vines curling out of every window like unruly back hair under a tank top. He sees the plots of earth missing from the roadside and chicken wire resting on the back gate. "Just what are you up to today, Cyrus?"

I explain my plans for sprucing up the Dixie Court. "You wouldn't believe what you can find along a roadside, Sheriff. It's like a buffet table for property improvements."

He doesn't have a response for that.

"All right for me to help myself, Sheriff Horton? I mean, it's not like stealing, is it?"

"No, you're fine, I suppose. Make sure you leave some for our inmates. Got them slated to clean up along this route next week and I'd hate for them to find nothing to do out here."

"You want me to put some back?"

"No, really you're fine. But are you sure you want to lug all that mess back to the motel?"

"It's valuable stuff," I tell him. "Didn't I explain that already?"

"Yes, but considering what's happened to the Dixie Court today…" He rolls his hand out toward me like I'm supposed to say something here. When I don't add anything, he says, "You do know what's happened to the Dixie Court."

"Afraid I'm not sure what you're getting at, sir."

His grin stiffens up. "Wouldn't believe it if I told you," he says. "You best get back home see for yourself."

ALL THAT ROOTING around in the honeysuckle produced a powerful thirst. I stop by Pal Wiggly's for a bottle of Nu-Grape and an orange Chilly Willy. I'm still not comfortable with this place, but it's the only one in town that carries Chilly Willies, and the only one with a soda machine stocked with Nu-Grape in bottles, and nothing tastes better on a hot summer afternoon than an orange Chilly Willy with a bottle of Nu-Grape from a soda machine to wash it down. Some people would have you believe that the greatest treat is a goober fizz, which is a bag of salted peanuts poured into a Pepsi. I don't know who came up with that mess and I've never seen anyone try such a nasty concoction, but I've read books where that's all people drink, that and peanuts in RC Cola.

No, for me it's an orange Chilly Willy with a bottle of Nu-Grape from a soda machine. And another thing, it's not a pleasure you can experience while driving or even riding a bike. That would be reckless. You got to sit in the shade, in a cane rocker on the porch if you're lucky, and you got to take in those two treats, perhaps the coldest elements on Earth, until the back of your head freezes up and sends ice aches down your backbone.

That's exactly what I'm trying to do now, but my mind keeps going back to that dream. It's weird because I don't usually dream about writing stuff for *Reader's Digest*. I usually dream about the acceptance letter I might get from them one day. I have all sorts of ideas for their "Life in These United States" department. Even a few for their "Humor in Uniform" section.

Here's one I got from Norman: A buddy of his got sent off to Oklahoma or Okinawa. Somewhere far off. And he wrote back to Norman, saying how crazy things were there. Like there was this guy who could do great impersonations of drill sergeants and every U.S. President all the way back to Nixon. They called this guy 'Winky' because every time he went to see his girlfriend, he came back with one eye swollen shut.

It really sounded hilarious when Norman told it.

I need to get around to sending my stories off one day, but I should probably stick to stories from these parts. Lot of funny things happen around here.

For instance, and this is unexpected, maybe a bad example, but Cal is hustling down the middle of the road right now. I'm sitting here on a clean swept porch, mat dog at my side for scratching, and frosty orange-grape goodness seizing up my central nervous system to protect it from the heat. All seems well in the world, but then something about Cal disturbs me and sends that ice ache right back up my spine. I can't place what's wrong, but I swear I can feel the porch sag under my rocker. Maybe it's his frantic pace or the dismayed look on his face. Maybe it's the fact that he's naked as an ape. Not a stitch of clothes or spot of paint on him. I don't know, but it makes me feel like I'm taking too long to get back home to see what Sheriff Horton was talking about.

Cars parked along the shoulders narrow the last stretch of road leading up to the Dixie Court Motel, but its parking lot is empty. That's really all I can say about the place before I'm at a loss for words. The sight of what's happened here, it's made my brain freeze up in a big way.

Mr. Patil is kneeling at the edge of the road, staring at his motel. Tears clean lines through the dirt on his face and he's sobbing to his many gods in one of the many languages he speaks. Could be using all the words in three or four languages, way he's carrying on. For all I know he could be speaking in tongues.

Lester is standing next to him, chomping on a Wiggly Burger, grease drizzling down his arm. I don't know whether to pity or loathe him until he starts complaining about all the noise, moaning about what a dump he's checked himself into. Then he sees me coming and he knows I've overheard what he's said. He retreats to his room before I can get my hands on him.

But it hardly seems important, way the place looks now. Sheriff Horton was right in questioning why I'd haul so much junk back here when there's debris scattered everywhere.

Saturday

For all the complaints Lester voiced over the noise yesterday, he sure is making a racket this afternoon. Lucinda Weckerling delivered his car and he is none too pleased with its condition.

"He is such a giblet," Mina says. "Why does he have to pitch a fit over every little thing?"

She's got a point. The Jaguar is near flawless. Not a scratch or dent on it. Waxed so bright it could guide aircraft down for night landings. Engine's purring, hubcaps sparkling, interior smells April-fresh in July.

But that's not good enough for old Lester. He jacked up his Jaguar and took a look underneath. He found Spanish moss tangled up in his undercarriage and it's stuck up there with some pitch and swamp goo. Hardly anything to get worked up over, but you'd think he found dead kittens up in there, way he's reacting.

His car's just like him now: All slick up front, but with a sticky, mossy, slimy underbelly.

We watch him through my kitchenette window. He's flat on his back and cussing up like common folk. And he's got his radio way too loud, playing that adult contemporary station. Not sure if I can name that tune, but "Little Red Corvette" comes to mind.

I miss the old guests. Not the ones who spun nunchakus and kicked down doors. Not the rowdy teens and unhappy husbands who made their ladies wait in the car while they checked in under false names, although any would be preferable to Lester right now. I'm talking the decent folk who had a reason for coming here, or at least stumbled across this place by accident and departed thinking it was fate.

I'm talking the Mount Carmel Baptist Church Bingo Bus that broke down on the way to Whitehead Beach. Some twenty-four senior citizens piled into this motel in the dead of night, packed themselves six to a room to save on rates. Next morning, they gummed down all the yogurt we had and drank up our orange-kiwi punch and drooled it back out. They stumbled around the pool deck, bumping into loungers and umbrella stands. Mr. Patil lost it, had to point and shout out posted rules: No diapers or bobby pins in the pool. They wouldn't listen, acted like they couldn't hear.

They hoarded soda bottles and plastic wrap and spoons, turned them back in with demands for nickel refunds for each piece. Mr. Patil had to remind them: "This is not a kind of scrap drive for your previous world war efforts. The homeland is well secured. You may rejoice in your victory, but I cannot afford to reward you for your frugal efforts."

So they collected complimentary soap and stationery like it was free. They wandered off into the thickets behind our grounds, set off on shopping excursions without their supervisors' permission, as if we have outlet malls in Pullman. And in their spare time, while Lucinda Weckerling did all she could to repair the bus, they challenged me to checkers at a dollar a game. I made out with nearly a hundred dollars before Mina explained to me why I had to let them win it back.

So I eased off my strategy, and they changed. Their faces blossomed in sheer ecstasy over a simple "king me." And when I handed their dollars back, they clutched the cash like it was the hem of Jesus' garment. That's when I got it, when The Light struck me in the head and filled me full of hope. It made me realize no matter how slow or dim you might be, you can still live to a ripe old age and still find happiness. I loved them for showing me that, and I about cried when they finally left. Hurt more since they took off with some hundred and eighty dollars of my checker money. You'd think they'd go easy on me, after I let them spread out three to a room without charging them extra, but you know what? The optimism they imparted was so valuable I often think they got the raw end of the deal.

And then, about a year ago, there was the opera singer. He showed up here at dawn's early light like some gangster on the lam, so dressed up you'd think his godfather died. He stayed for a week, maybe longer, but in that time he never ever left his room. I brought him meals on a tray. Daylight hours kept him quiet, but as the sun fell, his voice rose. It rattled walls and scattered bats. It was the kind of voice that could summon angels and keep the hooded vampires from your door. Same songs, over and over. I had to ask him what he was belting out. He called it *Mephistopheles*. I never understood a word of it, but if he had stayed a day more, I'd have learned the entire score. Sometimes I can still hear it rattling around my head, and it's all I can do to keep from belting it out myself.

Right now, I'd pay a dime a note just to hear him sing it again. Instead, we got Lester, the man I've been waiting for as long as I could read, and all he's doing is making a horrible racket out there.

Mina calls him Lester the Molester.

Mina says, "Make him stop before he disturbs the guests."

I have to remind her that he is our only guest.

"Make him stop, anyway. I've about had it with his mouth."

"Me, too. I'm about ready to drop a bucket on his head and bang on it with a ball-peen hammer."

"Cyrus! You wouldn't dare."

Of course I wouldn't, but I tell her, "You watch me."

Matter of fact, I am in no mood to confront him in the heat of the day. Not much else for me to do, though. All the great stuff I salvaged from the side of the road yesterday got carted off with the rest of the debris early this morning. They even took my dirt. Would've hauled off my car as well had I not stopped them.

I pour myself some Honey Comb in a bowl the size of a football helmet and head outside. Lester's legs poke out from under the engine. I squat down next to the front wheel and shout over his radio and his cussing. Through a mouthful of cereal, I shout at him: "Lester, you need to quiet down!"

"Sorry about that, Cyrus. Go ahead and turn it down. Change the station if you like."

Sorry? I wasn't expecting *sorry*. I wasn't expecting anything less than language I wouldn't repeat, words like GD and sh*t. But I'm not letting this opportunity pass me by. I jump in his car and tune in an old country station.

"Careful up there!" he call out with a nervous laugh. "Don't make this car fall on me!"

I ease out and watch his feet as I try to assess the situation, this amiable behavior he's perpetrating. "You feeling all right, Lester?"

"Yeah. Well, no. I didn't sleep much. Up working all night and I'm not exactly finished with my business here." I hear him drop a screwdriver and then he's trying to stifle more cuss words. "And now my car. Would you get me something with a flat edge, like a putty knife? Please, if you don't mind."

I go and fetch a putty knife out the back of my wagon, hand it under to him.

"Thanks, Cyrus. That's perfect."

I chew thoughtfully. "What're your plans for today?"

"Clean this up, a little more writing," he says, "but I'll be checking out soon."

"Don't you still have a demon to face? I mean, after you track him down?"

He scrapes at the muck under his car, then pauses to say, "I've faced it. Yes sir, I believe I have. As far as I'm concerned, my demon was in facing the truth, learning to accept it and convey it properly."

"Sounds a little hokey to me, if you don't mind my saying."

He says, "I never was much on speeches. That's why I'm a writer. But hokey or not, truth is a horrible demon to face, and you forced me to face it. I suppose, in a way, it can be said that you were my demon." Then he gets quiet, stops working for a moment and lays still. I'm about to walk off when he says, "Before I go, I'd like to impart some knowledge. Leave you with some advice on the world. As a kind of thanks." I've been reading his column for decades. I doubt there's anything new in the world he can tell me now, but I let him go on. "I don't recommend you go out and see it. It's hard and ugly out there and you're set up nice here. But it doesn't hurt to know about people from far away places, because one day they'll all be coming to Stillwater and you'll have to deal with them."

That's unlikely, but even if they do come here, I don't want Lester's badmouth to prejudice my views of them. "Lester, you shouldn't—"

"I don't have much time, son, so let's start with Canada."

"Canada?"

"The Great White North, only it ain't all that great. You know what the problem with Canada is?" He peeks out at me from under the car for a reference point. I'm still chomping down my Honey Comb, probably dribbling milk down my chin on account of the oversized spoon. It's not so much a spoon but a ladle. It came in a box of Honey Comb a long time back, features a mini telescope in the handle where you can spy in on the Honey Comb Hideout.

Lester says, "Consider breakfast cereal and I'll tell you how screwed up Canada is. You go and buy some cereal there, best cereal they got. You know it's the best because they make it for the Queen of England, her Mother and the Prince of Wales. Says so right on the box. Okay, forget that the Canadians are making cereal for British royalty. The messed up part is this is their best cereal and it has almost zero nutritional value. Far less than, say, your Honey Comb there. In fact, Canadian cereal has a hell of a lot more calories, but it tastes like that stuff you feed animals at the petting zoo."

"That's unfortunate," I reply. "But those Canadians, they make a mighty fine bacon."

He goes on like he didn't hear that. "Now down Mexico way, south of San Diego, we built a fence that stretches along the border, crosses the beach and goes way out into the ocean. Only reason we don't need to build it like that on the Canadian border is because the water's too cold there. But let me tell you why we need a wall that spans our entire northern border."

"Lester, I don't want to hear this. I've met plenty of Canadians, and most are decent folk." That's a lie. I mean the part about meeting plenty of Canadians. Truth is I've met only two, an elderly couple with a Winnebago and a basset hound named William. But they were decent folk, as I'm sure most Canadians are.

"All right then, let me tell you about the gooks."

"Lester! You need to—"

"Reason we call 'em gooks is this: During the Korean War, when General MacArthur made his daring landing at Inch'on, local children greeted his men with cheers of '*Miguk*!' See, *Mi* means 'beauty' or 'grace.' And *guk*, in this case, is 'nation.' Together, they mean 'America.' The American GIs, however, thought they were saying, 'Me, gook,' and henceforth referred to them as such. Gooks, that is. It really caught on." He coughs out laughing. "Funniest thing in Vietnam was hearing a Korean soldier refer to the VC as 'gooks.' "

"That's not funny."

"No, you don't get it. The Koreans thought it was an American word."

I get it. Hardly the kind of material I can use for the "Humor in Uniform" department.

He says, "All right then, let me tell you about the Arabs." He says it the old fashioned way, like it rhymes with bay crabs.

A lone figure lopes into the parking lot. I cut off Lester's Arab rant. "Hold that thought. We got a visitor."

I hear him scuffling around under the car to get a look, then I hear him drop his putty knife. "Oh sh*t," he gasps. "Sh*t sh*t sh*t. That's him." He rolls around and scooches farther under the car till his whole body's hid.

I don't know who he thinks it is, but I tell him, "That's Cal."

"You know him?"

"Who?"

"Kyle!" he whispers. "Kyle Barr!"

"What about Kyle? I'm talking about Cal."

"Kyle!"

"Stop saying that. We're talking about Cal there."

He huffs, catches his breath. "You know I can't understand a GD thing you're saying with all that crap in your mouth. Are you telling me Cal or Kyle?"

I swallow down what's in my mouth. "Cal as in Ripkin, not Kyle as in Petty. That's Cal coming this way. He's the local nutcase. Should've seen him yesterday, running around naked."

"That's Kyle Barr," Lester insists, "the meanest summabitch who ever stepped on a wrestling mat. I know. I still have nightmares about that face."

"Naw. Huh-uh. No way. That is definitely Cal and he is definitely harmless. You should get to know him. I'll introduce you." I wave Cal over. "Hey, Cal. C'mere a minute. Got a friend you should meet."

Lester hisses: "Stop that! I'm not ready to face him yet!"

He's cracking me up, acting so scared of Cal. "I told you, he's a harmless coot. Some people say he got struck by lightning six times in one afternoon, but I think all his problems come from knocking his noggin too hard some years back. Motored through three billboards and a tar house, was what I was told."

Music on the radio slows to a deep bass reverb, unmistakably Johnny Cash. Cal's reflection shimmers in heat puddles on the blacktop, mine bends across the fender and hood of the shiny red Jaguar. That's when a sense of danger seizes my heart. "Lester, you better get on out from under there."

"No, not yet! He didn't see me."

Cal gallops closer. I set my cereal bowl on the walkway, tuck the spoon in my back pocket. "Seriously. Get out now."

"He won't see me as long as I stay here. Tell me when he's gone."

Cal draws close enough for the red of the Jaguar to reflect in his eyes. It's got to be the brightest, shiniest paint job he's seen in his life and it sets him charging. I skirt round the engine yelling for him to back off. He's not slowing down. He catches me in the shoulder and bounces me hard to my left. I hit the ground tumbling. He hits the passenger side door, hits it like it's a drill sled and he keeps pumping his legs. Jaguar jolts sideways and the jack slides sparking to the walkway. Front tires touch down, rest of the car keeps falling til it bounces back up.

Lester doesn't so much as cry out.

Cal takes off like a deer in the woods.

I army crawl to Lester's side. His face is a pool of black oil and bubbling red sorghum, and he's twitching like a newborn kitten. I'm trying to shout for someone to call Sheriff Horton, but all the noise coming out of my head is a shell-shocked yell, and it's all I can do to keep from upchucking.

I scramble out from under the car and into the driver's seat, back the car off Lester. That moment, Mina and Mr. Patil bolt from the office.

Mr. Patil retreats to get on the phone with a dispatcher, but Mina stays stock still. Her gaze shifts between Lester on the ground and me behind the wheel. Through the fingers on her lips, she says, "Oh f*ck, Cyrus! What have you done?"

LESTER CURRENT'S RED Jaguar XJR remains in our parking lot, but all that's left of him is a bloodstain and an outline in pastel blue chalk.

"Why'd your deputy draw that?" I ask Sheriff Horton.

"Procedure," he replies.

"But he's not dead."

"We don't know that."

"He was breathing."

Sheriff Horton pushes the brim of his hat forward, wipes the sweat off the back of his razor burned neck. "Yeah, but he was lying still long enough."

He wasn't that still. His arms moved enough times to give him three arm outlines on each side. Looks like a Hindu god. Looks like Shiva died here. "This can't be good for business."

"I reckon not," Sheriff Horton admits. "But see, we got all this chalk and not that many people get killed around here anymore." His deputy carries a bucket back to the deputy car. A yellow bucket with pink flowers and hopscotch diagrams printed on the side. It's full of sidewalk chalk, says so on the lid.

Deputy returns to the scene of the accident with a disposable camera, snaps pictures of the outline, winds it up with his thumb, then snaps the dent in the car door.

Sheriff Horton done got his statements from Mina and Mr. Patil. Now he's asking me what happened here this morning. I've long since figured I'd dread this question. No way I can fib my way through it, can't say I put that dent in the door. But I can't rightly say who really did. Cal, Kyle—either way I'm sure Sheriff Horton would understand. Problem is, I don't. I don't know who he truly is and I dread to contemplate it much further, because it throws into question who I really am and what it'll make me if I rat him out.

"It all happened so fast, Sheriff. He came from over yonder, plowed into the car and took off like the wild man from Borneo." I squint off in the direction he fled, off toward the swing under the beech tree. "Hard to say who it was."

"Wild man, huh?" He strokes his chin like a detective. Clicks his pen a few times. "Was it Cal?"

"Yes sir." Oh good God, I am such a snitch. "But I heard Lester call him 'Kyle.'"

He nods. "Kyle Barr, aka Quiet Bear, aka Cal, aka 10-73. Poor bastard doesn't know who he is anymore." He sighs through his nostrils while setting a firm grip on my shoulder. I can't look him in the eyes. He signals his deputy. "All right, Vickers. Put away the yellow tape."

Vicker's got the tape tangled round Lester's car, strung out to his room and back. "But Sheriff," he protests, "the K-9 unit is on their way to sniff out the victim's accommodations."

"Won't be necessary. Call them off and wind up the tape. That roll needs to last us through the fiscal year." He turns back to me and says, "Can you handle Mr. Current's belongings? Pack it all up and send it where it needs to go?"

"Yes sir." I can, but it doesn't feel right. I don't feel right.

It's like when you're falling off a roof and all you can hope for is that no one will see you hit, because you know you look like quite the fool. And even if you get really hurt, you'll have no one to blame but yourself. I'm not sure what I mean by that, but that's how I feel right now. Like I'm falling, disgracefully, back toward the land where I spent my whole life.

MINA FOLLOWS ME to Lester's room, trying to cheer me up. "I didn't really think you ran him over, but I had to tell Sheriff Horton something and it just came out sounding that way for some reason."

"Don't worry about it, Mina."

"You look like you could use some rest. Why don't you let me clean up his room?"

"Naw, but you can help if you want. Wouldn't mind the company."

Turns out I don't need her help. Lester's room is as tidy as if we'd already cleaned it. His clothes hanging in the closet, bed made, towels folded, ashtrays and trashcans empty. He even replaced the phone book and the Bible.

On the table is a notebook. My notebook. The one where I keep my best stories. It's open to "Amitabh Patel's Story." And next to that is Lester's laptop. It's open and it's powered up. On the screen, there's a story. A "Current Adventures" article. Mina and I squeeze together in the chair and read:

Current Adventures: Fountains of Youth
by Lester Current

AT THE DIXIE *Court Motel in Pullman, the neon once shined bright, but road-weary travelers searching for it today will find the old lights extinguished and the motel displaced.*

Yet this is a story about shining optimism in the face of bleak odds. The optimism belongs to Amitabh Patil, who has spent his whole life, in a sense, to keep a beacon lit.

In that time, he has struggled to keep his dream alive with few on staff, fewer guests and a mess of a motel. But this is a story of hope, of optimism and keeping a dream alive.

"I am dreaming of one day when I can expand my motel into an attraction in itself," Amitabh told me upon my arrival here. "A structure so splendid that people will be traveling for miles and miles just to stay here."

His vision proved invisible to me. Just one day before I sat down to write this, his guests could've best described the motel as frowzy. Lumpy and dumpy might've sprung to mind as well. Service proved attentive and enthusiastic, but then so did the cockroaches. Water bugs, they call them here, and these water bugs were the size of pecans and the color of chestnuts.

These water bugs ran frantic, like rats on a sinking ship. They streamed out of the mossy bathtub drain and the sink overflow. They scurried up the cracked bathroom mirror and through an exhaust fan, startling a starling that had nested there for years.

Other bugs broke from their platoon and charged across the shag carpet. They used cigar burns for foxholes and camouflaged themselves in stains on the wood-paneled walls. Eventually, they all evacuated my room through a rusted screen and a gaping crack under the crudely hanged door, and they charged out into the night.

They trampled down a cracked cement walkway, toward what was once, long ago, a dining facility. Now it appeared more as cinderblock ruins with two simple functions: Holding down weeds and holding up kudzu, and it remained almost completely hidden in the pernicious vegetation, save for its roughly defined boxcar shape.

Amitabh had plans to restore the diner as an annex to the attraction in itself, but he never got around to cleaning it out and opening it up for business. Not that he could expect any business. Not even water bugs could enjoy such a horrible place. They streamed back in a great hurry and even greater numbers.

I followed the expanding ranks across a corner of the crumbling parking lot, past dead snapdragon vines, which managed to cling to a wall that had shed much of its paint. I followed them through a cobwebbed breezeway and into the central courtyard.

They surrounded the fading patio furniture, flanked the ashtrays and umbrella stands, then regrouped next to the swimming pool, under the diving board. They paused there, cautiously approaching what appeared in the night as pond water. And then, like frightened lemmings, they scrambled over the pool's edge, into the murky abyss.

They drowned en masse, in fashion of a suicide cult, burbling *in the algal morass. At that moment, when it seemed as though the oddity of events had peaked, I saw, by the moonlight, a creature, a silvery, scaled-down leviathan, churn the water and slice through the surface scum. It gobbled down the water bugs.*

Change Is Gonna Come

I DID NOT *know it then, but a change was filtering through the air on that sticky Thursday night. The water bugs must've felt it coming, for Friday morning, a new species of insect landed here. They checked in at dawn and didn't check out until well past midnight. These were no ordinary bugs. These were Pullman's own breed. Carpenter ants and busy bees, bustling like you've never seen.*

Pullman has never been known for bustling activity, but at six on a Friday morning it seemed like the whole town and half the county swarmed up to work at the Dixie Court Motel.

It began with the arrival of a dark man in dark glasses. A man with no visible form of transportation save for his wingtips and a feather in his fedora hat. This man said to Amitabh: "Someone's called in a favor for you."

Amitabh tried to refuse the favor, said no one owed him anything.

The man explained, "One who called it in owes you plenty. And I owe him. Now since the greater part of the county's population owes me, you might see how that's gonna come back around to you."

Amitabh continued his protest, causing the man to lose track of his accounting. "Don't matter," he concluded. "Everybody will get some out of it before too long. Besides, it's too late now. I already called it in. They already coming." He wasn't done saying that when they began to arrive.

They arrived in pick-ups and dump trucks, a moving van and a front-end loader. They also came by bicycle and fire engine and at least one long, black hearse. There was an ice cream truck and a mobile barbecue pit. All that seemed missing in the great flurry were news crews, but then I guess they knew that I was already here.

I thought to warn them that there was no point in trying to fix up the old place, that you can spit-shine an old trashcan for days on end and it'll still be an old trashcan, but I don't think they would've listened to me, such was the determination on their faces. I reckon with that much determination, they could've rebuilt Atlanta after Sherman's little visit.

They began their work, curiously enough, taking down the one thing here that functioned with any reliability: The neon lights. That's right, they kicked off the day dragging down the colors of Old Dixie.

They set up a surveyor's table on the east side of the courtyard, under rotting eaves. A self-appointed foreman, in flannel and overalls on what already promised to be a sweltering day, barked orders to men, women and children alike.

The rush for tools was as immediate as it was joyful. Even the littlest ones made a grab for grinders and power drills. Soon the air filled with saws ripping, jackhammers ratcheting, sledgehammers thumping, and sanders, well, sanding.

Contractors and plumbers, unaccustomed to donating their

time, got busy in the bathrooms. They tore out the yellowed fiberglass bathtubs and the rust-stained bowls and sinks with cigarette burns in the soap dishes. In their haste, they failed to spare the Rickie Tickie Stickies, those delightful daisy-shaped non-skid appliqués, and it's a shame. Bathtubs just aren't as cheerful or safe without them.

They stripped the floors of their faded linoleum and deep pile shag, found checkerboard tiles and smooth oak beneath. They stripped the walls of their Tru-Wood paneling and Brick-Look vinyl, painted the plaster underneath a sensible shade of alabaster. The outer walls received a paint job as well, a lovely robin red with touches of mockingbird gray.

They got rid of everything that lent unsavory character to the Dixie Court. Musky mattresses, germinating sites for many an ill-conceived hillbilly, are no more. Vanquished are the mysterious stains, the rank odors and heady man-stink. Where it once reeked like a truck stop, or milk spoiling in a dumpster, it now smells of apple blossoms, and maybe a little almond.

Hard hours of hard work resulted in real changes, but the miraculous transformations were yet to come.

Miracles in Metal

AN ELDERLY MAN named Noah Johnson performed the first miracle. It was both good and appropriate. Let me tell you why.

Noah Johnson was born the son of a preacher man, who himself was born the son of a preacher man. By all family accounts, Noah was destined to be a preacher man, too. He accepted the calling early in life and learned to read the Good Book in Greek, Latin and Hebrew by the age of fourteen.

After all those years of studying the Word of God, Noah was seized by a divine discontent. He couldn't shake his passion for a place he had grown to love more than heaven.

That place was Jerimiah's Junkyard, an auto salvage lot on the outskirts of Calloway.

He played there as a child, and helped Jerimiah scavenge, search for and sort out car parts in exchange for unlimited access to this Golgotha of automotive graveyards.

He brought a sizable chunk of his graveyard to the Dixie Court Motel. I asked him about it as he inspected the grounds. "Jerimiah's Junkyard was a city of the dead for cars," he told me. "But each piece here, see, is waiting for resurrection, for new life. Jesus told us not to put new wine into old bottles, but he didn't say not to put old parts into new cars—or anywhere else for that matter. That's what Jerimiah always told me."

Jerimiah passed away when his protégé was merely sixteen, leaving him in sole possession the legacy that was his scrap heap and the dogs that protected it. Noah then knew he had to choose between salvage and salvation.

He didn't hesitate.

"First thing I did is yank down the old sign, just like we done here today. Then I painted up a new one. One that said, 'Noah's Boneyard.'"

Then he got to work on building the thing he'd been constructing in his mind for half his life. He rounded up hubcaps and bumpers, alternators and axles, grilles and pistons. He took a blowtorch to the heap and created his own ark. Noah's Ark, replete with chrome animals. It got to be pretty famous. So famous, in fact, that famous people traveled for miles just to see it.

"Freddie Prinze, Jr. was is awe," Noah boasted. "He wanted

to buy a pair of animals and wouldn't leave until I let him go with the emus."

Noah has since replaced the emus and added several dozen other species to the menagerie. Currently, he's working on those that face extinction in our lifetime. He'll look at the fender of a Plymouth Satellite and see an Ethiopian wolf. He'll look into the rust-mottled hood of a Corvair and find the coat of an ocelot. And strange as it sounds, Dodge Dart taillights are good for the eyes of a variety of lemurs, provided they're enormous lemurs.

"I won't live long enough to build them all. It takes more than a lifetime to recreate Creation. But if I did, I'd still have enough materials left over to build and fill a second ark."

He said he has enough chrome alone to mirror the earth. "That's a good thing, too," he added. "Everything looks better with chrome on it."

That goes doubly true for American diners, which is why Noah Johnson, master craftsman that he is, readied himself to put his chrome touch on everything in and around Amitabh's diner. He might've completely encased the old establishment in chrome—or stainless steel where chrome proved too gaudy—*had not a preliminary cleaning uncovered the finest in diner décor already in place.*

Under the kudzu, they found a structure with rounded glass-block corners and a fine barrel roof. Inside, under the dust and dirt, they found porcelain tiles in aqua-lime colors and glass with art deco patterns. They uncovered red vinyl stools in need of but a little oil before they could swivel at a solid marble counter.

The kitchen, however, was a remnant of inexplicable cataclysm. I might guess it was a grease fire ignited in the heat of a fierce gunfight, but that wouldn't explain half the damage. Still, Noah Johnson set to work there, too. He built stainless steel counters and grills and ovens. He built a basket fryer so big you could flash-fry a pony in eight seconds flat. And still he had enough material left over to steel- and chrome-plate the exterior until it shined like a rocket ship.

It was a work of art beautiful enough to drop Amitabh to his knees and make him cry. In fact, last I checked, he was still crying. Well, he'd better dry those tears and write up some menus because he can expect some business now. What's more, they won't be coming to Pullman for bread alone. They'll be coming to take in the waters.

Miracles in Water

WHY, YOU ASK, would folks come to Stillwater for water when there are lovely beaches just one county over?

Well, let me tell you about the waters in Stillwater. I'll tell you what I can.

Nobody knows for sure where the waters begin. Nobody can explain what's in the waters or why they behave the way they do. All that's certain is these are no ordinary waters. These waters have powers.

Near as anyone can figure, the waters begin in the Odium Swamp as regular swamp waters. Nothing too special about them, except part of the waters turns colder than the rest. This causes them to sink deep down into a spring that runs under the swamp.

The spring carries the waters westward, where they filter through the sandy soils under the Dearth Hills. It's still all normal water at this point, but then it crooks back in a northerly direction and something strange happens.

Just north of the Dearth Hills are the Calypso Fields. Story goes, this was where the Gingaskin Indians buried their dead. For thousands of years they planted bodies here. All kinds of dead. Baby dead, war dead, elderly dead. Those who died in hunting accidents or drowned or just dropped dead. Gingaskin Indians had a habit of dying early and often, which helps explain why none are around today.

The ground got so full of death it couldn't take any more. It began rejecting the dead. It evicted their souls and bones, moved them on to find hallowed grounds. Old ones say whatever was in the ground rejecting mortality, it got in the waters.

But the waters don't stop there. They pick up momentum and flow toward Hunters. They stay deep enough underground to keep from disturbing the dead there, but every so often the waters rise. They seep into Mount Calvary, which isn't really a mountain, but rather a valley that holds Stillwater's biggest cemetery. The waters get in there and stir up the souls of the dead. And then there's trouble in town. Agitated souls prowl through homes, and stalk children and the elderly at night.

Nobody knows the trouble better than Tookie Harrington. Her twin boys have been dead for decades, but they keep coming back. Every time the waters rise, they start smashing things around her house, scaring her cats and chasing Tookie out into her yard. That's what Tookie will tell you, anyway. That's how she'll explain what she's doing when she's standing in her front yard at six in the morning, wearing nothing but black pajamas.

Like most folks in Hunters, Tookie has a bottle tree to trap wayward spirits. They're drawn to the colorful bottles like tourists to neon, and then they get trapped inside. But the bottles don't always hold, especially when the waters rise.

"*The waters, they're not all bad,*" *Tookie said to me at the Dixie Court.* "*I figured that out years ago. I figured anything with enough power to raise souls from the dead could be applied to useful purposes.*"

Tookie claimed that the rejuvenating powers of the waters have preserved her health and restored her youth. That much is evident in her looks. She also said that she uses the waters for her garden. As a result, she harvests okra the size of bananas, tomatoes like softballs, and peaches nearly as big as your head. Best of all, she's never had to replant a crop the following season. They just keep coming back.

Tookie showed up here on Friday morning just like everybody else, but with a very different plan in mind. But first, it helps to know what Tookie knows. She knows a lot because she's been around longer than anybody else in Stillwater, or at least anybody near as lucid as herself. That is to say, Tookie remembers the days of yore, simpler times and, some might say, better times.

She remembers a time before Noah Johnson took up studying the Bible, a time when his father, Reverend Johnson, had his run as Stillwater's favorite preacher.

"*People don't like to talk about how the Apostolic church was back then,*" *Tookie said, as if anyone else remembers.* "*Back when Reverend Johnson preached at the Unified House of Prayer for All People of the Church of the Rock of the Apostolic Faith. You might say he was a spell on the flashy side. That Reverend Johnson, they called him Reverend King Daddy Johnson, you know, on account of he liked to wear a tall crown made of all silk and jewels, and long flowing robes. And he carried a scepter. I remember that now. Big gold shaft with a bulbous end. Oh, but he was so handsome it hardly mattered what he wore.*"

Tookie also remembers that he couldn't baptize his people fast enough or often enough, and so saw fit to baptize with any waters he could lay hands on. "He'd dunk us in the Cottonmouth River," she said with a fond grin. "More than twice he marched us through a thunderstorm in Jesus' name, halleluiah. In the summer, he'd baptize us with fire hoses. Mind you, this was a long ways before they turned on the fire hoses in Birmingham."

But for all the soakings his congregation received, they still liked to take in what he called the Devil's Waters. These, of course, are the same waters that rise up to cause problems in Hunters, the same waters Tookie sometimes indulges in. Only back then, they weren't so elusive. In fact, they flowed straight to the Dixie Court Resort, where guests could enjoy the healthful and rejuvenating warm springs.

"I remember when President Franklin D. Roosevelt came down for a dip," Tookie said, her eyes shining with a distant look. "He had all kinds of men in suits and nurses and lifeguards to help him into the pool. But oh Lord, you should've seen the look on their faces when the President got up out the pool and walked himself to fetch a cig'rat. They had a look like he was walking on water. President's little miracle didn't last long though. Soon as he lit that 'rat, he went back to being an invalid.."

Reverend Johnson was not ready to compete with miracles, small, brief or otherwise. He therefore pronounced the waters as evil and the resort a Hedonistic playground for charlatans, nomadic harlots, mischievous imps, and promiscuous college students. When that failed to undermine its popularity, Reverend Johnson decided to dam up the waters, and he did so with a divining rod and a well-placed tombstone on the far side of Mount Calvary.

The stone reduced the waters to a trickle, with only the occasional overflow problems, and effectively shut down the Dixie Court Resort.

"There's some filtering through," Tookie said, sniffing the air. "You can smell it."

So if Tookie remembered right, and I'd bet *diamonds to doorknobs she could, a simple tombstone removal would restore the substantial flow of waters to the Dixie Court.*

But first, at Tookie's advice, her assistants drained the pool. I stood by and watched, hoping to see the leviathan from the night before. Turned out to be a school of carp, and no one knew what to do with them until the ladies from the Calloway Garden Club suggested a pond on the far side of the courtyard. What they had in mind was some sort of Japanese-style garden. Sort of minimalist, I heard one say. Well, that soon evolved along arabesque lines until what they had more closely resembled a mogul's garden with a Southern Victorian touch.

They replaced all chain link on the grounds with wrought iron fencing tall and sharp enough to impale pig heads. They trained Cherokee roses to climb the posts. They scored a pair of peacocks from Noah's chrome menagerie. Then they constructed a gazebo with an onion dome roof and brought in claw-footed lounge chairs. On every table, they placed sweetgrass baskets full of jasmine in bloom. As for the pond, it quietly occupies a corner behind the three-tiered fountain, and the carp seem content as ever.

The pool, drained and scrubbed, was now ready for its healing waters. It was just a matter of removing a tombstone and waiting for it to come bubbling in. Well, as it turned out, Tookie also had to remember exactly which tombstone appeared for no good reason shortly before the waters dried up. And as further testament to her keen memory, she got it right on the fifth try.

Resorting to Perfection

I HAVE SEEN *many a fine spa resort in my time. In the Black Forest town of Baden-Baden, I once seated my naked rump in a tub that oft washed some of the greatest minds the world has ever known: Victor Hugo, Dostoyevsky, Brahms, and Mark Twain, to name a few.*

In the clearest of Florida's artesian springs, I witnessed the Weeki Wachee Mermaids' somnambulant adagio. I have soaked away aches and ailments in Mexican arsenic wells, and drank the water to keep them from coming back.

But never have I enjoyed a spa like the one here in Pullman. It is a spectacle to behold. Had I not watched the townsfolk resurrect it in a day, I might justifiably wonder now if somewhere in the Byzantine world an emperor was missing his baths. I watched it all happen, but I still can't figure out how they did it.

At first glance, you might mistake the citizens of Stillwater for slack-jawed imbeciles, mean drunks, superstitious simpletons, and inbred, Bible-thumping ignorami, and you might easily be excused. But when they come to do a job, they come in a showy rush and work like the Amish on amphetamines. It causes me to shake my head in admiration.

What they created here is a thing of beauty, a joy forever, and certainly an attraction in itself. Truly blessed are the guests who stumble upon this place. For now, they might simply be folks looking to hideout for a spell and wayward travelers who got lost looking for a shortcut to the beach. Whatever their reason for coming here, Amitabh welcomes them all with his new neon highlights and a sign proudly shining out "Fountains of Youth Spa Resort." Surely without it they would continue to stumble

aimlessly into the night.
Shine on, Amitabh. Shine on.

Three Months Later
Diwali

First Day of Diwali:
Dhanvantari Triodasi

THIS HAS GOT to be the strangest time of year for me. Strange in a good way, I suppose. It's not even Halloween and Mr. Patel's got the place lit up like Christmas. It's kind of like Indian Christmas, only it's called Diwali.

I don't exactly get Diwali, but I do know what Mr. Patil expects from me. I'm supposed to make sure the rooms are extra clean, and then I'm supposed to bathe like I haven't bathed in a year. I'm supposed to wash with some kind of special bathing oil here, the same kind he's been giving me every year for as long as I can remember. Smells pretty, like toasted macaroons, and every time I use it, I can close my eyes and smell my way back to better days, when my mama was alive and Sonali was still here. It's better than that feeling you get on Easter when you eat Marshmallow Peeps.

We pray like mad during Diwali. We offer saltwater taffy to the beech tree out front and pray that nobody dies an untimely death. We also throw bones like it's Mardi Gras because all gambling is sanctioned by Goddess Parvati so that we may achieve the blessings of wealth and prosperity in the coming fiscal year. Strange thing is Mr. Patil won't let us gamble for money, says it's illegal. But I happen to know for a fact that he won the Dixie Court Motel on one Diwali night.

Toward the end of Diwali, on Bhratri Dooj, guys are supposed to visit their sisters and ask how they're doing. Since Mina, Arati and Sonali never had any brothers, Mr. Patil always asked me to stand in as one. I didn't mind, really, because it's a simple ritual, easier now that I only have to bother with Mina. She's cool about it, doesn't drag it out like Sonali and Arati used to. Ask them how they're doing and they'd respond with laments fit for Bronte sisters. You'd think I was their therapist, way they went on. They didn't want me to get by so easy because they knew as well as I did that the otherwise simple chore absolved me of all sin. Weird, I know. Like the opposite of a Catholic confession, and not at all a bad deal for me, no matter how long they whined and groaned about their lives.

Thing I love best about Indians is they have so many holidays. About a million in all, I think, which makes sense considering their deities number about thirty-three million and change. Diwali is the most significant holiday, and so much religious significance is tied to it that it takes five days to sort it all out. A whole mess of important things happened during Diwalis past: Mother Lakshmi emerged from an ocean of milk to bring wealth and prosperity to India, though that's not much in evidence today, from what I hear. Lord Krishna destroyed the demon Narakasur and made the world free from fear. Lord Ram returned from His fourteen-year exile. Fourteen years doesn't amount to much in the life of a god, so I don't get all the fuss. I don't question it either, because everyone gets presents.

Still, Diwali around here can get more complicated than the laws of cricket. That's because Mr. Patil, who grew up in his father's hotel, learned to celebrate the holiday according to the regional customs of his guests.

He told me that in the northern parts of India, Diwali is all about binge shopping. Buying presents. New clothes, kitchen utensils and recliners being the more popular items. In Delhi and elsewhere, a friendly game of poker can go on for three days and nights.

Meanwhile, the West Bengalis pay tribute to Kali, an aloof goddess bent on cleaning up societal corruption. This She attempted through the total annihilation of humankind, but the other gods wouldn't allow it. The destruction of humanity, I mean. I don't know where They stood on wiping out corruption. All I know is Shiva tried to stop Kali, but He ended up getting His butt stomped.

I'm not sure what the deal was between Kali and Shiva, but I think they had a thing going on. Some kind of love jones.

Kali gave up on her mission, but now She's got a popular following of thugs who aim to carry it out for Her. So I guess that's what they do for Diwali in West Bengal, set out on murderous rampages. We don't do anything like that here, though.

The most important thing about Diwali is the lamps. We get to light the place up. Like I said, it's looking a lot like Christmas. In addition to all the fancy new neon and reflective chrome, about a hundred *diyas* light up the windows and the walkways, and the pool and fountains. Diyas are these oil lamps made out of clay. Arati and I made most of them years back. We dug wagonloads of red clay out of the banks of the creek that runs out of Pullman Quarry and spent a whole weekend making diyas of all shapes and sizes. From afar they could be mistaken for jack-o-lanterns, so this place doesn't look entirely weird. In fact, it's right pretty, and with the weather as it's been, crisp enough for long pants and a windbreaker, there's no better night to sit out in a cane rocker and stare at oil lamps.

I must've been sitting out here for hours now, watching traffic go by and rereading *American Ethic* for the umpteen-thousandth time. *American Ethic* ran the "Fountains of Youth" story. Not the whole thing, of course. Mina and I made a few changes before e-mailing it to Ed. We cut out the references to kudzu and water bugs, things we didn't like. We also added a little section on our new open-air piano lounge. Lester didn't mention it because we don't have a liquor license or a piano player, but we can make any kind of juice, chai or yogurt lassi you can think of and enjoy it by the pool. Mina also wanted to mention all the marigolds they planted around the resort, but I wasn't comfortable with that. Marigolds aren't supposed to appear unless somebody's getting married.

Hardest part in editing the piece was Lester's fibs. I don't care so much that he took my work and played like he did all the research and interviews. Mina and I started that end of the deception. But that he just took it and ran with it, well, I suppose the old dog was too far-gone to change his habits and too tore up right now to worry about it.

But that left Mina and me to deal with as many fibs as we could catch—like changing that nonsense about Freddie Prinze, Jr. and the emus back to Sammy Davis, Jr. and the ostriches. Mina figured Lester was reaching for a younger audience, emus being more popular with the kids these days.

When we finished editing, we were proud of the piece, and Ed was quite proud of Lester, even though Lester doesn't remember writing it. He's what doctors call a blithering imbecile, doesn't seem able to keep up on current events like he once did. He doesn't even seem to mind that his Jaguar bounced on his head and smashed his face. He's so tore up, the nurses make him wear a mask. They had what looked like a hockey mask on him, made him wear it every day. He looked like Jason Vorhees. That creeped me out, so I brought him a couple of my old Halloween masks. Now some days he's Casper, other days he's Skeletor. Doesn't seem to matter much to him either way.

What matters is that story made Pullman famous. It ran all over the planet. It was on the wires and the Internet. *Stars and Stripes* ran excerpts, as did *Homeland, McHart's, Golden Years, RV Destinations* and *New Age Retreat.*

All kinds of folks from near and far come motoring here. Some for the waters, some just to marvel at the chrome. Everybody loves the food. They say, "That's the best catfish curry ever I did have!" And, "Boy howdy, that's some tasty lentil barbecue!"

They come from neighboring counties and states. Some from states with license plates I'd never seen before. Ohio. Oregon. New Mexico. I wasn't aware they had cars in New Mexico.

We get guests from other countries, too. Places like Canada and England. Had a young couple here from Korea last week. No kidding. They spoke Korean and everything.

It's a wonderful thing, seeing all different kinds of people coming here. Mr. Patil rejoices in welcoming them all, and everyone else in Stillwater has adopted his shining enthusiasm for hospitality. At Noah's Boneyard, Noah Johnson gives three tours a day, even though half his animal sculptures are gone. This guy from Washington, D.C., talked him into shipping them off to a place called the Hirshhorn. I'm not so sure that was such a wise idea, taking the creatures out of their natural habitat, but

Noah said he was honored and he still gets all his visitors. He put down his last two Jerimiah dogs so they wouldn't scare anyone off.

Moses gets a bunch more traffic coming through his place, too. Tourists on the way to see Noah's Boneyard can't help but wonder what the All-Seeing Eye is doing on the side of a tar house. They come in and see the sign, the one I helped write up about all the things revealed to you after you die. They're very curious about that, especially the one that goes, *The mistakes you repeated most frequently.* You'd think people would be well aware of anything repeated most frequently, but outside of radio tunes and movie sequels, they act painfully unacquainted with the repetitious patterns in their lives.

Tookie's a good example of that. For years and years, she let her boys tear through her house and scare her cats. She knew all along how to get rid of them, how to keep the waters from rising. She knew what would let souls all over Hunters rest for good. All she needed to do was pull up the right tombstone, and she went for decades like it was pulling a tooth. Give her credit, Moses says. She did undo her biggest mistake in her lifetime. Most people don't get to say that before they die.

So the waters don't rise in Hunters anymore, but I swear Tookie must have stored away barrels of it, way her garden still grows. She's growing older, though. You can see that as the months pass. Moses says she ought to be ready to see her boys again, this time on their terms.

Way things have changed around here so fast, seems like a bucket of months have passed. People all the sudden got money now. Money goes to fix things up, like the Stardust Drive-In and Stillwater County High. There's talk of putting up what's called an Imax theater, which is a theater with a screen as big as a drive-in's, but you sit in chairs to watch it. There's talk of constructing a big huge Harris-Teeter Supermarket in Calloway and a TCBY in Pullman and a TGIF in Hunters. Maybe a Hooters, too, which they say is a Halloween-themed restaurant with owls and trick-o-treat colors.

People are donating money to Historic Preservation Societies and Endangered Species Preservation Societies and other societies that didn't exist in Stillwater more than three months ago. Sheriff Horton's leading the drive on erecting a statue in Hunters, says it should be of our greatest military hero. His son Norman is currently stationed in Tegucigalpa, fighting the War on Drugs, so that pretty much qualifies him as our greatest military hero in anyone's best memory. I'm all for it, a statue of Norman Horton in the middle of Hunters. I figure since I passed as him when I used his license to buy beer, maybe people might mistake me for a military hero. I wouldn't mind that so much.

But then nobody is opposed to overall improvements around here. It's like they got some fixit bug when they decided to spruce up the motel. They tore down that old Dixie neon and didn't ever quit, like they just don't know the cure for fixit bugs. Whole place looks a far cry from the one Lester described in his first story on Stillwater. That's a good thing, I suppose, but I can't help but think they need to slow down.

Not like I have time to dwell on it, though. Place is getting crowded with tourists. You can spot them coming from a mile away, but you can't turn around without bumping into one.

Like tonight, it's the night before the harvest moon, I can tell from the way the horizon is screaming pumpkin orange, and there's a rental car, a white Chrysler Cordoba with tinted windows prowling up and down the road in front of our resort. People from far away places act like they're casing the joint before they finally decide to pull up. Farther away they live, the longer they take. I figure the Cordoba people must be from Sweden at least. Or maybe we'll get Zambians tonight.

I'd like to jump right out in the road and tell them there's no need to scout us out. This place is great, I'd tell them. Everything you read about it is true. The waters are fine all year round, but best on a cool night like this. The food is outstanding and worth the wait, but you better hurry because the diner is about to close for the night. Of course, if you're hungry, we'll whip something up. The staff is friendlier than the Superfriends, I'd yell, so stop staring at the place like it's a damn house of haints.

I'm about to do that on the Cordoba's tenth pass, but then it pulls into the lot.

I stay put, in a cane rocker next to the lobby door. Got a Nu-Grape in one hand, the other scratching Surya's head. I'm dying to find out where these people hail from, what new foreign words they can teach me, but I don't want to seem too eager.

Surya, however, hasn't yet learned proper resort etiquette and decides to go nuts. He wobbles to his feet and howls at the headlights. Takes three whole steps before keeling back on his left haunch. Old mat dog hasn't shown that much energy since leading Lester and me out of the swamp.

The car stops in the valet drop-off space, a few feet in front of me. Cuts the headlights, then the engine. Passenger side door pops open and I see who's sitting in the front seat. Arati, that's who. And next to her, in the driver's seat, is Sonali.

I am stuck in the cane rocker like a bat in the baffle, and all I can do is yell out for Mr. Patil. It takes him seconds to reach my side, but then and there he's struck with the same spell I got. We both feel pretty silly acting frozen this way, but the girls aren't doing much better. It's like we're watching each other on TV.

Sonali breaks the spell. She eases out from behind the steering wheel. She looks like a ghost in her white cotton sari, but she's oh so exotic. She says, "I brought mother home."

WE ALL EXPECTED him to grieve when Sonali carried the silver urn in outstretched arms and death-marched into the lobby. We expected him to tie a cloth around his head as though he has a toothache. We expected him to tie his big toes together and, somehow, his thumbs as well. We expected him stretch out on the floor, face up, head pointing south. We expected all this and more, but all Mr. Patil says is: "She said this place would be her tomb."

"She said you would say that," Sonali replies. "She believed it strongly. That is why she asked me to bring her back here." Her voice is different from what I remember. She has an accent, almost as soft and delicate as the way I imagine the way Mohini spoke. It's also dreamy in a way, like she's been in some kind of Krishna cult.

She sets the urn on her father's desk. A gone look dulls her eyes. She wipes her hands on the hem of her sari while asking him, "Where is Mina?"

Mr. Patil is locked on the urn, so I tell her, "Over yonder." I nod toward the window, toward that symphony in stainless steel where we serve up confections of the gods. "In the diner. You hungry?"

"Starved!" Arati blurts. Her voice comes back to her in the somber silence. She cringes, adjusts her glasses, whispers, "But I can stay here with Bapa while y'all eat."

"No," Mr. Patil responds, snapping out of his gaze. "There will be no staying here with Bapa while stomachs are pining for sustenance. Now come along, we shall all dine together."

Sonali checks her watch. "I've got noon, which means—" She counts back on her fingers. "—it's now nine o'clock last night. Haven't you eaten yet?"

"Of course we have eaten." He embraces both his daughters. "You must be knowing there is never hunger in our home; and likewise, there is never a time when we cannot eat again."

I'm still trying to wrap my head around the fact that it's now nine o'clock last night. It's as if Sonali came to us out of the future, out of a distant, exotic land where the past is older than Creation and the future is now.

THE WURLITZER IS blasting rockabilly tunes all over the diner. Mina's facing it, mop in her hand. She's mopping the same swath of checkerboard tiles over and over and she step-slides to the left, shakes it there, step-slides to the right, gyrates, all the while belting lyrics into the mop handle.

Her groove is infectious. First Arati backs her up with a step-slide and shake. Then Sonali's drawn in. Step-slide and gyrate. Then Mina leads them into a spin, followed by a scream and what looks like jazz hands.

"You scared the pee out of me!" she gasps, clutching her belly. And then she wants to know, all at once, how long they've been dancing behind her, and when did they get in, and why didn't they warn us, and what they're doing here, anyway. And they reply with a flurry of hugs and kisses and pulling on her arms to punctuate answers.

Mr. Patil and I are floored with the spectacle of his daughters' reunion. It takes us back, not to simpler times or better times, necessarily. Just back in time, and that's enough to cheer us up in a sad, sorrowful way, a way that lifts our hearts and pits out our stomachs and fills us with wonderment and what-could-have-beens. Mostly, it makes us wish it could stay this way forever.

Mr. Patil rocks back on his heels and says, "I should be beating the two of you with a rattan cane. How long has it been since either of you thought to write home?"

Sonali and Arati hang their heads, while Mina takes on an uncharacteristic look of self-righteousness. The three of them scooch together in one side of a booth. Mr. Patil and I take the other side and stare them down. He says, "Mina, go into the kitchen and begin with the preparing of suitable food for your sisters. They are so skinny now they look as if they might snap like some kind of skinny stalk of dried bamboo."

Mina smoothes over her own tummy, sucks in her gut. She's gained a few pounds since we opened the diner. As she shuffles off toward the grill, I tell her to fry me up some okra. She sticks her tongue out at me before rounding the corner.

Arati takes her father's hand. "I'm sorry," she says. "I couldn't write you. I was so unhappy with Coloco that there was nothing else I could think of saying. I didn't want to worry you."

He studies her eyes for a moment. "What is going on at this Coloco pharmaceutical company that is making you so miserable?"

She draws in a deep breath, holds it. Puffs the air out in an unsteady flow, like a stutter. "I invented a new medicine. I even got to name it. I named it Caliban, after crazy old man Cal, you know, the guy who painted everything? Is he still around?"

"I'm sure he is," I answer. "But nobody's seen him since July. Why'd you name a drug after him?"

"The way the lab rats behaved before I cured them, mostly the way they ran into things, that sort of reminded me of Cal."

"So what, exactly, is the purpose of this Caliban medicinal drug?" asks Mr. Patil.

"It's a cure for brain cancer."

"Why have I not been hearing about Caliban on the TV and in the newspapers?"

"It's still in the developmental stages. I mean, it works. Everybody at Coloco knows it works. Only there are some problems." She sips on the tea Mina's brought us, sips on it like she doesn't need to say anything else.

But we're waiting for the aforementioned problems. She knows we're waiting, so finally she blurts it all out: "For one, I made Caliban out of natural substances, regular old plants. So until they develop a synthetic alternative that they can patent and monopolize, they're going to let it sit, which serves them just as well, since research shows they'll make infinitely more money if they wait for an epidemic. They're banking on an epidemic."

Mr. Patil reaches across the table and takes her hand. "Arati, my sweet, have I not warned you against the flagrant quackery that is Western medicine?"

Arati lowers her gaze to his stern, steady hand. "Yes, Bapa. Many times."

An idea crosses my mind. "Hey, so if I get brain cancer, you can fix me up, right?"

"Need a brain to get brain cancer," Mina says, dropping a basket of fried okra in front of me. I have to let that one slide. She did bring me okra, and there's a lot more food on the way. She'll be bringing out catfish curry and lentil barbecue with a side of chard slaw. She even learned her father's recipe for the now legendary mango chutney.

Sonali picks at my okra, sniffs it, tosses it back. Sighs. She says, "Mina, I don't know how else to tell you, but mother has passed."

Mina says, "So?"

"Mina!" her father scolds. "Show some respect!"

"Hell she ever do for me, besides leave?" No one has an answer for that. "And how is it you know this tragic news before us? You got some kind of Indian news channel on your fancy cable TV in Wilmington?"

Sonali bobbles her head, a distinct Indian gesture I've always found inscrutable. "I no longer live in Wilmington, Mina. I haven't lived there in years." She parts her lips to say more, but her eyes widen instead, as though she's grown woozy from head-bobbling and no longer trusts herself to speak.

As with Arati, we wait for her to gather and explain herself. She apologizes, blames her discombobulation on jetlag, but doesn't add anything more. Her father sips on iced chai and smiles at her with all the patience of a drunken fisherman caning for crappie in a dry creek bed.

Mina and I, on the other hand, are about to blow rivets out of our foreheads. We grow exhausted with the waiting and lob a few questions at her. Sonali bats them down, but over the next two hours we manage to coax, prod and provoke answers out of her.

In short, the interrogation reveals this much:

Her career as a starlet in Wilmington's cutthroat celluloid industry was short lived. Actually, stillborn is a better word. Closest she came to see her name on rolling credits was as "third rumble victim" in a Jan Michael Vincent movie that never got finished. After that, she landed photo shoots with cars and drivers at the Wilmington Motor Speedway. Some of her pictures ended up on calendars. I mean big-time calendars, nationally distributed though Tommy Torque Hardware and Auto Parts Emporiums.

Way she talks, the fame wore her out. All that fan mail to answer, all those appearances she had to put in at racetracks and family restaurants, not to mention every Tommy Torque Emporium throughout the South. So after six years of photo shoots, she quit the calendar racket and set out for her dreams of Bollywood stardom. However, instead of heading straight for Bombay, she decided to hit the opposite seaboard to pay her mother a visit.

Mohini lived alone in Orissa, all of her family long dead in the skirmishes against the Patels. She lived in hunger and constant fear. She begged Sonali to bring her home to Stillwater. Sonali could not afford it. She couldn't even afford to take her to Bombay, but certainly wasn't prepared to leave her mother in a dirt hovel in rural Orissa. So she compromised, and the two of them moved to Calcutta.

"It seemed like a good move," Sonali says. "Calcutta has a decent movie industry. It is very avant-garde," she says, tapping her index finger to her temple. "Far more sophisticated and artistic than Bombay. In Bombay, they made fifty-eight Indian adaptations of *Ghost*, plus thirty-two sequels—all of them musicals." She presses her hands to her face and moans: "I'm telling you, I could have starred in half of them."

So while Calcutta lacked the glitter and glamour of Bombay, Sonali figured avant-garde cinema might very well launch her career. And while waiting for her break with Calcutta's art-house cinema, she took up modeling.

She modeled as various Hindu gods and goddesses, the kind that often appear on Indian calendars. She flips one of these calendars on the table and says, "I guess I was destined to be a calendar girl, but at least this way I'm also a god."

Better than that, she's many gods. She's a pantheon.

Way they got her dressed up and in a different color every month, you can't tell it's her in every picture. But I can. I can see right through the glam-rock make-up and candy-colored skin tones. Her scalp, revealed in the part in her hair, is much lighter than her face, and it shows in the pictures. Her left eye has two freckles beneath the pupil and is a shade lighter than her right. That shows, too. The mole above the bow of her lip is concealed, but I can see it, if only because I know it's there. And of course the rest of her face. It's *her* face on Brahma, on Kama, on Indra and Agni. On Yama and Surya and Kali and Dwapara. She could be any one of the thirty-three million *devas* and she'd look just as hot.

Mr. Patel's eyes grow ever wider with each passing month. "These certainly appear more risqué than the gods and goddesses I am used to seeing on my calendars."

"It's blasphemous," Sonali huffs.

"No, no. Not at all. It is quite stunning, and you must be knowing that I am very proud of you. Very proud of the both of you. In fact, I am disbelieving that my two daughters are finding frustration in their successes."

"Hey, *three* daughters," Mina objects. "The success of our resort is getting a little frustrating for me without the extra help we need."

"When I read about the resort, I could not believe it," Sonali says, admiring the diner's sparkling chrome and tile. "I never imagined it could be this beautiful, this palatial."

"You read about it?" Mr. Patil asks. "In India?"

"Of course."

"And your mother? She read about it also?"

Sonali nods.

"Well? What did she think?"

Sonali bites her lower lip. "She didn't have much time to think. She read it. She had a stroke. She died the next day. Her last words to me were, 'It's mine. It was a gift to me. Take me back.' I told her no, her ashes needed to be scattered in the Ganges. She cried. She said she wanted her Taj Mahal. She kept saying, 'It's mine,' and 'Take me back,' all the way up to her last breath. I couldn't say no to that."

An idea crosses my mind, a really cool idea about masks. Wouldn't it be great to have masks modeled after Hindu gods? I'd like to be Ganesh, the elephant-headed god who rides around on a rat. No, better: I want to be Lord Hanuman, the monkey god.

Wait, that's not my idea. Well, it is, but I have a more important one. This idea is about my agreement with Moses Jefferson. He said if Sonali comes back first, I can go on and marry her. But if Mohini returns first, I stick to the arrangement. My idea is this: In the event of a tie, side with the one who's still alive.

Second Day of Diwali:
Narak Chaturdasi

LORD HANUMAN NEVER wears a shirt, just a whole mess of gold chains around his neck. He also wears this little skirt, like a mini-sarong, or more like a kilt. He keeps his hair up in a bun, librarian style. Hardest part about the costume is the face. Not sure how to make my face look like a monkey's, but I have an idea.

I should be thinking more on Krishna. The second day of Diwali, Narak Chaturdasi, is dedicated to Krishna. But I don't want to be a Krishna. I want to be a monkey god.

I dig through my costume chest of Halloweens past. Gold chains surface from the year I dressed as LL Cool J. No chance in finding any kind of skirt in here, so a flannel shirt tied round my waist will have to suffice. I'll do without a bun in my hair. The important thing is the mask. I might've left it at the hospital for Lester. No, wait. Here it goes: My Cornelius mask. Long time ago I was Cornelius from *Planet of the Apes*.

So now I'm loping around my room, bare-chested except for the gold necklaces. Got the plaid flannel skirt tied around my waist, ape mask strapped to my face. I'm wondering why I didn't think to merge Halloween with Diwali in previous years. And at that moment, as I'm screeching and clawing for something to swing from, Sonali walks in, which wouldn't be so bad except that she catches me mid-lope and sees I'm not wearing anything under my kilt.

She waves it off. "It's nothing I haven't seen before." She's talking about when I was little. I had a penchant for running around naked until I was five years old. "I even had to change your diapers once." Somehow that makes me feel worse. I should've dressed as Lord Krishna. He's far more handsome. "What are you doing, anyway?" she asks.

"Getting ready for both Halloween and Navu Varsha." This year the fourth day of Diwali, which is called Navu Varsha, or Vikram New Year, falls on Halloween. That's just two days away. I should've spent more time today preparing for the new holiday combo. Instead I lounged by the pool with Sonali. Actually, she did the lounging. I mostly fetched passion fruit lassis for her and other guests. Somehow, that exhausted her. She complained about jetlag and turned in just after sundown. I figured she'd sleep through the night, but here it is, nearly eleven, and she's revved up and looking sprightly. A day in the waters can have that effect.

"So…" I hop off my bed, push my mask up on top of my head. "You're up late. How are you doing?"

"You're not supposed to ask until Bhratri Dooj."

"Right, but just remember, I already heard your laments last night, so don't waste our last day of Diwali with more bellyaching." She promises she won't. "Didn't think you would," I tell her. "You look like you're doing pretty good." She looks better than that. She's got on a long red T-shirt, comes halfway to her knees, and she's wearing a silver ring on her left ring toe.

She says, "You look good, too, Cy." She presses her forearm against mine. "You're so dark."

I look down at her forearm. We're about even in the tanning department and I feel pretty good about that. But then she laughs at the mask on top of my head, which is now grimacing straight at her. She pulls on it and lets it snap back against my scalp.

I gaze into her eyes. "Yeah, okay. I'm dark. But that's it? What about tall and handsome?"

She steps up close to me, her breath hot on my nose. "I'm still taller than you, but you don't look all bad."

"You neither."

"Yeah?" She grins. "I saw the way you were looking at my calendar."

"I was admiring the way you could represent so many gods."

"You were lusting over it."

"Was not!"

She strikes a godly pose and asks, "Was I sexy?"

I sit down on the edge of my bed, squeeze my knees together. "Yeah, I suppose."

"Even as Shiva? He's quite masculine, you know."

"Didn't appear that way to me."

She sits down next to me, her bare thigh touching mine. "Well, if you liked the calendars, maybe I ought to show you my video."

"What video?"

"I did a movie in Calcutta. I didn't say anything earlier because I don't want anyone else here to know about it."

"Why not?"

"Well, it was supposed to be something, I don't know, artsy. The script was based on an important play. *Salome.* It was an avant-garde version of *Salome.*" She tugs the hem of her shirt to her knees and frowns. "But now I'm afraid it's just sleazy."

"No. I don't believe it. Nothing you could do would turn out sleazy."

She nods. "I'm afraid it's true."

"I'll be the judge of that. Let's see it."

Something akin to suspicion passes over her face. "Perhaps later."

Sonali. In a movie. She must be famous in India. That means like a billion people know her name. "Hey, you remember when you told me that when you got famous, you'd come back for me and we'd live in your movie star mansion?"

She scrunches up her nose and shakes her head. Her hair whips across my face. It smells of marigolds. "Not really, but remember when you used to help me practice for meeting celebrities so I wouldn't seem like a demented fan when introduced?"

"Yeah, you'd say something like: 'I'm sorry, Mr. Cassidy. I'm looking for a more mature costar. What's your brother David doing these days?'"

She rocks back and laughs, fans her face with her hand. "No, no! I was more like: 'Yes, Mr. Travolta, I've seen a few of your song and dance routines. But if you really want to impress me, try doing a Hindi musical. No, seriously, you could pass. Just get a tan and apply some eyeliner.'"

She's cracking herself up in a big way. I should be laughing, too, but I'm not. I can't get my mind off what might be on her video. "Sonali?"

She shakes her finger at me and says, "Fonzie, you might be a teen heartthrob now, but that nephew of yours—"

"Can we watch the video now?"

She takes a sharp inhale, turns her gaze to her hand. That's when I realize I'm holding it. She pulls it free and wobbles her head in that cryptic way.

Third Day of Diwali:
Diwali

A LITTLE BACKGROUND info for all you heathens who skipped out on Sunday School: Salome was the sluttish daughter of Herodias and stepdaughter of Herod Antipas, Tetrarch of Galilee. Dysfunctional families abound in the Good Book, but this one beats all. Salome's real dad was Herod's brother, Philip. It gets worse: the brothers' shared wife was also their niece. And if that's not enough incest, Herod lusted after Salome as well. John the Baptist condemned this joyless union. Incensed, Herod imprisoned John, but was afraid to have the well-known prophet killed. Salome, of course, lacked such hang-ups, and demanded his head on a platter. And when she got it, she smooched on it.

She also had this thing about dancing with seven veils, a talent which some say makes her the hottest babe since Helen of Troy.

Murder, incest, strip teasing and heavy drinking—it's all about family values in Galilee, but I don't really get it.

I'm trying to explain all this to Mina, and she doesn't really get it either. "Sounds like something from a daytime talk show. Someone actually wrote a play about it?"

"Yeah, some guy called Oscar Wilde," I tell her in my most knowledgeable voice. "He thought this New Testament drama made a neat story and wrote up a shocker of a one-act play. This was like a hundred years ago when people were still really uptight, so it got banned from a lot of places."

"People do this stuff on stage?"

"Movies, too."

"I'd kinda like to see that."

I figured she would, way she got off on those *Friday the 13th* flicks.

We're washing dishes, cleaning up the diner after the breakfast rush. She looks a mess. Circles under her eyes, hair frazzled. You'd think it was her who stayed up till dawn, not Sonali and me. To be fair, Sonali is still in bed. I went to fetch her from her room before breakfast. She told me to sod off. I'm not sure what that means, but it didn't sound nice, so I let her sleep.

Mina says, "I came by your room last night."

"Really? What time?"

"Just before midnight."

"Why didn't you come in?"

"You already had company."

I fight back a grin. "Yeah, Sonali stopped by."

"So I heard. Sounded like you were having a ball. What were y'all laughing about so much?"

I shrug. "Just talking about the old days."

"Oh, bull." She squirts me in the face with the sprayer. "You spent the whole day with her, and then she had to see you late at night, too?"

"Yeah? So?"

"So y'all were making fun of me, weren't you? You were laughing at me."

"What? No, Mina. I swear your name didn't even come up."

She growls something under her breath and sprays me again. "Then what were y'all doing for so late?"

I wish I could tell her. She might be a brat sometimes, but she's the one I can talk to better than anyone, except maybe Moses Jefferson. I can't tell either of them about last night because Sonali insisted on total secrecy, made me swear on it before she left my room. Made me swear on my mama's grave.

I cock up an eyebrow in an enigmatic, smart-ass way.

Mina plunges a pair of juice glasses into the soapy water. "You think she's so hot, especially since she's a calendar girl. I could be a calendar girl, too, you know. I could be a god."

"Sure Mina. Whatever you say."

"Tell me the truth. Look at me and tell me. Don't you think I could be a god?"

I can't believe she set herself up like this. I look her dead in the eyes and I tell her: "Yes, Mina, you could be a god."

She cracks a smile, first one of the day. "Really?"

"Honestly, it's not said often enough: You could pass for Lord Hanuman, you monkey-face freak."

Oh man, that was a good one. What a slam. I hold up my hand for her to high-five me on that one, but she leaves me hanging. What's worse is she busts out bawling, sobbing all over the sink and boo-hooing so hard she blows a snot bubble.

"Mina? What's wrong?" I rub her back, but she shrinks away. "Mina? It's not like I haven't called you a monkey-face freak a hundred times before." That doesn't seem to help. She cries harder, calls me a bastard.

Ouch, jeez, that hurt. She hasn't called me a bastard since she first found out what the word really means. But what hurts worse is I haven't seen her cry this hard since her prom night. I don't know what her date did to her, can't even recall his name, but I beat the living crackers out of him and that made her feel better.

I can't think of anything to make her feel better now and it's breaking my heart. Hurts so bad it feels like it's thumping and bumping and beating the crackers out of me. I say, "Mina, look here." She won't face me, so I grab her by the shoulders and turn her around. She hammers on my chest, but I just look at her. I stare at her hard and deep. What I see lights a fire in my mind. I see—despite the frazzled hair and tears and tired eyes, despite the fact that she never wears makeup or any jewelry besides a beaded friendship bracelet that matches mine, despite how familiar her face has become in the decades I've known her—I see she's actually a hottie, too.

"What?" she says defensively. "What are you looking at?"

I'm looking at her tears, looking at them like diamonds are falling out of her eyes. I'm looking at her mouth, more specifically, the tiny crease in the middle of her lower lip. And her jaw, the way it hangs open slightly in curiosity. And her neck, smooth and long. Finally I look at her shoulders beneath my hands and I realize how good it feels to be touching her.

This is bad. I pretty much went through all this last night with Sonali. Difference is I understood that. I'd been saving up for that moment more than half my life, and in all that time I didn't ever think I'd feel this way for Mina, too.

It's a breathless revelation, finding out I've had this love in me for Mina all along. It's like finding out that I've had brain cancer growing inside me for years and years without knowing. Well, no, not as bad as cancer. It's more of a good thing.

This is more like, I don't know, what's the opposite of cancer?

This is more like enlightenment, the discovery of truth, joy and beauty. This is what Diwali is all about.

I can't help but tell her: "You're gorgeous."

"What?"

"You dazzle me." The surprise in my voice is about as strong as the tremor in her shoulders. I lean in to kiss her, but she pushes away from me. She backs into the counter and knocks over a pitcher of milk.

It spills to the floor and pools up over the tiles.

It's Diwali night. Typically, we'd all be throwing bones, betting candy on the outcome of our rolls. We should be praying and singing Diwali carols to Mother Lakshmi and Lord Shiva. None of this is happening now because a blue funk has settled over everyone.

Everyone except Mr. Patil. He's decked out in his finest kurta pajamas and he's setting off fireworks all over the resort, all the while trying to figure out why neither his daughters nor I are celebrating with him. "What has come over you people?" he asks me. "Everywhere I look is gloom, like some kind of gloomy Gus. You are all sitting around like somebody has died."

That's when it occurs to him. I sometimes get the blues on Diwali, partly because my mama isn't here to celebrate with us anymore. She loved this holiday more than any other, more than Thanksgiving and her birthday and Mother's Day combined. She loved the story of Mother Lakshmi emerging from an ocean of milk.

But now that story runs kind of the opposite of what my mama did. The ocean was in turmoil that day, the Dunes County sheriff told me, whipping up whitecaps that looked like frothy milk. I'm still stuck with a mental picture of her submerging in a sea of milk.

Mr. Patil understands this, probably better than myself. He lost his family back in Orissa. It's a wonder he can still celebrate Diwali at all, what with all the memories it brings. I asked him about it once when I was too young to know better than to ask questions like that.

He said he'd be fine as long as he didn't think about the Diwali customs that are practiced only in Orissa. He recalled with the sadness of remembrance about the sailboats his family would build on Diwali. They'd fill the boats with mustard and asparagus and wild creepers, things like that, then light the whole thing on fire.

Sounds like a blast, I know. I'm sorry we can't do stuff like that.

And then they'd pray like this, the way he whispered to me: *"Bada badua ho, andhaara re aasa, aluwa re jaa."* That means something like, "O forefathers, come to us in this dark evening, we light your way to heaven."

He couldn't pray that way any more, he told me long ago.

I wish we could. I wouldn't mind calling up my dead ancestors, or my mama for that matter.

At least he's always willing to allow me my space to grieve, but he has no idea how bad things have become.

Fourth Day of Diwali:
Navu Varsha / Halloween

I CAN'T REMEMBER the last time Halloween fell on Navu Varsha, the Vikram New Year. Might never have happened before in my lifetime. I have twice the reason to celebrate, but I can't muster the spirit. Likewise, you'd think finding love with two beautiful women would give you twice the reason to rejoice. It doesn't work that way.

Not much of a day for festivities anyway. Started out with rain howling down all over us. Seemed like it was raining all over the world. It doused our diya lamps and about guaranteed to wash out the trick-o-treaters as well. It washed away all the blown-up firecrackers. Before the rain, charred confetti swirled around the grounds and the smell of gunpowder clung to the heavy air. Mr. Patil seemed to enjoy that more than the bursts of fire and noise. Now it's all drained away in wet clumps. Despite that, I'm still trying to conjure up a holiday mood. I went ahead and dressed up like Lord Hanuman because it's my coolest costume ever, but I feel like quite the fool.

Sonali still won't talk to me, won't even leave her room. I've brought her meals, but all she tells me is to leave them at the door and come back later to pick up the dishes.

Mina acts like she's afraid of me. Every time I pass her she cringes like I might jump her bones and leave her with hickeys. I want to say something to her to make it better, but nothing comes to mind and I end up following her around like a lost dog. You might call it stalking.

I kind of understand their behavior. It makes sense to me if I try to think like a girl. What I don't get now is Arati. I wished her a Happy Navu Varsha and she ignored me. Wished her a Happy Halloween and she grunted at me in disgust, like I just dragged my butt across her carpet.

I catch her alone in her room and I say, "Arati? What's with you, girl?"

She tells me to figure it out, then tries to slam the door in my face. I catch it before it can do any damage to my mask. I say, "Come on, talk to me."

She tells me to take off my ridiculous mask and go put some clothes on. Then she'll talk to me. Five minutes later I'm back in her room wearing my favorite blue jeans and an orange sweatshirt. She says that's better, but she doesn't know I'm still wearing the chains.

She sits up on the dresser, pulls her knees to her chest, wraps her arms around her shins. Looks me over. She says, "You need to grow up, Cyrus."

I plant my fists on my hips. "Funny, Sonali told me the same thing the other night, only I knew what *she* was talking about."

"You know what I'm talking about. You can't play around like this."

I snort out a laugh at her.

"Don't pretend you think I don't know what I mean, because I know what's going on."

"Why don't you tell me then?"

She leans forward, says in conspiratorial whisper: "You and Sonali and Mina—"

Mina chooses this moment to trot by the window, ponytail wagging next to the beat up sneakers tied at the laces and dangling over her shoulder.

Arati eases off the dresser, adjusts her glasses. "Let's go for a walk."

We walk along cotton fields that nobody bothered to harvest this year, money coming in too easy for hard work like that. Arati strides at a brisk, I-mean-business pace, making me struggle to keep up. Silence stays with us until we reach the woods on the near side of Pullman Quarry. Long time back, Arati and I saw a yearling bear here. It rubbed and scratched up against a hollow maple. We came close enough to lob acorns at its head, didn't consider for a second the trouble we'd be in if its mama happened by.

I'd like to see that bear today, or one as small as it was, but the only sign of life I hear is a woodpecker rattling away on high, well out of sight. Our footsteps are quiet over the bed of damp leaves. The storm pulled them down by the bushel, whole branches in places, but for every leaf on the ground there are hundreds yet to fall. Bulldozer yellow and hunter orange and shotgun-shell red—so many leaves and colors that the clear blue of the sky, the small patch I can see, appears like faded denim.

While I stare up above, Arati continuously scans the ground for rare plants. I break the silence warning her that she's about to walk into a stand of wild azalea. She responds with, "That all you have to say to me?"

"I was waiting for you to talk next. That's where we left off, with you talking."

A stray wind kicks up, some slowpoke, lollygagging remnant from the storm that moved along hours ago. It blusters up her hair, obscuring her eyes. "Well, seeing as you actually might not be playing dumb, I'll walk you through this. Tell me what you said to Mina to make her cry."

"Called her a monkey-face freak."

The look she gives me says that's the wrong answer. "Then what?"

I crane my neck back, focus up at the leaves. "I can hardly begin to explain what I said next."

"I'm not asking you to explain yet. Just tell me what you said."

"I said she looked good."

"Good?"

"Gorgeous."

Arati hums in thought. "Yup, that's what she told me you said. She thinks you were being sarcastic, and then plain mean when you tried to kiss her."

"Hey, she tried first," I protest. Then, to Arati's look of doubt, I explain, "Back in high school, at the drive-in. She got drunk and practically tried to rape me."

"Let's stick with recent history. What happened with Sonali?"

"Can't tell you that. She made me swear on secrecy."

Arati shakes her head, clears the hair out of her face. "Sonali's already told me everything."

"She didn't!" I knew she would. The snitch keeps secrets like fireflies in a tiger cage.

"I need to hear it from you now," Arati says. "It's the only way I can help you."

I reflect back on the night, the way Sonali looked in my room, sitting next to me on my bed, her hand in mine. She said, "You know, Cyrus, I used to think one day you would be old enough to be my boyfriend, but you just seemed to grow younger and younger. For a while, I worried that maybe you were somewhat slow in the head and you'd never grow up."

I ask Arati, "Can you believe she said that to my face?"

"I can understand why she might've thought that," she replies.

Sonali also said she thought I might never grow up if I never left home. She said, "In Wilmington, so many actors work in surf shops while waiting for their big break. They're young, beautiful people who act so strong and confident. They walk their own walk, dress fashionably out of style, talk like they have their own language. It's like they know exactly what's going on all around them. Then you realize they do know, because they're locals. They've lived in that town their whole lives and they still live with their parents. Then you realize that they're pathetic losers, little punks too scared to go anywhere else in the world."

Arati tells me that Sonali doesn't see me that way.

"I know." I walk to the quarry's edge, chuck in a rock.

I know because Sonali told me that everything is different in India. Growing up does not require leaving your hometown or your parents. You can stay as long as you like and nobody cares if you live with your mother.

"But then nobody knew what I had to do to support us," Sonali told me. And that's when she showed me *Salome*.

"*Salome?*"

"The video," I remind Arati, only she still looks confused.

"Sonali did *Salome* on video?" Arati gasps.

"Well, more like a Hindu version of *Salome*. A kind of Kama Sutra *Salome*."

"Oh," Arati says, getting an image. "So, um, how was she?"

"Not bad." In fact, she sizzled. If Sonali was red hot as a calendar god, she was thermonuclear as Salome.

Sonali had asked me, "You're not ashamed of me for doing this? You're not repulsed?"

Smooching on the severed head of John the Baptist was a little over the top, but I'd seen worse. I told her, "Hey, I know what kind of horseplay goes on in the world. I get a pretty good idea from cleaning out motel rooms. Plus, I'll have you know I have some pretty wild blood running through my veins. Don't forget it was me who bought the Wiggly Burger."

Sonali then whispered in my ear: "Don't forget it was my idea."

"I've got a better idea," I said. That's when I kissed her. I kissed her neck while tugging up her red T-shirt.

She said, "Whoa, Cy, you'd better save that idea for your dreams."

I said, "You're right, you're right." I sucked in air and tried to slap my senses back together. "I need to wait until we're married."

She laughed like I was kidding. "Married? What makes you think—" And then I could see a more startling thought crashed through her mind. She said, "Cyrus? Are you still a virgin?"

I nodded. "Of course."

"Because you've been waiting for me? All this time?"

"Yup."

And then she just kind of melted back into my bed, and her T-shirt kind of slid away.

The details on what happened next, it wouldn't be right to spell that out, gentleman that I am, but I'll say this: It was like nothing I'd ever imagined, and I have imagined quite a lot, what with the things I find cleaning out motel rooms.

But Sonali wasn't into vacuum pumps and bulbous tubers. She had other business in mind and she knew what she was doing. I'm glad one of us did, otherwise I think it might've been awkward. At first, I figured she knew from reading some of those Hindu texts that explain variations of these things.

Krishna's renowned exploits with shepherdesses comes to mind.

But then partway through I reckoned she didn't learn this from any book. You don't learn how to race stockcars by reading about them. It takes practice. It takes experience. She had enough of that for both of us, which took a lot of pressure off of me that night.

So that was the night I became a man. That's what Sonali told me by the dawn's early light. She said, "Well now, Mr. Slant. You're all grown up now. How does it feel to be a man?"

I thought about it, looked around, saw my Hanuman costume strewn across the other bed. I said, "I feel like a god."

The god I felt like was Shiva. Not Shiva with the big lingam, though I did feel like that earlier. The god I felt like was Shiva after Kali got through with Him.

Kali's a big bad mama the color of a thundercloud. She wears nothing but a garland of fifty human skulls and a girdle of human arms, even though she's got four arms of her own.

She's the one who wanted to rid humanity of our corruption by destroying us all.

She likes to hold an axe, a trident, a severed human head and a bowl of blood. She's all heavy metal, sticking out her tongue, drooling the blood of her enemies.

She's often portrayed standing on the body of a vanquished Shiva. That's the Shiva I felt like after Sonali got through with me. I felt like I got blindsided and trampled over by a goddess on an apocalyptic rampage. Tell you what though, it doesn't feel as bad as it sounds. It's a good kind of hurt, like the satisfying soreness you get after a rousing game of dodge ball.

I'm telling all this to Arati before realizing it's all new to her. I ask her, "So what did Sonali tell you?"

Arati takes off her glasses, wipes the steam off of them. "She said you got all hot and bothered looking at her calendar. She said you told her to dance for you, and when she didn't, you, well, made unwanted advances. Then when Mina told me you tried to put the moves on her, well, I thought—"

I place a finger over her lips, tell her softly, "Hush. I understand. You feel left out. But my love is divided between the two of them. Besides, you and I—we could never be together."

Next thing I know, Arati's twisting my finger around backwards and calling me something like an arrogant bastard. I'm not sure. It's hard to hear straight when someone's trying to snap off your index finger.

She says, "You pissed me off because you're messing with my sisters."

"I'm sorry. That wasn't my intent."

She lets go my finger. "You can't play with their hearts," she warns. "You need to choose." To let me know she's serious, she grabs a fistful of my sweatshirt, and in doing so, gathers up my chains as well. "What's this? Are you still wearing those stupid necklaces? Give them here."

My head hangs low as I remove the LL Cool J chains. She snatches them out of my hand and tosses them into the quarry in one quick motion. Turns out my gold chains aren't real gold. They float.

Arati says, "I don't know what to do about you, Cy." This worries me. I've never heard her confess ignorance on anything before. She asks me: "You really got with Sonali?"

I nod.

"I knew she was lying to me," she said and then added quickly, "And she was your first?"

I nod.

"And now you say you love both Sonali and Mina?"

I nod like a mule.

"Okay, what you need to do is," Arati says, choosing her words carefully, "sit your butt down on that rock right there and listen to me."

I set myself down on a block of granite, dangle my legs over the quarry's edge. Drop in a rock. I can count to six-Mississippi before it hits the water.

Arati tells me to close my eyes and breathe. I know exactly where this is going. She's taking me on a guided meditation. She'll ask me some simple question and suddenly I'll learn something great, like how the circle of life can be viewed from the side as a downward spiral.

She's wrong about that. Life forever spirals upward.

She'll ask me about a full bowl of Honey Comb and an empty pitcher of milk, and I'll understand that an abundance in life means nothing if you don't have the basics. She might be right about that one.

This time she asks me to go on a journey, far away to a place I've always wanted to see.

I close my eyes and I'm halfway there. That's how good she is with this guided meditation.

"But it can't be India," she says.

I have to start over.

She asks me if I'm alone. I tell her yes. She says that's good. Am I afraid? No. That's good, too.

And it is good. I sail over Odium Swamp, past Dunes County and beyond the ocean of milk. I approach an island of marigolds. From up here, it looks like a campfire in the snow. The marigolds are big as trees, shading the boulevards beneath them.

The boulevards are wide. People are driving motor scooters. They wear black berets and drink wine at cafés with red-checkered tablecloths. Elderly gentlemen offer red balloons to charming little schoolgirls in the park. Scruffy men in striped shirts paint pictures of sunflowers and marigolds. Everyone is as happy as a drunk. Happiest of all is my mama. She's running down the street with a handsome man in a gray suit and a skinny black tie. They're both wearing sunglasses and the paparazzi are chasing them.

Somewhere in an alley, someone is playing the kind of jazz that doesn't require sheet music.

"Where are you?" Arati asks.

"Must be Heaven," I tell her.

"Perfect. Now you get to invite someone to join you. You can share this most perfect place with anyone in the world. Quick, who is it?"

"Mina," I say, and I open my eyes.

Arati claps her hands and shows her palms to the sky. "That's your answer," she says. "You love Mina most of all."

"Of course I love Mina most of all. I already knew that. I figured that much out when I made her cry till her eyes swoll shut."

Arati says, "Oh. Well, then, um, so what do you think?"

I think hard. An idea comes to me fairly easily, but I struggle for the right word. "I think I got a hankering for a croissant."

"I mean about Mina," she huffs. "I think you should marry her."

"Oh, no. That's where you're wrong. See, we got set up in an arranged marriage, and that has nothing to do with love. Besides, if I marry Mina, then Mr. Patil has to pay the dowry, and I don't think that's right." I also think maybe what I need is a croissandwich, you know, with ham and cheese. Mmm ... the thought of it makes my jaws leak.

"Arranged marriage? What dowry?" She presses her fingers to her temples, the way Wonder Woman does to summon her invisible jet. "Cyrus, what are you talking about? And why are you drooling?"

I wipe my jaw and explain about the night Moses Jefferson came to visit my mama and Mr. Patil, how all they came up with the arrangement. "See, I know I'm supposed to marry Mina. It's what my mama wanted, and a boy's gotta do his mama's bidding. But I tell you what: I ain't a boy no more. I'm a man now, see? And besides, Moses said I could marry Sonali if she came home first."

Arati soaks this in for a moment, then responds: "They came home pretty much the same time."

"I know." I hunch over and scratch Mina's initials into the dirt. "I still need to get a ruling on that."

Arati takes a knee next to me, draws Sanskrit letters in the dirt. "Look, Cy. You do know that Mina is in love with you."

No, I was not aware of that.

"Madly, hopelessly in love. Haunted and unrequited love. With you."

"You think so? Since when?"

"Oh, I'd say since she was about ten years old." I hate it when she uses that snippy voice with me. "So, are you going to ask her to marry you?"

I close my eyes and meditate on a response. It comes out like this: "*Un croissant avec hambone et fromage.*" Ladies love it when you speak French. Drives them crazy. I can tell it's working on Arati. She's thumping her palms on her forehead like she's gone insane.

MINA. MADLY, HOPELESSLY in love. Haunted and unrequited love. With me.

Once I get food in my belly, the reality of Arati's words sink in my head and heart. So Mina's had the opposite of cancer all along, too, only she was wise to the fact.

How could I be so blind? Why did it have to take Sonali's homecoming for me to see the truth? When did life get so complicated?

I'm beginning to understand why Lester liked to tell stories of simpler times, and why he liked to obscure the truth. I'm tempted to believe the light of truth isn't always the best thing, just like a burned out bulb in the middle of the night isn't necessarily a bad thing.

This is a disturbing, if not blasphemous thought during Diwali.

Diwali isn't just about presents and firecrackers. It's about leading ourselves from falsehood to truth, from darkness to light. That's what all the clay lamps are for. I get that much.

But with all these gods and goddesses, you'd think one could come down here and tell me what I'm supposed to do with this light and truth.

But then, I never asked.

So that's what I decide to do. I'm fixing to summon a god.

I retreat to my bathroom, turn off the light. I stand there in the dark and face the mirror. I stare into the mirror until I see Hanuman.

No, wait, that's just me.

I stare longer and I say, "Hey Lakshmi? Jesus? Anyone? Look, if y'all want something from me, just give me a holler. Anytime. Really, I'm up for it."

I listen. I stare.

Nothing.

I grip the edges of the sink and whisper, "In the meantime, could someone pop down to give me some advice? It's about Sonali and Mina."

I stay put and I wait. I count to six-Mississippi.

And then I see Her. Mother Lakshmi. Emerging from a sea of milk.

Funny, she looks just like my mama.

Fifth Day of Diwali: Bhratri Dooj

THIS IS THE DAY I'm supposed to visit with my sisters. Not like any of them are my real sisters, of course, but it's part of the family tradition.

I don't know if Sonali will even see me. She has to. She has to hear me ask about her well being and I have to listen to her answer or I won't be absolved of all my sins. And lord knows I have sinned.

Not that I'm too tore up over it. I woke up early, took a swim in the pool. Waters in this crepuscular hour are dark and slippery. I emerge from the pool feeling superhuman, almost godly, but shivering cold. The cool air mops away my warmth sooner than I'm ready. It braces me for the day to come. I've got a good hint this day will go well. Fall colors go spastic the day after a hard rain, like the colors of a million gods. They're on my side, I can feel it.

I know Lakshmi is. She has a plan for me.

My heart is racing, racing heavy, like I've been running figure eights all around this resort. I creep into the office and steal away the keys I need, then make a pit stop in the diner, throw some things together.

This isn't part of the plan. These added touches, they're my idea.

Mina's room is three doors down from mine. I tiptoe along the walkway, balancing a tin tray and some flowers I've been saving up with my share of undiluted waters.

I touch the key to the lock. Door clicks open at a nudge. I reckon now her door's never locked any more than mine is.

I set the tray and flowers out of view. A breeze folds the curtains within. Mina stirs in her sheets. I edge in. This is not stalking, as far as I'm aware. This is love. I watch her for a moment. Then I wake her with a kiss.

She kisses me back before she's fully awake.

I whisper: "Good morning, gorgeous."

She smiles, burrows her head under her pillow. "Cy! What are you doing here?"

"Come to ask how you're doing."

"Miserable."

"What's wrong?"

She curls up under the sheets. From the outline, I'd say she's gnawing on her knees and squeezing her toes. "I'm in love. Madly, hopelessly in love. Haunted and unrequited love."

"So I've heard." I peel a layer of sheets back. "Is that all?"

She talks to the wall. "That about sums it up."

I stand and dust off my sleeves. "Well, then I guess my job here is done."

"Where are you going?"

"I need to see Arati, ask how she's doing," I announce. "Then Sonali. Busy day for me." And I march out of the room.

She sits bolt upright, scattering dust angels throughout the rays of early light. "Wait!"

I'm already out the door, but I poke my head back in. "Problem?"

She tugs the sheets up to her neck, tries to act all nonchalant. "Little hungry, no biggie."

"Hungry? Well, now, we can't have that." I kneel down to hoist up the tray. I swear it's heavier now, fast as those flowers grow. They're just marigold, but their stalks are thicker than sunflowers' and their heads are the size of basketballs.

I ask her, "You like croissandwiches?"

Her eyes light up. "*Avec jambon et fromage?*"

I tell her, "*Oui,*" and she just melts.

As I approach with the tray, a most curious thing happens. The marigold petals, now the size of oak leaves, shed all over her bed. They rain down on top of her like blessings from above. She says, "Cyrus, are you proposing?"

"Sorry, I should've asked you a long, long time ago, but it's taken me this long to come to my senses." I offer her a ring made from a clover flower. "So what do you say?"

She says yes.

Yes. I heard it clear as a gunshot, and it set me running like a fawn in heavy wood. I bounced out of her door, skinned my knee on the walkway, and tumbled into Arati's room with blood on my shins.

"She said yes!" My voice cracks as I struggle to suppress my whisper. I somersault over her bed, tunnel under her covers. She shivers from the cold I sucked in with me.

"This couldn't wait until a warmer time of day?" she asks.

No. It couldn't wait. And Surya agrees. He shambles through the open door, scoops under the blanket, nuzzles his cold nose against Arati's ankles.

Clearly this is a glorious day.

"You were right," I tell Arati as I roll over her and wrestle her for warmth. "Mina loves me! We're getting married!"

"I'm ecstatic," she grumbles. "Now why don't the two of you get together and write your vows."

"No time for that now," I tell her in my most urgent superhero voice. "It's Bhratri Dooj."

"Praise gods."

"Serious now. I need absolution. I need to ask how you're doing."

She tosses over on her face, arms spread out like Jesus on the cross. Why she would want to block out such a pristine sunrise is beyond me. It shimmers through her curtains like a searchlight through mango sorbet. "I'm dead asleep, Cy."

I jump up to make a trampoline of her mattress. Surya barks at the commotion. Arati grabs hold of the headboard and whines: "What do you want from me?"

I straddle her back, shake her hard. I yell in her ear: "How ya doin'?"

She pushes herself to her knees, presses her head to her pillow. "I don't know, Cy. You tell me."

"Glad you asked." I bounce to my feet. "Because I think you're fed up with Coloco."

"No duh."

"Quit that job," I tell her. "Stay here with us."

She flops over on her back. "I didn't earn an alphabet of degrees to spend my life tending to a motel."

"Nothing wrong with tending to a motel. Besides, it's a resort now. We got gourmet food and a health spa. You could contribute a lot to that."

"Like what?"

"Well, like maybe you can find out what's in the waters that makes them behave the way they do. I don't know. Whatever you want to do, I'll make sure you are rewarded for your services."

"You will?" She sounds interested. "And how's that your responsibility?"

"Oh, it ain't just yet. But when I marry Mina, I get this place. The whole place. Mine to run as I please. That's the dowry Mr. Patil and my mama agreed on."

Now she's full-tilt awake. I know because she sits up and let the covers slide down and I can see what I suspected when I first crawled under her covers. She sleeps in the raw.

She says, "You can't take this place away from him! It's all he's got!"

Engaged gentleman that I am—fiancé, if you will—I adjust her covers up to a point of decency. "It's all he ever had," I remind her, "which is why he offered it as the dowry." I stand with my back turned so she can dress herself. Strange, I see in the mirror, how she goes for her glasses first. "Not my decision and I won't defy him." I cross my arms and shut my eyes as she reaches for her undies. "Last time he got in a dowry dispute, his family slaughtered Mohini's entire clan. I won't allow Mina and me to get caught up in that same mistake." And I stride for the door.

"Cyrus, wait!"

But I can't wait. I'm on a mission of absolution, and I've got just one sister to go.

I'm on a roll.

My PLAN NOW is to burst into Sonali's room like a firecracker and swan dive into her bed.

Problem is, her door is locked.

By the time my shaking hands get the key in the lock and the door pushed open, she's found refuge elsewhere. In the bathroom. I can hear her emptying her guts in the commode, or somewhere near it.

Change of plan.

Dawn has blossomed into full-blown daylight. It radiates throughout her room like a snapshot of a forest fire. It prisms through tiny bottles, the kind sold in bars when the county outlawed liquor by the drink. The kind served free on international flights or available at an exorbitant markup in hotel minibars. Must be dozens of that kind of bottle scattered around Sonali's room. Strange, we never installed minibars.

I call out, "Sonali? How are you doing?"

"Sod off, Cyrus!"

I still don't know what that's supposed to mean, so I tiptoe to the threshold of her bathroom door. She's hunched over the sink with her forehead pressed against the mirror.

She retches out a dry heave, collapses to her knees and bawls. "What are you doing here?"

"Came to ask how you're doing. It's that day, you know."

She wipes her forearm across her mouth, gathering spittle and snot on her wrist. "I hate you for seeing me this way."

She wasn't too comfortable with me seeing her as Salome, either, but that turned out all right, so I press on with my mission. "Sonali, work with me here. I need absolution. Just tell me what's wrong and I'll be on my way."

She squeezes toothpaste over her fingertips, smears it across her teeth and tongue. With her eyes swoll shut, she feels her way to the bathtub, slides in. Her red T-shirt darkens with the moisture it absorbs. She tucks her chin to her knees and cries. Blubbers all over herself. It prickles my heart, but I need to be strong for her and I won't let it dampen my mood.

I sit on the edge of the tub, stroke her matted hair. "Don't be like that, sister. I've got great news."

She props herself up on an elbow. A wisp of hope cracks in her voice: "Tell me."

"Well, I'd planned to tell you a better way, but Mina and I, we're getting married."

She breaks out coughing. Not like she's going to be sick again, but more like she's laughing. "Brilliant," she says. "That's exactly what I need to hear right now."

I pat her back. "Yeah, isn't it something? You and I—we're going to be brother and sister for real."

Her elbow slips out from under her, face drops to the floor of the tub. She lays there with her nose pushed sideways and toothpaste foaming out her mouth. I can't recall seeing her this ugly. I ask her one more time how she's doing.

"I'm pregnant."

Well, I asked. She told me. And now I'm absolved of all sin. That's how Bhratri Dooj works. I'm on my way out of here.

She pulls herself up the side of the tub, rests her chin on the edge. "Cyrus. Wait."

My back turned, I ask her, "How far along are you?"

"Oh, I'd say less than three days."

That spins me round. "Well, I'm no doctor, but it's possible you might be wrong this early in the game"

She gives me a look that says she knows better. She knows from experience because she's made this mistake before. "This isn't a game," she says. She curls her arm under her belly and says, "I am certain of its presence."

"Well, if you're so certain, maybe you can tell me if it's a boy or a girl."

"I don't know, Cy. In fact, I don't care." Delirium muddles her voice. "Either way, my child will take the surname of the most brilliant actor of all. That's all that matters."

"Really? You'd name your child 'Bacon'? Cause I wouldn't name my dog that."

She raises her head, looks at me as though I'm dim. "No, not Bacon.

Phoenix, as in River, the most talented actor who ever lived and died."
She breathes an adoring sigh. "My child will be a great actor. I am certain
of that, too."

I'm frightened by the prospect. I don't know how to raise a child, much
less an actor. Suddenly manhood has lost its appeal. Godliness is out of the
question. I want to retreat to the pool and start this day all over again. No,
I want to go further back than that. I'd like to turn back time, back to the
place where everything was right. I'd like to tear up her calendars and replace
them with ones from years long past. Like the calendars Mr. Patil keeps.
They're still valid in a cyclical way. They spiral up out of better times and
seem to say the past will always be with us. I find that comforting. But I look
at Sonali and I see only the future is at hand.

The Future,
As I See It

EVERYTHING YOU READ about Fountains of Youth Resort is true.* The waters have powers. It can preserve your health and restore your youthful vigor. It can enhance your crops, protect against pestilence and frostbite, too. Pour a bucket on your car to get rid of rust and restore its factory shine. Put a few drops in your gas tank. It'll triple your mileage.

It'll remove gum from hair and upholstery. It'll mend torn trousers and broken hearts alike. It'll soothe aching muscles, strip your floors, lift your spirits, improve your memory, and keep collectors from your door.

It'll bring back the dead if that's what you want, but you may find that unpleasant.

Yet for all the miracles the waters might yield, it cannot turn back time. And where the waters might let you down, booze will fail you worse. I drank myself into a sorrowful state learning that lesson. Ended up on a bender, a Lester-like binge, for the better part of eight hours. Put away a six-pack of Mickey's Big Mouths on my own. I got soused. My head about caved in when I pulled out of that one, and now I know there's a mistake I won't be repeating often.

---

* Results may vary. These statements regarding the waters at the Fountains of Youth Resort have not been verified or approved by the EPA, the FDA, or any independent laboratories. The Management of the FoY Resort cannot accept responsibility nor be held liable for consequences, or the lack thereof, resulting from the use of our facilities.

On my road to recovery, I turned to prayer. I repented the way I learned in church, crying to Jesus for a second chance. Then I prayed the way Mr. Patil showed me, going *om om om* and blessing every living creature on earth. I stuck my fingers in the flame of a diya and smudged my forehead. I offered saltwater taffy to the beech tree and apologized profusely to Lord Hanuman for any disgraces implied or inferred.

It was too late. The future, while never within your immediate grasp, is already set in motion, and no amount of waters or booze or prayer can set the course different once you make a mistake. Mr. Patil used to warn me about that. He cautioned me against temptations in the world. He said you can endure the pain of discipline now or suffer the pain of regret later. The pain of discipline, he said, is a demon, but it's a demon you know. You'll meet him often. The pain of regret, that's a demon you never want to meet.

Once you make a mistake, you can look for someone else to blame. You might find him and beat the living crackers out of him. Look hard enough, you'll find a whole crowd. You can blame demons and the government and the father you never knew.

You can dismiss your mistake as the result of a passionate moment or you can point the finger at your whole hardscrabble life. You can repent, flog yourself into redemption and find absolution for all your sins. But in the end, you just got to take your share of responsibility and deal with what the future holds. Though I suppose, in some cases, that can mean finding ways to put it off or fudge around it.

I consider myself lucky, because I have befriended a reverent seer who can offer sage advice on dealing with the future.

Moses Jefferson's door is always open, but it's unusual to find his screen door propped open, too. His house is as dim as usual, still smells of tar and cigars and Jockey Club cologne. Also stinks of cat pee.

He's not in his usual chair, at the end of the long dark table. Instead, he's clattering around the kitchen. Sounds like he's swinging a frying pan. It strikes like a gong, he curses, and two fuzzy brown creatures dart under the table.

"Need some help, Moses?"

"If you think you can get them rodents out my house, then hop to it."

I peek under the table. Two pairs of eyes glimmer back at me. "Look like kittens to me."

"S'what I said," he grunts. "Can you git 'em or not?"

"Gonna need some light." I draw back the curtains, raise the blinds, flip up all the light switches. For the first time in my life, I can see the full extent of the mess Moses lives in. He keeps newspapers and magazines dating back to 1963. I ask him about that, going, "What is all this for? You can't read."

"I use them to swat flies."

"I don't believe you."

"You right," he confesses. "I like the comics. They smell funny."

"Come on now, seriously."

"Sometimes people can't afford my services. They bring me magazines instead. I give them a reading, they read to me in return. It's a fair deal."

Dirty cups on every available surface look like they've been sitting there since Carter took office. Red pencils are scattered across the floor. Mason jars are stacked precariously in every corner. The list of *Things Revealed to You after You Die* is peeling off the wall, and his motto, the sign that reads, *When life shuts all the doors in your face, God opens a window somewhere,* is so covered in dust that it appears to say: *life shits in God s wind.* I figure what that means is maybe I need to open a few windows around here.

I tell Moses, "Place is so dirty it's blasphemous."

He pokes his head out the kitchen door, sniffs around. "What you gone do, clean it up for me?"

"Damn straight."

He nods. "All right then. Just make sure you get them rodents out while you're at it."

"You're lucky you don't have possums and coons in here." I kneel down to inspect the kittens. They're shivering and rheumy in the eyes. Their fur is not so much brown as plain dirty, as though they've been rolling on bare dry earth and rubbing up against posts oily with tar. They approach me on wobbly legs and squeak out cries like a chew toy. "How long they been here?"

"About a week. I was hoping you'd come by earlier and chase them out for me. Where you been?"

"Sonali and Arati came back. They brought Mohini with them."

He draws heavy on his cigar. "Who got through the door first?"

"I guess Mohini, seeing that Sonali carried her in." I scoop up the cats, set them in one of the cardboard boxes I use to carry Moses' groceries. He doesn't have to know about that.

"What's wrong with Mohini she can't walk on her own volition?"

"She's dead."

"Sonali's carrying around a dead lady?"

"Well, yeah. In an urn." I fetch a saucer of milk from the kitchen to set in the box. I figure the kittens for feral and wormy. They put off a stink like peaches gone bad, so I set the box out on the porch.

Moses frowns and says, "I reckon that gives you a choice then."

"Already made it."

His straightens out of his slouch and beams out a smile. "That's marvelous, son." His arms outstretched, he calls me over for a pat on the back. In his embrace, I feel something slipping away from me, a feeling that I'm trying to hold on to for as long as I can hide it, but his hands draw it out of me like waters leaching away an illness. He turns serious and says, "You want a cigar?"

I tell him no and get back to straightening. He finds a seat out of the way and starts up on this: "I got a story you need to hear. It's the story about a young lady come in here with a problem," he begins. He shifts round in his chair til he finds a comfortable keel. Lifts his hat and scratches his scalp with the same hand. He says, "This lady, she was pregnant. Father gone off. She didn't want to raise a bastard, but then didn't have much of a choice. I told her to make the best of it. If the father wouldn't show himself, that left her options wide open. I told her, 'Pick him out a daddy. Got a world of choices, so pick him a good one.'"

"Who'd she pick?" I ask.

He answers with another question, the way wise men often do. "Who would you pick?"

"I don't know. When did this happen?"

"Let's say this was back around the time you came along."

"That makes it tough." I clear cobwebs out from the upper corners of the room. "Couldn't have been a whole lot of positive role models to pick from then. But if I had to choose, I'd say Joe Greene. He seemed decent. Brought a decade of terror to the field, yet stayed cool when stalked by a soda-pushing runt."

"Fair enough. But that's not who the lady chose. Instead—"

"Too bad. That'd be pretty cool growing up thinking your daddy was Mean Joe Greene."

"Something to be said for a more realistic choice, you know."

"I don't know. I'd say it's okay as long as the kid doesn't grow up to learn that his father is really the village idiot, because let me tell you: That's no fun at all." I run a dust rag along the windowsills, thinking how I haven't seen a mess this bad since Lester trashed his room.

Arati once accused me of being a compulsive cleaner, said I was as bad as Cal with his paint. I don't agree with that assessment. For one, I don't go crashing into furniture after a good dusting. I've always kept the rooms spotless because that's my responsibility. I've had to earn my keep.

Some hours later, after I got the place tidy as a display case in a doll museum, I lead Moses around by the hand to let him know where everything is. He protests, telling me he can figure it out on his own. All he cares about right now is where the kittens are being kept.

"On the porch," I tell him as I check on their well being. They done finished the milk. When they see me peeking in on them, they turn circles and purr. I scratch one on the scruff of the neck. "I'll name you Wormy."

Moses says, "Get rid of them."

I scratch the other. "And I'm going to call you Little Mo, after that nice gentleman in there."

"Don't make them feel welcome here."

"I'll drop them at the pound on my way home." I give Little Mo a tug on the tail, just enough to start him crying. That sets Wormy off crying, too. "The pound will take care of them."

Moses shifts in his chair, clears his throat and says, "Naw, leave them be. I'll take care of them."

"Hear that kitties? Moses Jefferson is your daddy now."

PUTTING MOSES' PLACE in order—cleaning it up, airing it out, letting in light—that somehow lifted a burden off of me. Made me forget why I went to see him in the first place, and I walked around for weeks feeling like I had scapula wings that nobody could see. I always feel better after a visit with Moses, but it was different that time. Everything seemed better. Even the future started looking as good as it used to be.

Sonali learned to let go of the shame in her life. The calendars, the film, the way she seduced me like a Jezebel—none of it bothers her, least not enough to drive her to drink. We've still got consequences to deal with, but we're working on that, and she's got her whole family for support for as long as she stays with us.

Mr. Patil took the news with equal parts stunned silence and reluctant elation. The silence which defines his ill mood—that came first, mainly for my contribution to her pregnancy, and he realized in time the pointlessness in lecturing a daughter who's all grown up. His mood soon lifted as he considered the prospect of grandfatherhood. He did insist, however, that he would not allow another rapscallion bastard to run amok around here. I don't blame him. It's no fun being a bastard. But like I said, we're working on that.

The best part is Sonali has decided to stay. She put together a lounge act for evening entertainment at our Fountains of Youth Resort. She'll sing and dance, and when she gets too bloated in the belly, she'll hide behind the piano and play rockabilly tunes that Mina can sing and dance to.

Arati has decided to stay as well. She'll help out in the kitchen and advise on the menu. She says we don't need to change anything, really. Catfish curry, barbecue lentils, chard slaw—it's all good, but we can charge three times as much if we call it "fusion." That's what they do in all the trendy restaurants in Colorado, she said. She told me that people in Aspen will pay thirty bucks for mayonnaise on a cracker if you call it "fusion."

She's also got some ideas about adding a health spa and clinic to the resort, offering our guests therapeutic massages and ayurvedic medicine. She can teach them how to line up all their chakras and astras, and then she can take them on guided meditation trips that will blow their minds. Folks pay top dollar for that kind of treatment.

As for me, I'll stay on to help where I can, but I won't have as much time to contribute, now that I've finally answered my calling. The *Stillwater Mercury* posted a help wanted ad. They needed an editor for their "Milestones" department. In addition to the standard application and resume, they required three writing samples, one each for Deaths, Weddings, and Births.

This is what I gave them:

> *CURRENT—Lester Current passed away peacefully in his sleep on December 19, after a courageous struggle with injuries sustained in an auto-related accident. He leaves behind legions of loyal readers, but no immediate family members. A Dunes County native and veteran journalist, Current was best known for his syndicated column, "Current Adventures." A Rosary will be held on Thursday, December 22, at 7:30 p.m. at The Church of the Risen Savior. The Funeral Mass will be held on Friday at 10:00 a.m. at The Church of the Risen Savior followed by internment at Mt Calvary. Bethel Mortuary Services is handling the arrangements.*

> *PATIL-SLANT—The wedding of Mina L. Patil and Cyrus R. Slant took place March 10, at the Unified House of Prayer for All People of the Church on the Rock of the Apostolic Faith. The bride is the daughter of Amitabh and Mohini Patil of Pullman. The bridegroom is the son of Gloria Grace Slant of Hunters. The matron of honor was Sonali Patil. Flower girl was Arati Patil. Bridesmaids were Dee Durham, Holly Danneger and Holly Phyler. The best man was Moses Jefferson. Both the bride and groom graduated from Stillwater County High School. Cyrus is the owner of The Fountains of Youth Resort in Pullman. He is also a staff writer here at the* Stillwater Mercury. *Mina is the assistant manager at The Fountains of Youth Resort. The couple, known as Mr. and Mrs. Cyrus Slant, are residing in Pullman.*

> *SLANT—Cyrus and Mina Slant are pleased to announce the*

> *first addition to their family, Phoenix Slant. She arrived in this world*
> *on July 31, at the Fountains of Youth Ayurvedic Clinic in Pullman.*

None of those things have happened yet. I didn't even dream they happened, but they will because that's the future as I see it. No, I'm not a seer. Not yet, but I'm getting close. The *Mercury* was so impressed with my writing skills that they might let me pen the Astrology section as well. I can do that. I might need Moses' help at first, but I'll learn along the way. I managed to write this one on my own:

> *CANCER (June 21- July 22) Today you will receive a cryptic message*
> *from your ancestors. You may mistake it for a calling back to your roots*
> *when in fact they are directing you toward your destiny. Listen carefully for*
> *key words like "ameliorate" and "resonance" and "fiasco" —basically*
> *any words you might need to look up in the dictionary. Write them down.*
> *Use them in a sentence. Try them out in casual conversation. The better*
> *you understand the definitions, the more clearly defined your destiny will*
> *become.*

I read that back to Moses and he said it was marvelous. He said he couldn't have taught his own son any better, even if he had one. He said, "If you could keep coming by, I'd teach you some real magic."

I beamed back a smile so bright I'd swear he could see it. And I told him of course I'd keep coming by. Why would I stop? I got cat food to bring him now in addition to his usual dry goods and sundries. And who's going to carry those kittens to the vet for their shots? Not Noah. He still smells too much of Jerimiah dogs.

As proud as I was for earning Moses' approval, nothing compared to the surge in my heart when Mr. Patil got through reading my samples. He called them brilliant. That's what he told me. Brilliant. He's fiercely proud of me, said so himself.

First he said, "Brilliant!" Then he said, "You are finally a journalist, and for that I am fiercely proud. More so, however, I am very, very happy that I will finally have a son."

I replied, "I'm so happy I'll finally have a dad."

He poked me in the chest and said, "You must call me Bapa."

And so I will.

That's what life has become here in Stillwater, and that's how it should be.

"As THE YEARS wind down, the past becomes lost and irrecoverable. But what you gain is far more precious, as every passing moment runs you closer to The Light." That's what Moses told me the other day, and I believe him.

I know the moments can't stay this way forever. If they did, you couldn't call them *moments*. They'd be more like *eternities* and you'd be stuck in these little slices of time forever and ever. That's just way too long for me.

I mean, even if these moments were my birthdays and first kisses and *Gunga Din* all rolled together, I'd still cringe at the idea of getting stuck there forever.

I've been thinking on this a lot lately because of what Moses said about every passing moment, about how they're running me closer to The Light. He said it like he was giving me the Standard, same way he gave Lester the Standard, slipping in that key word—*run*—like I don't have much time left.

So I'm about to have things revealed to me, things like the mistakes I repeated most frequently. But I already know about that. No huge surprises in my eternity. I can't say I'm looking forward to it as much as I once did. Whether it's an eternity of Glory and Grace or wailing and gnashing of teeth, I've decided I'm not cut out for getting stuck there.

I think Amitabh had it right all along and that's why I was born in his motel. He never wanted to raise a bastard, but Destiny forced his hand. Now he's my bapa. It's a clear sign: God doesn't want me in Heaven. He wants me to go Hindu. It all makes sense now.

Funny how clarity doesn't kick in until your final moments. Well, okay, it wasn't all that funny for Mohini and Lester, but it works out nice for me. I'll soon die, and I can accept that because I'll be right back. I'll rise from my own ashes as a cardinal or a bear or some completely different person who is in essence still me.

And if the Circle of Life does me right, it'll spiral me back down here to Stillwater, where I can live my life all over again, only without the all the mistakes. Truths and lies, paths and pitfalls—I'll know what to look out for in the next life because I spent this one sorting it out and getting it all written down.

Hideki Kanno

Stephen Ausherman is the author of two award-winning books: *Restless Tribes*, travel stories, and *Typical Pigs*, a novel. He was the 2005 Writer-in-Residence for Buffalo National River in Arkansas, Devils Tower National Monument in Wyoming, and Bernheim Forest in Kentucky. Born in China and raised in North Carolina, he now lives in New Mexico.